MY SON'S NEXT WIFE

Book 3 My Son's Wife series

[Scan barcode w/mobile device for more information]

ISBN: 978-1-944643-24-9

Library of Congress Number on File

MY SON'S NEXT WIFE

Book 3 My Son's Wife series

Dedication

To those who need forgiveness, healing, redemption, and a new chance in life.

Acknowledgements

Thank you, God, for every good and perfect gift that comes from above. Thank you to all of the book clubs and individual readers who acknowledge me, support me, review my books, and provide constructive criticism with much love. To family, friends, and loved ones, far too many to name: thank you.

To my sons, grandchildren, great grands, sisters, and my mother: I love you all so very much. I thank God for a family that is close and interconnected with a love like ours. To those who are not family by blood but by love and acceptance: I thank you for helping me, holding me up, and going out of your way to see that I am well taken care of. Thank you, God, for sending such beautiful people my way.

To life and living life . . . I thank you, God, for allowing me another moment, second, hour, and day to live my dreams now because that truly means you still have work for me to do.

Praise God from whom all blessings flow.

God's Amazing Girl,

Shelia E. Bell

1

*"Death is not the greatest loss in life.
The greatest loss is what dies inside us while
we live."* Norman Cousins

Pastor struggled to mask his grief and heartache. He understood that everyone had to die, but the last thing he expected was for Audrey's diabetes to lead to her demise. It was still such a bitter pill for him to swallow. Not many people understood the magnitude of losing a loved one unless they'd experienced it firsthand. It didn't matter that it had been over a year since Audrey's death. It didn't matter that for everyone else life seemed to go on, because nothing could mend the agony he felt each time he lay in bed and saw the other side empty. Audrey had been more than his helpmeet, more than the first lady of Holy Rock, more than the mother of his children; she was his heart, his encourager, his lover, and his best friend.

Francesca had started to call far more often since Audrey's demise, but even that didn't make Pastor feel better. Well, maybe it did a little because his baby girl sounded more bubbly, more alive, and happier than he'd heard in a long time—years, in fact. It's funny how death can bring such grief to one and barely affect the life of another.

As for Stiles Graham, well, it was a different story. Stiles had found comfort and solace in God, of course, but it was God's gift of a woman that Pastor believed was the healing salve for his son's loss. The woman was Detria Mackey. Detria had remained a constant presence in Stiles' life. Their relationship started before Audrey's shocking death so it wasn't a real surprise when the two of them came to see Pastor three weeks ago to announce their official engagement.

Pastor smiled on the outside at hearing the news. He thought about Audrey. She had told him a few weeks before she died that she believed Detria would make a good wife for their son, Stiles, and an even better first lady. She couldn't be as great as Audrey Graham had once been as far as Pastor was concerned, but Detria was acceptable in Audrey's sight. Pastor, I'm so happy. God has smiled on my baby. I believe He's brought a real helpmeet into his life—nothing like that she-devil that train-wrecked his life. Pastor's mouth turned upward in a smile as he recalled her words while he sat in his favorite recliner in the family room. Judge Mathis was on the television making one of his comical remarks to the plaintiff. But it wasn't Judge Mathis who brought the smile to his face. It was the thought of Audrey.

Pastor pictured Audrey running around, making preparations for Stiles and Detria's upcoming wedding. Knowing Audrey as well as he did, Pastor understood her need to control things, to be the best of the best. Audrey was not one to be outdone. A tear finally streamed down Pastor's ever-wrinkling face. He may have been still approaching the sixty-year mark, but grief was taking a toll on him. He stared at the television like he was hypnotized. He didn't try to hold back his tears. There was no use trying anymore because they always returned.

The ringing phone was the only thing that forced Pastor away from his internal turmoil. He reached to the side of his chair and removed the ringing phone from the charging base.

"Hello." Pastor's voice sounded weak.

"Pastor, how are you?" Francesca asked.

"I'm fine, dear. How about you?"

"Oh, I'm blessed. Blessed and highly favored," she said in a joyful voice.

"Good, darling. Praise God for that."

Hearing Francesca give God praise was definitely evidence that she was on a new and better path. Her days of fighting against God seemed to be over. Francesca was involved in her church, had made new friends after she moved from Memphis to Newbern, Tennessee, and despite some major health concerns, she considered herself to be blessed.

"Pastor," she said in a voice that overflowed with joy. "I was calling because our church's child advocacy ministry will be in Memphis this weekend. I was wondering if we could make plans to see each other."

"Francesca, I'm your father. You don't have to ask permission to see me. You're welcome here any time. Honey, you know that."

Francesca remained quiet for a second or two. "I know, but I wanted to make sure you were going to be around and didn't have other plans," she explained.

"I don't have anything going on that will keep me from seeing my one and only baby girl." That was a given. However, it did bother Pastor sometimes to think that it took Audrey's death to bring his daughter back into his life. But, on the other hand, Pastor was a man who didn't question God's timing. He understood that God had His own way of doing things. "What time do you plan on being here?"

"We're leaving Saturday morning around ten. We're coming on the church van, and I suppose we should be there around noon. But I won't have a chance to see you until Sunday. We're going to hit the ground running as soon as we get there. I was thinking that we could meet for brunch after church. I know it's not much, but I don't want to come to Memphis without seeing my daddy, you know. Even if it is for just a little while."

"Of course, no problem," Pastor said. "Is it a conference of some kind that your group is attending?"

"No, more like a weekend retreat. Several church groups in our district that have the same ministry are meeting to discuss ways to provide better shelter and protection for battered, abused, and molested children. We're doing that from the time we get there until late Saturday evening. The following Sunday morning, we're going to join in a special worship service at Centennial Fellowship

4

Church." Francesca's voice was full of passion and excitement.

"I've heard of Centennial. It sounds like a great ministry." Pastor's heart swelled with thanksgiving. The transformation he heard in his child's voice was more than enough to lift his spirit, if only for a little while. Francesca sounded like the love of God was radiating from the inside out. "Honey, you don't know how grateful I am to hear you talk about your ministry. You've finally discovered your purpose in life. I can't wait until I see you."

"Good, then let's plan to meet Sunday around two o'clock. That should be plenty of time for both Holy Rock and Centennial to have ended Sunday service. We're supposed to eat at The Olive Garden on Winchester. You know the one that's right off the expressway at Germantown and Winchester?"

"Yes, I know where that one is, sweetheart. I'll see you Sunday."

"Okay, Pastor. Well, I've got to go. I have a ton of things left to do." Francesca paused. "Pastor?"

"Yes," he answered.

Francesca spoke slowly. "I love you, Daddy. I know you're still lonely, and you're missing Audrey, no doubt. I hear it in your voice every time I talk to you. But remember that you're still here. That means you still have work that God wants you to do."

"You sound like a preacher's kid, my child." Pastor chuckled for the first time in weeks. "You sure you're not supposed to be in somebody's pulpit, sharing God's Word?" he quipped.

"No, at least that's not what I believe God has called me to do. I'm supposed to be out in the neighborhoods sharing the love of God with the unsaved, the wounded at heart, the same kind of people I can identify with. The most important thing God wants me to do now is to help save the children—to let them know that there's somebody who cares. All of the stuff I've gone through, every mess I've ever made and every wrong that was done to me—I understand it, Pastor. I believe that if I hadn't been molested and raped, or a castaway and locked up, then I wouldn't be as effective with the children I counsel every day at my church. It's more than an outreach." Francesca spoke with deep-rooted conviction. "It's about others seeing Jesus inside of us through our actions and deeds. Not that we can work ourselves into heaven. I'm not saying that."

Pastor cleared his throat and choked back his tears. "Baby, I'm so proud of you. Take care of yourself. Keep doing what God has called you to do. I'll see you in a few days."

"I plan to. Buh-bye, Pastor."

"Good-bye, baby." Pastor hit the end button on the phone and returned it to its charger.

The last half of Judge Mathis was on. Pastor focused his attention back on the show. He munched on vanilla wafers and slices of bologna that he'd prepared before the show came on. It was another one of the things Pastor was accustomed to Audrey doing. It hurt, but at the same time, it gave him a bit of comfort. He pretended that Audrey was sitting in the chair next to him. He laughed out loud when Judge Mathis made another one of his humorous quips. He took a vanilla wafer and another piece of bologna and popped it into his mouth.

2

"There are no classes in life for beginners: right away you are always asked to deal with what is most difficult." Rainer M. Rilke

Pastor prepared for the ten-thirty Sunday morning service. Being able to attend church was one of the most important things in his life. Listening to Stiles deliver the Word Sunday after Sunday had been Pastor's saving grace. He attended noon midweek praise services too. Pastor's vision was affected because of his past stroke, and he was limited to driving during daylight hours.

Although he was retired from preaching, Pastor sat in the pulpit, one of the things Stiles had insisted upon. He listened as Stiles delivered a soul-stirring, life-altering message about the power of God's love.

"You can hear Christians saying all of the time that God is all-seeing, all-knowing, and that He is everywhere. You hear us talk about love and how we should love our neighbors as we love ourselves. We hear the Word preached that perfect love casts out fear. We listen to the children say time and time again that Jesus loves me . . . I know because the Bible tells me so." Stiles walked down the two steps leading from the pulpit and began to pace across the length of the sanctuary, talking into his wireless mic. "Yes, we talk a good talk. We play a good game. But what happens to all of our talk when something tragic happens in our lives? What happens to 'God is good all the time—and all the time God is good'? What do we do when death knocks on our doors and claims our loved one, perhaps a husband, a wife, or even a child? Where do your faith and your talk stand then?" Stiles preached strongly, with beads of sweat forming on his forehead.

Detria sat on the second row reserved for the family of the pastor. Her sister, Brooke, and brother-in-law, John, sat next to her, followed by her parents. Detria wasn't a flashy dresser like First Lady Audrey was, but she could hold her own. She listened intently to her husband-to-be's message.

Most of the time, Detria thought she would enjoy her role as first lady. But she felt somewhat inadequate when she was expected to attend various church functions. She and her family had been members of Holy Rock for years, but Detria never thought she would be sitting on the pew reserved for the pastor's family. She was more reserved than Stiles' mother. As for Stiles' ex, Rena, Detria felt that she already had garnered far more respect than Rena ever had, considering Rena's sordid past with Stiles' sister.

When the scandal about Rena and Francesca spread through the church, Detria had not yet returned to Memphis. But Brooke had filled her in on what transpired during that time. It had left Stiles shaken, ashamed, and devastated. Detria did her best to make sure she was worthy of soon being first lady. Though quiet in nature, she was determined to stand by her man.

Pastor listened as his son continued to prick his spirit with the powerfully anointed message God had placed on Stiles' heart. The church had continued to grow by leaps and bounds. The ministries at Holy Rock were not just talk, they were active, working ministries with a purpose to reach people and proclaim God's power to change lives.

"Y'all know, at least most of you do, my mother passed away almost two years ago. That was one of the hardest times of my life," Stiles said. "I didn't believe God's anointing was still over my life. I cried, and I hurt so badly. The pain was like none I've ever experienced. This was the woman God had blessed me with to raise me, to help mold me and shape me into the human being who stands before you today." Stiles turned and looked back at Pastor. "My father, Pastor Graham, and my mother were married over thirty years. Can you believe that? Thirty years. I've seen my father grieve over my mother's death. He may not want me to say it, but I have to preach what God gives me to preach. I've seen my father weep, break down as if there is no tomorrow without his first lady, Audrey Graham. I understood his grief, but I don't think I quite related to it in the same way he did. You see, she was my mother, but she was his helpmeet. Oh, you don't hear me now."

Several congregation members responded with, "Amen," and "Preach, Pastor."

"I know my father is a man of God. I know my father loves God more than life itself. But when his beloved wife died, it did something to him. He's a changed man now. It saddens me that I can't do anything to relieve his loneliness and his desire for my mother."

Pastor sat still with his eyes focused on Stiles.

"But what I can say to you, Pastor—" Stiles looked back over his shoulder at Pastor again—"and what God has told me to tell you—" he looked at the congregation—"He said He knows what He's doing. God says, 'Do not fear. One day the sting of death will be no more.' But for now, God wants me to remind you that if your loved one dies in the Lord, then you will surely see him or her again. He wants me to let you know, just in case some of you have forgotten, that He is the author and the finisher of our faith. He is the beginning and the end. He wants me to remind you that precious in the sight of the Lord is the death of His saints. Pastor, I just want to let you know that though your heart weeps for your helpmeet, everything is going to be all right. First Lady Audrey Graham is at peace now."

Pastor spoke up with a slight wave of his hand, and a "Thank you, Lord" poured from his lips.

Stiles was deep in the throes of preaching. "She's moved on to her eternal home. If you don't have your life in order, if you haven't given your life over to the One who is the giver of eternal life, I suggest you do so today. Right here, right now. We don't know the second, minute, or hour when our number will be called and death comes to greet us. You don't have to wait until you're doing better, or until you have your act together, or until you stop cussing or stop your sinful lifestyle. God wants you to come to Him just the way you are. He said that while we were yet sinners, Christ died for us."

At the close of service, several people came forth and gave their lives to Christ.

Detria stood next to Stiles at the exit doors of the church, shaking hands and greeting members of the congregation.

"Pastor, do you want to go out to dinner with me and Detria?" Stiles asked after the crowd of members in line to shake hands with him, Pastor, and Detria finally dissolved. Stiles wrapped his arm comfortably around Detria's waist. "I know you told me that you'd spoken to Francesca and she'd said something about the two of you meeting up at, was it The Olive Garden? Is that still a go?" he asked as they departed the almost empty sanctuary and entered the parking lot.

"Yes, she called before I left for church to confirm that I was still coming. She's leaving this afternoon around four-thirty heading back to Newbern," Pastor told Stiles. "I'm meeting her at the one on Winchester near Germantown Parkway."

"Do you want us to go with you? That's a pretty long drive to take by yourself."

"Stiles is right, Pastor," Detria told him.

12

"You don't need to be driving that far by yourself. If you don't want us to stay with you, the least we can do is drive you to the restaurant. Stiles and I can eat somewhere close by and then come back to get you. All you have to do is call."

"That sounds good. But I don't see why y'all can't have dinner with us," Pastor suggested.

Stiles spoke up. "We can. It's no problem for me. I just don't know what frame of mind my darling sister is going to be in, and since she hasn't called me in some time, I don't want to intrude on your time with her. I'm just glad to know that she's reaching out to you more," Stiles said.

"Me too," Detria agreed.

"Your sister has changed. I don't see her having a problem with you all taking me to where she is and staying to eat. I'm not an old man, not by a long shot," Pastor joked, "but I do need a little assistance here and there."

"Then it's settled." Stiles looked down at Detria and tightened his grip on her waist. "Honey, do you mind driving Pastor's car to the house? Pastor and I will follow you, and off we'll go to Olive Garden.

"Sure. Pastor, will you give me your keys?" Detria asked.

Pastor reached inside his pants pocket, pulled out his keys, and passed them to Detria. "You're going to be a wonderful wife to my son. I thank God for you," he told Detria.

Detria leaned over and kissed Pastor softly on the check. "Thank you, Pastor. It means a lot to have your blessing. I'll see y'all in a few minutes," she said and headed to Pastor's shiny black Buick.

Stiles walked slowly next to Pastor, looping one arm inside his father's. Pastor used a quad cane. It was a blessing that he could still drive himself places. Stiles led Pastor to his Chrysler sedan parked under a reserved, covered space. He remotely unlocked the car and assisted Pastor as he slowly climbed inside.

They drove the short distance to Emerald Estates. "I can't wait to tear into that bottomless salad and bread they have at The Olive Garden," Stiles said and started licking his lips.

Pastor chuckled. "You always have loved to eat. After hearing God's Word today, I feel like I can eat a little something myself. I'm proud of you, son," Pastor told Stiles and reached over and patted his hand.

Stiles shifted his gaze momentarily over to Pastor. "Thank you, Pastor. You've been a great example to follow," he said and returned his focus on driving, but he kept up his conversation. "I praise God for your wisdom and guidance." Stiles' voice softened. He watched as Detria drove in front of them. "I know today's message may have been somewhat difficult for you because it was hard for me to preach it, but like I said, and you know this better than anyone, I have to be obedient to God."

"Yes, I know that, son. God knows exactly what He's doing. I do miss your mother. I'll miss her for the rest of my life. That's a given, but death is something we all have to face one

day. Thank God my dear Audrey was ready."
Pastor's voice weakened and trembled slightly.

Stiles changed the subject. "We're finalizing
the wedding plans, Detria and I."

"When is the wedding again? I forgot the
date."

"Next month. On the twenty-first. I'll be
jumping the broom again. But this time, I
believe the Lord has given me another chance
to be the husband I should have been when I
was with Rena. I've learned a lot from the
mistakes of yesterday. I've learned how to be
more forgiving, more loving, and more
accepting."

"God doesn't waste any opportunity to teach
you, son. No matter how bad the situation,
God can use it and work it out for your good. I
have to remind myself of that sometimes when
I'm in the house alone and I'm thinking of your
mother. But, like you said, we all have to
answer the call of death. I just wish I'd been
the one to go first."

Stiles heard Pastor's voice break. "Pastor, I
haven't mentioned this, but I guess this is as
good a time as any," said Stiles. He turned
behind Detria as she entered Emerald Estates.

"What's that, son?"

"Detria and I have been looking at some
houses."

"I already know that. Are you getting
absent-minded like your ol' man?" Pastor
asked and grinned.

"No, I know you know that. But that's not
what I wanted to tell you. We're going to stay
close by in Whitehaven, so we'll be near the

church."

Pastor nodded.

"We want you to think about coming to live with us. And before you say no—" Stiles waved one hand and pulled in the driveway behind Detria—"tell me that you'll pray on it. That's all I'm asking."

Stiles put the car in park and shifted his body toward Pastor. Pastor returned his son's gaze with a questioning look. "Son, you don't need an old man living in the house with you and your wife. I can take care of myself. I do just fine. And whether you believe it or not—" Pastor looked at Detria as she stepped out of the car and reached back inside for her purse—"Detria is not going to want me hanging around." Pastor laughed.

"That's not true. Detria is fine with it. As a matter of fact, it was her suggestion." Stiles and Pastor waited for Detria to get inside the car. "We know you're capable of staying alone, but that's one of the reasons Detria and I—" Stiles patted his chest—"think you might begin to feel better if you're around family a little bit more. We're family, Father."

Detria opened the back door and climbed inside. "Honey," Stiles said as Detria closed the back door.

"Yes, what is it?" Detria responded.

"I was just telling Pastor about our discussion concerning him coming to live with us after we get married."

"Oh, yes, I hope you'll give it some serious thought, Pastor. We'd love to have you with us. I can prepare your meals, and you can have your own father-in-law wing." Detria sounded excited.

"Son, what are you planning to do with your house? Have you decided to rent it out or sell it?"

"I'm selling it. It's already on the market. My realtor said we have someone who's put a contract on it. I hope, if it's God's will, they'll get it. Actually, it should have been up for sale soon after the divorce, but it never became an issue between Rena and me," Stiles explained. "But all of that's in the past. When the house sells, Rena and I will split the profit down the middle. That includes furniture and everything." Stiles waved his hand. When she moved back to Andover, she never addressed the specifics of the divorce, and neither did I." Stiles spoke in a serious, monotone voice.

Detria spoke up. "But all of that will soon be in the past, and Stiles and I can be free to move on with our lives together. Isn't that right, sweetheart?" She leaned forward and looked at him with eyes shining like diamonds.

Pastor chuckled lightly. "See, that's what I mean." Stiles and Detria both looked confused. "You two are moving ahead into your future. You don't need me around putting a damper on things."

"Pastor, please." Detria patted his right shoulder. "We want you with us. Don't turn us down without at least considering it," she urged.

Pastor looked over his shoulder at her. "Okay, I give in. I've always been a sucker for a beautiful woman. And you, young lady, remind me of my darling Audrey. When that woman had her mind set on something, nothing could make her change it. She became stubborn as a mule," Pastor said, and the three of them laughed. Pastor turned back around and rested his head against the headrest. He sighed before he said, "I tell you what. I'll definitely pray on it. But I will say this: I am truly blessed. God is showering me with His favor. Who knows, once you two get married and return from your honeymoon, you might change your minds and decide that you don't want this old man around after all." Pastor laughed again.

Francesca looked awkwardly surprised when she saw Pastor walk in with Stiles and Detria. As they neared the long table where she and her church group were seated, Francesca actually smiled. No use getting bent out of shape about my brother and his new lady coming along. Might be kinda nice.

Stiles approached the table with Pastor and Detria right behind him. "Hello, Francesca," he said and leaned down to kiss his sister. "Hello, everyone," he said to the eleven other people gathered in the small family room of the restaurant.

"Hi, Stiles. Hi, Pastor, and I'm sorry, is it Detra? Detria?" Francesca asked politely.

"You got it right the second time. De-tri-a," Detria pronounced.

"Well, come on around. I'll ask the waitress for a couple more chairs. I wasn't expecting the two of you."

Stiles gestured with his hand. "Don't worry. I'll handle it. Just get Pastor seated, and I'll go get chairs for Detria and me.

"She can take my chair," said one of the men at the table. "I'll go with you to get the chairs."

"Thank you," Detria said and went to the empty seat the man pulled out for her.

Pastor sat down. He was equally glad there was a gentleman at the table who knew the proper etiquette when it came to women and men.

Francesca waited until Stiles and the church member returned with two chairs. Once they sat down, Francesca asked everyone to introduce themselves. After introductions, lunch was ordered while everyone munched on salad and breadsticks.

Surprisingly, Francesca had a great time. There was no bickering or backbiting. Stiles, Pastor, and Detria interacted extremely well with everyone. Francesca felt proud, and it seemed to show in the way she talked openly at the table about her ministry.

"Francesca, I hope you're going to be at the wedding," Stiles stated more than asked.

"I plan on it. I think you've found a nice woman," she said. She didn't smile. Instead, she looked at Stiles eye-to-eye.

"I know I've found the right woman," Stiles returned with just as much seriousness, but not in a defensive manner.

"Yep, I think he's got a winner here," Pastor chimed in.

"I'm happy for you then," responded Francesca.

The group continued to laugh, eat, and talk for at least two hours until the bus driver said it was time for them to get on the road.

Everyone expressed their gratitude for having met Stiles, Pastor, and Detria. Francesca stood up from the table while Stiles opened his wallet and placed enough money to pay for his, Pastor's, Detria's, and Francesca's meals, plus he left a generous tip.

"Thank you for bringing Pastor and for paying for my lunch," Francesca told Stiles.

Stiles looked with gentle eyes at his sister. It was like he could see the pleasant change in her. She looked happy, sounded happy, and the permanent limp she sustained as a result of her car accident wasn't as pronounced as it used to be.

They all hugged one another. "Francesca, anytime you're down this way, you have to come by," Detria offered and stepped up to hug Francesca.

"I will. I most definitely will," replied Francesca. She felt good about Detria, and she was sincerely happy for Stiles.

Next, Francesca hugged Stiles, and then saved the best for last. "Pastor, I'm so glad to see you. You look well. And I'm so glad you came. What do you think about the ministry?" she asked.

Pastor placed one hand on Francesca's shoulder. "Darling, I'm so proud of you and the work you're doing for God. You're a changed woman. And only God can do that." He took the back of his hand and lightly stroked his daughter's cheek. He leaned in and kissed her on the same cheek. "I love you, sweetheart. And I'm so proud of you. Now, you be careful, and we'll see you in a few weeks."

Francesca walked slowly toward the exit.

"Hold up, Francesca," said Stiles. "There's something I want to tell you before you leave. Detria and I asked Pastor to move in with us after we get married. We thought it would be a good idea because that way Pastor would have someone around most of the time. What do you think about it?" Stiles asked.

"I think that's a fantastic idea." Francesca turned to Pastor. "And you? What do you think about it?"

"I'm praying about it. That's all I can say right now," Pastor answered.

"Well, like I said, I think it would be good. We wouldn't have to worry about you so much. You could put the house up for sale or rent it, whichever, but we'll talk about it. I need to get going," she said when she saw the rest of the group heading toward the bus. She pecked Pastor on the cheek again. "I love y'all. We'll talk again soon, Pastor. You too, Detria and Stiles." She blew them a kiss and left to join the rest of her church group.

3

"For it was not into my ear you whispered, but into my heart. It was not my lips you kissed, but my soul." Judy Garland

With each day that passed, Detria found herself more excited. The thought of becoming Stiles' wife was like a fairy tale. She believed it would include living happily ever after. If only Audrey was still alive, then everything would be perfect.

Detria was on her way to do some shopping at the local mall with her three bridesmaids, Lisa, Shanté, and Sonia, and Detria's sister, Brooke, the maid of honor. The wedding was less than three weeks away, and Detria still had quite a few things to finalize.

"I don't know what I would do without y'all," she told the women as they rode in Brooke's Infiniti sedan. "I would fall apart," she said nervously. "I know it." Detria searched inside her purse until she pulled out a bulletin from Sunday's service. She began to fan herself.

"Girl, what's wrong with you?" Brooke asked. "I know you aren't having hot flashes already. You're still in your twenties." Brooke giggled and so did the other women.

Detria kept fanning. "I told y'all, but you don't believe me. I've got the wedding jitters or something." The air conditioner was on inside the car, but Detria felt sweat forming on her forehead. It was the first of July and hot outside, but no one else was perspiring. The four of them sat comfortably in the luxury car with the air blasting and the radio bumping to a Tye Tribbett tune on the gospel station.

"Detria, everything is going to be fine," Lisa told her.

"Yeah," said Shanté. "You do have wedding jitters. It'll pass once you say I do."

"What?" Detria turned toward the backseat and focused on the three women with a frown. "Are you telling me that I'm going to feel like this until after I get married? Now I'm really freaking out," Detria said. The others laughed.

Brooke came to the rescue. She leaned over enough to touch Detria's hand as it lay on the console. "Sis, it's really not going to be that bad. Take it from me. I have been married for five wonderful years. When I was planning my wedding, I went through the same thing you're experiencing right now. You should remember that."

Sonia nodded in agreement. "You're marrying a fine-as-wine, eligible bachelor. Who wouldn't be nervous? And you're a prize for him. Remember what his first wife put him through?"

"From what I've heard, she was a downright slut and a lesbian. How nasty is that?" Lisa chimed in.

"I don't like to pass judgment on anybody," said Detria with a slight frown on her face. "God made us all. And we all have something that we're battling against. So I refuse to talk negatively about his ex or anyone else for that matter. All I know is that I love Stiles. He is the man of my dreams. I'm not thinking about what his ex-wife did or did not do during their marriage, or any other mess that happened when the two of them were together. It's me that I'm concerned about. I want to be a good wife and a good first lady, like First Lady Audrey. Now, nobody is going to tell me that woman didn't have it going on."

"Yeah, you're right about that. I don't go to Holy Rock, but I've seen Sister Graham a time or two in her heyday," Sonia agreed.

Brooke whirled into the crowded parking lot and drove until she reached the middle entrance of the mall. She drove slowly with her eyes fixed on the parking lot.

"See, that's what I'm talking about." Detria turned and faced forward. She didn't look in the backseat at all.

"I'm confused," Brooke said. "What are you so uptight about?"

Detria answered the question. "Because I will be the first lady. I don't have the least idea what's expected of me. I've heard my share of horror stories about the problems other first ladies encounter—late night phone calls from church members, not having their husbands around much, and knowing that the church will always come first." Detria twisted her hands nervously. "I pray that I can do it. I pray that I can be all I need to be in Stiles' life, you know?"

Brooke pulled into a parking space and turned off the ignition. "Detria, what you're worried about is what I call a needless pain.

You are going to be a great wife and an even better first lady. Believe me, if anyone was made to be a preacher's wife, it was you." Brooke smiled as the three women in the back nodded.

Detria placed her hand against her chest. She drew in a deep breath. "I hope so. The last thing I want to do is make Stiles an unhappy man like he was when I first met him." Detria's face reddened as she thought of how hurt Stiles had been over the breakup of his marriage to Rena. Detria wouldn't admit it to her friends, but she still felt a bit of insecurity and jealousy when it came to Rena because she knew Stiles had really loved her. Now here she was getting a fraction of his love because part of his heart would always belong to Rena. Stiles had never told her any such thing, but Detria believed that women knew these types of things without being told.

The friends got out of the car, and the subject of Detria's butterflies was quickly forgotten. With the summer just beginning, the air was thick and humid. The five women dashed into the mall and chattered freely, going from store to store. For well over three hours, they strutted back and forth through the mall, revisiting some of the same stores. They shopped for token gifts and a few additional accessories, and picked up a handful of whatnots.

One of their stops was at Victoria's Secret. One of the bridesmaids bought something blue, while another searched for the perfect garter for Detria. Brooke and Detria studied the lingerie.

"I want something soft, silky, and sensuous-looking for my wedding night."

"You mean to tell me that out of all of the gifts you received at your bridal shower, there was nothing that you liked for your wedding night?" Brooke asked.

The bridal shower her friends had thrown for her a few weeks prior yielded plenty of gifts that Detria adored. Some of the presents coordinated with her wedding colors of burgundy and cream.

Detria waved her hand slightly then returned to searching for lingerie. "I love the gifts I received. And believe me, I plan on wearing every set of lingerie I was given, even the trashy ones," Detria laughed. "But I want to choose for myself what I'm going to wear on my wedding night. I'm not experienced in this sort of thing, so I want it to be my choice— something special." Detria looked up at her sister as if she was waiting for a response.

Brooke placed her arm around her younger sister's shoulder. "Look, you're going to be fine. I know you're a virgin and Stiles most definitely is not—"

Detria jerked at her sister's remark about Stiles.

Brooke held on to her. "Hold on, don't get all uptight. All I'm saying is that I believe Stiles is going to be gentle with you. You've told him you are a virgin, and I don't believe he would hurt you for anything in the world. You'll be just fine." Brooke reassured her and lightly squeezed her shoulders. "So come on, let's see what we can find."

Detria smiled. "Thanks, sis. I love you."

"Me too," Brooke responded.

They left Victoria's Secret and continued their shopping trek.

"Now, doesn't this make you feel better?" Shanté asked and placed an arm around Detria's shoulder as they strolled through the crowded mall.

All of the women walked next to one another. They looked at Detria and waited for her response.

"Yes, I feel great," she said and giggled out loud. "This is fun. I love you all so much. Thank you," Detria said and looked teary-eyed.

"Please, don't get all mushy on us," said Brooke.

"Yeah, save all of that for the wedding," Shanté added.

The women went into another store that sold jewelry. They found earrings and necklaces to match the wedding color theme. Though each pair was different, the jewelry had the same color pattern. When they left, Detria wanted to stop at Macy's to purchase a bottle of Chanel. She'd always wanted a bottle of the perfume but had never taken the time to buy it. They went into Macy's and tested several Chanel fragrances, plus a few others. Detria smelled breathtaking scents, but she remained fixated on wearing Chanel on her wedding day. She decided on Chanel Chance, a floral scent merged with sensual, sweet, and spicy elements. She treated herself to a .25 ounce bottle plus body moisturizing lotion.

"And you say you're worried about whether you're going to make a good wife to Stiles and be a good first lady," Sonia said and laughed while Detria paid for her purchase.

"Yeah," Lisa said. "Girl, you already got it going on. You already know what your man likes."

Detria blushed. "I said I was nervous. I never said I was a prude." Detria giggled as the clerk placed her purchase inside a personalized Chanel bag.

From there, the women trotted off to the shoe department at Macy's.

"God's favor is all over me," Detria said out loud to her friends. "We are finding all of the things we need without a problem."

The women tried on identical pairs of shoes, which pleased Detria even more. Detria found two pairs of sexy shoes for herself. One pair she'd wear with her wedding gown, and the second pair she'd wear at the reception.

"Are we finally finished?" Brooke asked as she scanned the women's faces.

"I guess so. I can't think of anything else right now," Detria replied. "What about y'all? Did we get everything?"

"Yep," Shanté remarked, and the others echoed her in agreement.

"Okay, then it's off to the bakery we go. I want to make sure that there will be no mistakes about the cake I ordered. I was looking at the wedding cake show on Food Network a few nights ago. This one couple had ordered a wedding cake, and when it was delivered just hours before the wedding, the bride peeked to take one last look at it, and it was not the cake she ordered. Talk about a nightmare," Detria said in a stressful tone as they exited the mall and headed toward the car.

"You worry too much," Brooke told her.

They arrived at Eden's Bakery a few minutes later. Detria was assured and reassured by the owner that her five-tiered cake would be perfect. Detria had chosen what the baker called a wedding dress cake. It reflected the color scheme of Detria's wedding as well as the detailed lacing and ribbon down the back of her gown. The cake was to have rich butter cream frosting. She also wanted burgundy rose petals and other custom decorations placed strategically on the cake. Detria looked at the picture of the groom's cake Eden's was going to make for Stiles. It was in the design of a pulpit, complete with a dais in traces of burgundy, and a couple of minister figures sitting in the pulpit looking at their Bibles while a figure slightly resembling Stiles stood at the podium holding a Bible and a mic.

Detria clapped her hands as she and her wedding party oohed and aahed over the sample cakes.

When the entourage left the bakery, they made a final stop at a Mexican restaurant and ate until they couldn't eat anymore. Detria was pleased with the day's events. Brooke dropped off each of Detria's friends first. Detria thanked them. Brooke then drove to their parents' house. The sisters retrieved their packages and went inside.

Detria and Brooke showed their mother most of the things Detria purchased, leaving the lingerie for Stiles' eyes only. Detria and her mother talked while Brooke went to chat with their father for a few minutes before she left for her home. After about a half hour, Brooke re-entered the great room where Detria and Mrs. Mackey sat watching an episode of Bridezillas.

"Oh, no. Please tell me you aren't taking advice from that show. I am not going to put up with a bridezilla sister," Brooke said with both hands placed on her hips.

Mother and daughters laughed. "If I act like any of the ones I've seen on this show, I give you permission to whip my behind like you used to try to do when I was a little girl." Detria laughed while she spoke.

Brooke walked over to where her mother sat and kissed her on top of her head. "Mom, I'll talk to you tomorrow. I've got to get home to my husband and give him some attention. He's had the boys all day, so I know he's probably worn out."

"He's good with Jayce and Jayden. He can handle those boys better than you," her mother told her. "You're the one they run circles around."

"I won't argue with you on that. Thank God for daddies—and good daddies at that. Anyway, I'll talk to y'all tomorrow."

"Okay, baby. Be careful," her mother instructed.

Detria stood and walked with her sister to the door. She hugged Brooke.

"What was that for?" asked Brooke.

"For being the best sister in the world."

"Girl, puhleeze, I'm your only sister."

"Yeah, I know," Detria told her. "But seriously, you've been a big help to me. I couldn't have planned this wedding without you."

"Aww." Brooke smiled and then pinched Detria on her cheek like she used to do when she was smaller. Except back then, Brooke did it to taunt Detria. This time it seemed more like a show of sisterly affection.

Brooke opened the door. "I'll talk to you tomorrow."

"Buh-bye," Detria told Brooke. She stood in the doorway and watched until she saw her sister safely drive off. "Mom, I'm going to go check on Daddy. Do you need anything?"

"No, darling. I'm going to watch the rest of this episode, and then I'm going to lay this body down and rest."

Detria got up and checked to see how her father was feeling. She spent some time with him, talking about the grand day she'd had and discussing some of the things they'd done. She spared him most of the girly details. She hated to see her father and mother in less than perfect health, but between her, Brooke, Brooke's husband, and the home health aides who came to their home, Detria didn't worry about her parents like Stiles worried about Pastor. Her parents had a network of family and friends who checked on them almost on a daily basis. They were still rather young, in their early sixties, but both of them had hypertension, and her father had diabetes. He was now on dialysis too, and that was a concern for Detria.

Detria had told her parents about Pastor Graham moving in with her and Stiles after they were married. They didn't readily agree with the decision, but they respected it.

"Have you and Stiles talked to Pastor about moving in with you yet?" her father asked as Detria sat on the edge of his bed.

"Yes, sir. He basically said that he would, but he's still going to pray about it. He said he doesn't want to be a bother to us because we'll be newlyweds."

Her father nodded. "Pastor Graham is a wise man. He was the leader of Holy Rock for a long time—still is in my eyes. And that's not for you to take negatively," he interjected before her lips had time to part in response. "It's just that I feel the same as Pastor. The two of you need some time to learn how to live with each other first. You need your privacy. As long as Pastor Graham can make it on his own, I say the best thing is for him to stay at Emerald Estates. Y'all can work out something for him like you have for us—home health aide, a monthly nurse visit, and all of the other services we get."

"But, Daddy, Pastor's health is not that good. He's had more than one stroke."

"Honey, your mother and I aren't in the best of health either, you know."

"I know that, Daddy, but the difference is that you and mother have each other for support. Pastor doesn't have anyone. Of course, he has Stiles, but you know that being the pastor of a church is no easy task. And with teaching at the university too, Stiles has his hands full."

"That's exactly why you need to look into some services for Pastor Graham. It's going to be more pressure on you and Stiles to take care of him. You're about to become a new bride and a first lady. You work every day too. Tell me, when will you have time for your husband, let alone time to help care for his ailing father?" Mr. Mackey tilted his head against his pillow and lifted his eyes. "Lord, I don't mean any disrespect. I'm not trying to tell my child that she shouldn't be concerned about the sick and the lonely."

"Daddy—" Detria laid her head on her father's chest—"I understand what you're saying. And I love you so much for being honest with me." She lifted her head slightly to meet his huge, deep brown eyes. "Pastor hasn't agreed to anything, and knowing him, he won't accept our offer. But we do want him to know that he has someone who cares about him. He's part of my life, too, because he's Stiles' father, and Francesca is too far away to do anything, not to mention that her health isn't the best either."

Mr. Mackey rubbed his daughter's soft, natural hair as she rested her head back on his chest. Silence momentarily filled the room. "Honey, all I ask you to do is to pray. Seek God for guidance. Your mother and I are going to support you in whatever decision you make. You're our baby. We just want what's best for you."

Detria rose and sat upright on the bed
again. "Thanks, Daddy." She covered her
mouth with her hand and yawned.

"Looks like my baby girl is ready to call it a
night."

"Yes, sir. I'm tired. Is there anything you
need me to get you before I hit the sack?"

"No, baby, I'm fine. Your mother will be
trotting in here once she's done watching her
shows." He chuckled lightly, and then
coughed.

"She said she was tired too, so don't be
surprised if she comes to bed early." Detria
stood. "Anyway, I'll be in my room if you need
me." She pecked her father on his thick lips.

Detria went up the hall to her bedroom and
closed the door behind her. She dived straight
away on her queen bed. She was in love with
the man of her dreams, the man she prayed
that God would send her way one day. In a few
weeks, she would become Mrs. Stiles Graham,
first lady of Holy Rock Church.

Detria placed her hands behind her head
and daydreamed about the life she would have
with Stiles. Her future looked promising, and
she couldn't wait to start her new life.

4

*"The most important thing in life is to learn how
to give out love, and to let it come in."*
Morrie Schwartz

Stiles called his father from the church
office. It was a little less than two weeks before
his wedding. He was filled to the brim with joy.
"Hello, Pastor," Stiles said when Pastor
answered.

"Hello, son. How are you? Nervous?" Pastor
chuckled in his one-of-a-kind manner.

"A little, but it's a good kind of nervousness.
I can't wait to have Detria as my wife."

"Well, that day is swiftly approaching," said
Pastor. "What's on your mind?"

"Detria and I are going to look at our house
today. We wanted to invite you to come along
so you can see your living space. We're going to
be closing in two days, so this is our final walk
through."

"Son, I've been praying about what you and
Detria offered. And I don't want to interfere on
a newlywed's marriage."

"Pastor, it won't be—"

"Hold on, let me finish," Pastor interrupted.
"I'm not an old man, but I realize I do have
some major health concerns. That last stroke I
had took a toll on my body. I understand that.
I don't want to be the kind of father-in-law
Detria will come to despise by having me

around her house all the time."

"Pastor, I told you, Detria wants you with us. It'll be much easier on her if you're there. We both can look after you. We'll put Emerald Estates up for rent, and you can make some money off of it too. I'm telling you—" Stiles said, trying to persuade his father—"you're not going to cause a problem."

"If you would have let me finish, I was going to say that I believe it'll be a good idea. I don't need all of this space anymore. And so as long as you two want me around, I'll be there."

Stiles felt overjoyed. His voice changed quickly to a tone of anticipation. "Pastor, you don't know how glad I am to hear that. I'll swing by there to pick you up in an hour. How does that sound?"

"Sounds like I need to start getting ready," Pastor replied. "I'll see you soon, son."

"Bye, Pastor." Stiles ended the call, and then called to tell Detria the good news.

The three of them arrived at the newly built house. The home builder had gone into foreclosure, so once again God's favor had showered over Stiles and Detria. They were able to get a great deal from the bank on the 3,600-square-feet, four-bedroom house. It included a humongous family room, wood-burning fireplace, bonus room, four-and-a-half baths, patio deck, beautifully landscaped grounds, and a three-car garage. One side of the house would be reserved for Pastor. He would have his own bedroom, a small area to use as an office or sitting room, a full bath inside his room, and the added bonus of having a side entrance that led to the three-car garage, so he could come and go as he pleased. There was a beautiful lake on the back of their property, which added to its beauty, and emitted an aura of serenity and peace.

As they toured the property, Pastor remarked, "This is a beautiful house."

"Thank you, Pastor," said Detria as she twisted slightly, stood on her tip toes, and kissed her soon-to-be husband on the cheek.

"Hey, what was that for? Pastor is the one who gave us the compliment." Stiles smiled.

"Okay, here you go, Pastor," said Detria and planted a light kiss on his cheek. "I can't wait until we close. We have so much to do before the wedding. We have to get the furniture delivered—that's the main thing."

"I'm going to use the furniture I already have," said Pastor. "No need to buy another bedroom suite, and I have my favorite chair and my own TV." Pastor lifted his hands and shrugged his shoulders. "Seems like all I have to do is get my clothes and get someone to deliver my furniture. If there's anything you all want out of the house, feel free to get it," Pastor offered.

"No, I think I got the things I wanted after mother's death. Maybe Francesca would like to get some of the things you'll have left. If not, then we'll just rent the house as furnished, or sell it, maybe even donate it to someone less fortunate. There are plenty of options, and we don't have to worry about that right away. I mean, your house is paid for, so you can take your time looking for someone to rent it. We can start that process after this pretty lady here and I become officially wedded." Stiles pulled Detria against him and kissed her on the top of her head.

Detria glowed with a plastered, genuine look of love.

Pastor smiled.

It was the day of the wedding, which was being held at Holy Rock with Pastor officiating as planned. The music began to play, and the guests rose to their feet for the entrance of the bride. Stiles stared with a sparkle in his eyes that could have outshined the brightest star.

Francesca was at the wedding, which made Pastor and Stiles proud. She really was trying to make a change in her life, and it showed. She looked rather pretty. Her jet-black, short double-strand twists rested along her neck. She seemed to have on just the slightest bit of makeup, and wore an elegant wine red and cream pantsuit with rhinestone buttons and satin French cuffs.

With his arm intertwined in his daughter's, Mr. Mackey proudly escorted Detria down the carpeted aisle. Detria looked stunning in a pure white strapless gown with a flowing, layered train following behind her. Her dress was made of silk, organza, taffeta, and chiffon, and had bits of lace strategically placed. The veil was made from the same material and was adorned with delicate embroidery. Her ears displayed the most luxurious pair of white gold earrings with swinging freshwater pearls.

Stiles couldn't seem to keep his eyes off the woman coming up the aisle toward him. He appeared to be mesmerized. The guests stared at Detria with looks of awe and pleasure. Detria stopped at the wedding altar along with her father, and the ceremony proceeded.

Pastor looked teary-eyed as he sat in the chair that was specially decorated for the wedding and for him to officiate. He started off with the traditional procedures of the wedding, and Detria's father took his seat at the proper time.

When the couple recited their vows, there was barely a dry eye in the sanctuary. Stiles said his vows with a voice that rang with honesty and, most of all, love for the woman standing in front of him.

Detria refused to cry. She did not want to ruin her makeup. She wanted everything to be perfect for the man she loved. She exhaled slightly when they said the words "I do," and Pastor introduced them to the guests as Rev. and Mrs. Stiles Graham.

"You may salute your bride," Pastor told his son.

Stiles inched in slowly and lifted the veil from Detria's head. He placed his hands on each side of her tiny waist and gently pulled her to him. He kissed her with passion, not rushed, but lingering. Detria did the same in return while some of the guests oohed and aahed.

Afterward, Stiles and Detria interlocked hands then turned to face the church full of guests. With smiles as large as half-moons, the couple made their way down the aisle and off into their future. What that future held, no one knew exactly. Whatever it brought, the newlyweds would discover soon enough.

5

"No man is worth your tears, but once you find one that is, he won't make you cry." Unknown

Detria stood at the mantle and surveyed the wood-burning fireplace in their upstairs bonus room. "Stiles, I love it here. Now that fall is settling in, I can't wait for you to start our first fire in this lovely fireplace." She inhaled deeply. "I can imagine it now—the smell of fresh-cut wood, embers popping." She closed her eyes. "We'll be sitting in front of it, cozy and snuggled up, sipping on hot cocoa or spiced tea." Detria exhaled and opened her eyes.

Stiles was within inches of her. He smelled her minty fresh breath, wrapped his arms eagerly around his bride, and began kissing her passionately. His hunger for her was evident as he groaned and moved his hands over her curvaceous body. Stiles picked her up and carried her into their master bedroom suite. Gently, he laid her on the bed and mounted his body on top of hers. He continued to caress her, stroke her, and she met his desire with that of her own.

Saving her virginity for marriage had been the right thing to do. On her wedding night, she was able to give herself to her husband totally and completely. And like Brooke had told her, everything turned out fine. Stiles was a gentleman. He took his time with her. Now, they were here at this moment, in their home, with their bodies burning as hot as the fire that would soon be ablaze in the fireplace. The rise and fall of their bodies were in tune with one another. Her cries of pleasure rang throughout the house.

It was one of those times that proved to be perfect because Pastor was not at home. Two of the deacons had come by earlier to pick him up to take him with them to a birthday party being held for one of their wives. Stiles and Detria had been invited but declined so they could use the opportunity to bask in their newlywed status.

The couple devoured each other until their needs were satisfied and they lay spent on the king-sized bed.

"I love you," Stiles told Detria as he held her in his arms and her head rested on his hairy chest.

"I love you more," she told him and lightly planted tiny kisses on his torso. "God has blessed me beyond measure."

He lifted his head enough so he could kiss her while he embraced her tightly. They drifted off into a light sleep.

Detria was aroused from her sleep when she heard the door downstairs close. She eased from underneath Stiles' grip and went inside the bathroom to take a shower. Afterward, she slipped into a pair of flannel house pants and a pullover tee, and then went downstairs.

"Pastor," she called, and then wandered downstairs toward his wing of the house.

Pastor appeared in the hallway. "Hey, there." He had a smile on his face.

"How was the party?" Detria asked him.

"It was nice. I had a great time. Where is that husband of yours?"

"He's upstairs taking a nap. Would you like something to eat? I can make you a sandwich and some soup if you'd like."

Pastor waved his hand and shook his head simultaneously. "No, that won't be necessary." He patted his flat stomach. "I had plenty to eat at the party. One of the ladies even fixed me a care package to bring home with me. I just put it in the fridge."

"Oh, so is this one of the ladies that has her eye set on capturing you?" Detria teased.

Stiles came downstairs and appeared before the two of them yawning. He had on his bottom PJs and was shirtless.

"What's up, Pastor? Did I just hear my amazing wife talking about you and another woman?" he said gleefully as he approached Detria, wrapped his arm around her, and kissed her cheek.

"No, it's nothing like that. I'm afraid those days are over for me. No one can replace my Audrey," Pastor said, and a soft smiled formed on his thick lips.

"You never know what God has in store, Pastor," Stiles told him, and then changed the subject. "Did you bring any leftovers from the party?" Stiles turned and walked toward the kitchen with Pastor and Detria following.

"There's a plate in the fridge one of the ladies fixed for me. You're welcome to have some. I'm sure there's plenty of stuff on it."

"No, I was just joshing with you. I'm going to take Detria out to dinner this evening."

Detria gasped. "Oh, I didn't know that." A pleasant look of surprise rushed over her countenance. "Where are we going?"

"Anywhere your heart desires, my lady," Stiles answered.

"Well, let's see. Let me think about what I have a taste for while I go and get changed into something else." She flippantly turned around, but before she raced to her room, she pecked Pastor on the cheek then ran up to Stiles and gave him a whopper of a kiss on his luscious lips.

Stiles and Pastor laughed lightly as they watched Detria dash off down the hallway and out of sight.

"How long has it been?" asked Pastor.

As if he could read Pastor's mind, Stiles answered without hesitation, "Three months and seven days."

"You've got it bad, and that's a good thing. The Word of God says, 'He who findeth a wife findeth a good thing and obtains favor from the Lord.' You've been given a second chance to be the husband God desires for you to be." Pastor walked to one of the bar stools parked in front of the kitchen island and sat.

"I thank God for Detria every day. She has been a blessing in my life."

"Mine, too. I can't thank you two enough for wanting to have me here in your home. I honestly thought I would be interfering in your marriage, and that's the last thing I want to do."

"Pastor, we love having you here. You seem to be feeling better, unless that's in my mind."

"Nope, you're right. I do feel better. I think moving from Emerald Estates was a good thing. There was so much there to remind me of Audrey. And don't get me wrong, that's not a bad thing, but it kept me from being able to move on and grieve healthily. I don't feel as depressed as I had been when I was there alone in that house. I'm enjoying getting out and spending time with some of my friends. I think it's good for my health too."

"Definitely. Detria told me that when she took you to the doctor last week he said your blood pressure was better, not as high as it has been. That was good news," Stiles told his father while he walked to the refrigerator and removed a bottle of vitamin water. "Want one?" offered Stiles.

"No, I'm satisfied. How are things going at church with the new ministries you're trying to start?" Pastor asked. He liked to sit and talk with Stiles, and hear his plans for reaching out to the community through various programs and ministries at Holy Rock.

"I think the men's ministry is one of the best. I'm sure you've noticed that we've had an increase in men joining the church."

Pastor nodded.

"And the youth ministry is also growing," Stiles added. "Ever since I brought on the new youth pastor, I've been hearing good things. His weekly youth jam meeting has been a huge success. Every Friday night, he has something planned for the youth. Whether it's going to a Grizzlies game, a lock-in at the church, a special youth speaker—whatever it takes to keep our young people interested, that man seems to be doing it. He told me the other day at staff meeting that he's had several new volunteers who've signed up to help with the youth."

"Now, that is impressive. To God be the glory," Pastor said.

"Yes, to God be the glory. The favor of God is pouring all over my life, Pastor, and spreading through to Holy Rock." Stiles took a big swallow of the vitamin water and rested one palm on the granite countertop while he leaned his sleek body against it.

"Well, you better decide where you're going to take your lovely bride, and then go get ready," Pastor told him.

Stiles took two more swallows and finished off the water. He placed the empty plastic bottle in the recycle bin located on the other side of the kitchen door that led to the garage. He walked over and hugged Pastor. "Thanks, Pastor."

"For what?" Pastor raised his eyebrows.

"For being you." Stiles didn't wait on a response. He walked out and went in the direction of where Detria had gone.

Stiles and Detria prepared to go out for their dinner date when the landline phone rang.

"I've got it," Stiles said. "You just keep getting your pretty self ready." He laughed and walked to the table and picked up the phone.

"Hello," he said.

Detria continued to get dressed but stopped when she heard Stiles' end of the conversation.

"Things are good," he said. "No, Pastor is fine too. He's living with me and my wife as a matter of fact." Stiles paused for a moment.

Detria stood still next to the walk-in closet.

"We had a small wedding," Stiles said. "How are Mr. and Mrs. Jackson? That's good. Thanks for calling. Maybe you'll be saying I do next." Stiles laughed into the phone. He sat in the bedroom chair with his back turned to Detria and chatted like he was having the time of his life. "Ha, ha, we'll see. Well, I better let you go, or this newlywed might end up in the doghouse. No, she's nothing like you. She doesn't take any mess." Stiles laughed. "Okay, bye now." He hung up the phone, stood, went to the bed, and picked up his freshly dry cleaned shirt.

"And who was that on the phone?" Detria asked in a pouty voice.

Stiles could tell from the look in her eyes and the dry sound of her voice that Detria wasn't too pleased about the phone call.

"Sure didn't sound like anyone from church," she added.

Stiles paused. "No, you're right. It wasn't anyone from church. That was my ex-wife. She was calling to congratulate us on our marriage. That was nice of her, don't you think?" he said to Detria while he put on his shirt and started buttoning it.

"Funny, I don't exactly see it that way. A card would have been fine. And how did she get this number anyway?"

"Detria, don't go there. You know our phone number is available to the public. One of the things Pastor taught me is to always be accessible to the congregation. But you know this already. So what's the big deal?" Stiles answered in an aggravated tone and rubbed his forehead.

"I don't have a problem with you being available to your congregation. But she's not part of your congregation. So there's no reason for Rena to be calling you, me, or anyone in this household for that matter. She's your ex-wife. Remember what I said—ex. How dare she take the liberty to call here, and how dare you sit over there like a schoolboy," Detria said harshly. "You were practically blushing."

"Look, don't do this. It was an innocent phone call, Detria. I didn't know you were the jealous type."

"I'm not jealous, but when my husband's ex-wife feels she has the right to call my house and speak to my husband like the two of you are the best of friends, then that's a problem." Detria's voice escalated and her disapproval was apparent.

Stiles walked over to where she stood. "Hey, it was nothing. You're my wife now. Not Rena. And you know how she betrayed me with my sister, so why do you think I would be the least bit interested in her." Stiles tried to smooth things over.

"I didn't say anything about you being interested in her, but I'm a woman, Stiles. I know how women do. You may not be interested in her, but that doesn't mean she's gotten over you. You told me she didn't want the marriage to end in the first place. It was your decision to divorce her. I'm telling you this one time and one time only." Detria pointed a finger in Stiles' face.

Stiles frowned. He didn't like the side of Detria he was seeing.

Detria turned around swiftly, but Stiles caught her by the arm. "Wait," he said.

"Turn me loose," she yelled and then she hit him with force in his chest with her petite, balled up fist.

Stiles was stunned.

"I'm not going to say this again. I do not want that woman calling my house ever again. Can you handle that or do I need to take care of it myself?"

"Hold up," cautioned Stiles. "You've taken this way out of proportion. I love you." Stiles pointed at her. "I married you. Forgive me, please? But she really was trying to be nice."

Detria exhaled. "Sure. You're right. I'm sorry. Maybe I did overreact."

"That's my girl," Stiles said and then pecked her on the lips. "Come on, let's forget about Rena, the phone call, everything, and go out and enjoy dinner."

"Okay," Detria agreed.

Detria and Stiles went to Bonefish Grill. They laughed, enjoyed fun conversation, and dined on a delicious meal. Detria showed no signs of still being upset about Rena's earlier call.

"Stiles," Detria said between bites of food.

"This spinach bacon salmon is superb. I've heard about this restaurant. Now I know why people rave over this place."

"Anything for my baby," Stiles told her and reached over to squeeze her hand. "You should taste a bite of this Lobster Dorado. It's wood-grilled, ummm. It's topped with sweet lobster, and see this?" Stiles pointed with his fork. "That's crab with a creamy sauce and a hint of sherry." Stiles placed a portion on his fork and put it in front of Detria's mouth.

Detria opened her mouth and allowed the delicatessen to rest on her tongue. She sat quietly and seemed to be taking in the flavor before she said, "Ummm. That is superb." Detria savored the last bite of the food.

At the end of their meal, they returned home to a quiet house. Detria checked in on Pastor, whom she found sleeping soundly in his bed.

"He's asleep," Detria whispered as Stiles snuggled her on the side of her neck. "Stop it." She affectionately tapped him on his wrist.

"Time for us to play," Stiles told her in a seductive tone. Slowly his hands moved downward and skimmed both sides of her body to her thighs. He swooped her up in his arms and carried her into their bedroom. Her body meshed against his. He kissed her until they reached the bed. They spent the remainder of the night in each other's arms, the evening's earlier drama long forgotten.

6

"Have the courage to live. Anyone can die."
Robert Cody

Pastor's day had gone well. He couldn't have been feeling better. He'd had lunch with one of the women from church who had insisted on preparing a meal in celebration of his fifty-eighth birthday, which was the following day. He had plans to spend his birthday with Stiles, Francesca, Detria, and Mr. and Mrs. Mackey, and he looked forward to the celebration.

Francesca had been so much more present in Pastor's life, even though it was mostly by way of telephone. Pastor was thankful for the closeness of family. Detria had been an important reason for all the positivity that had been pouring over the Graham family. Detria was the kind of woman who loved family because she was extremely close to hers. She basically forced Francesca into liking her with her always positive words. She often initiated calls to Francesca to check on her.

Detria, Pastor, and Stiles had gone to Newbern to celebrate Francesca's birthday three weeks prior. Francesca had several of her friends over, and everyone had a blast. Now that it was Pastor's birthday, Francesca readily agreed to attend the gathering of the Graham and Mackey families, and some of Pastor's friends. She and Detria planned most of the celebration by talking back and forth on the phone and texting each other. There was going to be plenty of food and lots of fun.

Stiles arrived home around two-thirty Saturday afternoon after picking up Francesca for the party later that day.

"Hey, sister-in-law," Detria said and immediately greeted Francesca with a hug. "I'm glad you made it here. I know how that brother of yours gets road rage."

"I do not. How do you think that would sound to my members if they heard their pastor had road rage issues?" he said and looked at both Francesca and Detria.

"It's not something they don't already know," Detria responded.

"Boy, no use in questioning your wife. She's just telling you what God loves—the truth." Francesca and Detria started laughing, leaving Stiles with his mouth poked out.

"Y'all are just teaming up on me. But that's all right. Wait until Pastor comes in here. He'll take my side."

Pastor walked slowly into the kitchen where they were gathered. "Take your side about what?" Pastor asked. "Man, don't be too sure. Depends on what it is. I know betta than to get on the bad side of my two favorite ladies. Hey, baby," he said to Francesca and stretched out his arms. She walked into them and received his tight, affectionate hug.

"Detria was talking about his road rage," Francesca said to Pastor as she remained by his side.

"Well, son, if she said that you have road rage, then I have to agree with her. You know you can make even the devil cringe when you get behind that wheel." Pastor coughed hard when he started laughing.

Francesca patted him on his back. "You okay?" she asked him.

"Yeah, I'm fine. Just got choked."

"Pastor, I see where you stand," Stiles said. "But that's all right. I'll be in this by myself, but I know one thing, y'all were sure ready to jump in a car with this road rager," Stiles said.

"That's because I have sense enough to realize that God is the pilot. He wouldn't dare leave it up to you alone to drive." Pastor started chuckling again, but his laughter was once again cut short by a hard cough.

"Pastor, sit down. Let me get you something to drink. Maybe that'll help that cough," Detria told him. She poured a glass of water for Pastor and took it over to the island where he sat.

Pastor took a swallow of the water. "Okay, let's leave my boy alone. You see he can't take it." Everyone laughed again.

Francesca ambled over to where Detria stood. "Let me help you get the deviled eggs made. They're my specialty."

"I heard. So do your thing."

"You've done the hard part, and that was boiling all of the eggs and peeling them. The rest is simple," remarked Francesca.

"Mostly everything you need is in the fridge. And look in the top cabinet over there," Detria pointed, "and you should find a platter for the eggs. The seasoning is in the bottom cabinet."

"Gotcha," replied Francesca.

"Pastor, why don't we go in the family room and get out of the way of these two beautiful women," Stiles suggested.

"I think that'll work." Pastor stumbled slightly when he stood.

"You sure you feel all right?" Stiles asked his father.

"Just because I'm fifty-eight years young today doesn't mean I'm an old man. Just to let you know, I have a lot of fire in this engine, and it's not from road rage either. God has been good to me."

"I heard that. All I can say is amen. Honey, call me if you need me to do something," Stiles told Detria.

"Don't worry. If she doesn't, I will," Francesca said.

Detria giggled. "Tell him, sister-in-law."

Pastor's birthday celebration turned out to be a fun event for everyone. The Graham and Mackey families, along with some of Pastor's closest friends, enjoyed laughter, food, and fellowship. Pastor managed to share some happier memories of the years he and Audrey spent together. Francesca was pleasant. She agreed to spend the night and go home the next day, which seemed to make Pastor beam with happiness when Stiles told him of the plan.

Some three-plus hours later, Stiles and Detria were in their bedroom snuggling. Stiles turned toward Detria and rested his lithe body on his elbow. "Thank you, First Lady."

Detria blushed. "For what?"

"For making my life remarkable. For being good to my family and to me. I love you, girl. And I'm so grateful to God for bringing you into my life." Stiles kissed her with intensity and smothered her body with his.

Between kisses and hugs, Detria told him how much she loved him too. "Stiles, you've made me the happiest woman on earth." She eased away from him and sat up in the bed. Stiles' eyes questioningly lingered on his wife. "I love you, love you, love you," she continued to say as she searched longingly in his eyes. "That's why I'm so glad—"

"Glad, about what?" Stiles looked at her. He used the back of his hand to lightly stroke the side of her face as he spoke. "What is it?"

A broad smile consumed Detria's glowing face. "We're going to have a baby," she said quickly. "I'm having your child."

Stiles sat up like a drill sergeant calling his troops to attention. His thick eyebrows rose, and his mouth fell open.

Detria stared at him, not sure if what she saw was happiness or confusion. She waited for some response from her beloved husband. "Stiles? Did you hear me?"

"Of course I heard you." Suddenly both hands flew up in the air, and he pounced from the bed and jumped so high his head almost touched the ceiling. "A baby? Me?" He pointed at himself. "And you?" he said. "Oh, my God, my God, my God." Tears formed in his bright eyes, and he placed both of his rough hands against his cheeks.

Detria threw her head back and laughed almost hysterically. Stiles reached over on the bed and gently pulled her up until she was on her knees. He reached down and held her close, and kissed her forehead, her red cheeks, and on to her lips. He mouthed words of love to her, and fresh tears poured from both of their eyes.

Stiles felt the rapid beating of Detria's heart pressed against his torso. He pulled back and rubbed her hair from her face. "I love you." He looked down at her tummy and gently began to rub it in a circular motion. He leaned her back down on the bed and sat next to her and started rubbing her belly again. Next, he lay with his head on her tummy. "A baby—our baby is inside of there."

"Yes, it is."

"How long? How long have you known?" He looked up at his wife.

"I suspected something when I missed my period, of course, but then I thought maybe my cycle was just late. I haven't been feeling sick or nauseated, so I didn't think I was pregnant. But I mentioned it to Brooke the other day and asked whether I should be concerned about my cycle, you know." Detria stretched out both hands in an I-don't-know gesture. "She told me she would buy me a pregnancy test kit and bring it to me at work. She said I should take the test during my lunch. I laughed at the thought, but you know Brooke."

"Yeah, I do. That woman can be persistent. I think I saw her flashing you some weird glances earlier during Pastor's birthday party."

Stiles tucked in his lips and nodded.

Detria tapped him on his arm. "No, I believe you're just imagining things now. But anyway, let me finish the story. So Brooke went to the pharmacy and bought me a pregnancy kit a couple of days ago, and just like she said, she brought it to work, and we took it. Well, rather, I took it, with her standing outside the stall waiting on me." Detria giggled.

"A couple of days ago? And you're just telling me?"

"Hold up, listen, will you?" she said and laughed at his obvious excitement. "I took the test, but I didn't believe what it read. So yesterday after I got home from work, I took another one."

"Ahh, so that's why Brooke was over here yesterday when I called you from church."

"Yes, that's why. Anyway, I took the test . . . and oh, Stiles, when it came back positive again, I couldn't believe it. I was so nervous. I thought there was a mistake or something, but leave it up to my sister, she had bought three kits!" Detria lifted three fingers and gathered her legs Indian style on the bed, and then bounced her buttocks up and down with joy on the pillow-top mattress. "Stiles, I took the test all three times, and all three times I got the same result: positive."

"We've got to get you to a doctor. You need to rest. And all of this work you did for Pastor's birthday . . . oh, baby, you should have been resting. Who else knows? Does Francesca? Your parents?"

Detria placed her hand over Stiles' mouth.

"You are so silly," she said. "No one knows other than Brooke. And she promised not to tell anyone anything until I told you first and we went to the doctor to be sure."

"Good, good." Stiles jumped out of the bed again.

"Where are you going?"

"I'm going to get you a warm glass of milk. You need to relax and get some rest. I'll call the doctor's office first thing tomorrow morning and get an appointment."

"Stiles, tomorrow is Saturday. We'll call Monday. And you have to get Francesca home tomorrow anyway. I'm going with you."

"I don't know. I think you need to stay here and rest. I'll get Francesca home and hurry back here."

"Stiles Graham, will you calm down? I'm fine. I am going to go with you in the morning, and I don't need any milk. I'm fine. Now that I know how happy you are, I can rest."

"Did you doubt that I would be anything other than happy?" he asked her and returned to sit on the bed again. "I don't know how to show you how much I love you, but I'm going to spend the rest of my life trying." He caressed her face again, kissed her belly, and then climbed in the bed next to her and gathered her in his arms. "Lord, thank you. Thank you so much."

"Amen," Detria said and cuddled in closer to Stiles. The two fell asleep in each other's arms with smiles plastered on their faces.

The following morning, Stiles awoke early. The sun had barely risen, but thoughts of what

Detria told him last night had him energized. He looked over at her, still sleeping soundly. He quietly maneuvered around the large master bedroom and into their bathroom. The bathroom looked like it could have been a middle-sized bedroom because it was so massive. God had truly spread favor over Stiles' life. Stiles turned on the shower and allowed the multi-spray jets to warm while he gathered towels from the bathroom closet.

"And what do you think you're doing?" The voice behind him startled him momentarily.

"What are you doing is the question?" Stiles asked Detria as she approached him and automatically stepped inside his arms.

"I thought I heard something and turns out I was right. Is my baby daddy trying to run out on me?" She smiled.

"No, I got up early, and I tried to move around, so I wouldn't wake you. You looked so peaceful and beautiful. I am so full of praise right now, Detria. God is just so good. So good."

"Yes, He is. We are truly blessed," she said in agreement.

"Do you want to join me?" Stiles leaned his head back toward the shower.

"Sure, how can I say no?" She slipped out of her robe and unveiled her naked body before her husband. Stiles gasped at her beauty. He could have sworn he saw her round belly protruding just a little, and he smiled with happiness. The couple stepped inside the spacious shower, and the bursts of steam and gentle jet streams caressed them as they washed each other.

Stiles and Detria dried each other off after they completed their shower, and then Stiles went to the enormous walk-in closet and chose a pair of jeans and a polo shirt. "Baby, it's still early. Why don't you stay up here and take it easy. I'm going to do my morning meditation, and then I'll fix breakfast for everyone. How does that sound?" Stiles asked as he looked on his smiling wife.

"I think I'm going to enjoy being pregnant if this is the kind of treatment I can expect. But you go on and do your meditation, and I'll prepare breakfast this time. I promised Francesca that I'd make her some of my homemade buttermilk pancakes. And, honey, I feel great. I'm pregnant, not an invalid," she told him with her hands now on both of her hips.

"Are you sure you feel all right? I don't want you to be doing anything that can hurt the baby. We haven't seen a doctor yet, and we need to be careful."

"I'm not a porcelain doll, sweetheart. I'm not going to break. And I feel fine. I promise to tell you if I feel the slightest bit uncomfortable." Detria crossed her fingers.

"Well, okay. But after we take Francesca home, we're coming back here, and we're going to see about finding an OB/GYN for you and our baby." He dressed while he talked.

"Okay, I won't argue with you about that. Now go to your study, and I'll go downstairs as soon as I finish putting on my clothes. Francesca will probably be waking up soon too.

I think she said she's an early riser."

"I can't believe that, but then again Francesca has made such a positive change in her life that it astounds me at times." Stiles walked over to the side of the closet where Detria stood, patted her on the butt, and kissed her again before he retreated out of their room, closing the bedroom door behind him.

As soon as Stiles left, Detria looked upward, and then she went to her knees. "Oh, God, how I thank you. You are so awesome, so marvelous, and so mighty. Thank you, Father, for this child I am carrying. Bless this child." She looked down at her tummy. "Bless Stiles and me to be the kind of parents that you would have us to be. I pray that we will find the right doctor, and that all goes well with this pregnancy. Amen." She got up off her knees, stepped back into the closet, and pulled a jogging suit off its hanger.

Detria finished dressing, made the bed, and tidied the bathroom. Last, she patted her hair lightly with a hand towel, put some hair butter in her hand and massaged it until it smoothed out. She massaged and pulled on her curly curls with her fingers and styled them to perfection. She patted her tummy, and then left out of the room, down the stairs and in the direction of the kitchen.

"Thank you, Lord . . . I just wanna thank you, Lord," she sang softly as she prepared turkey bacon, sausage, scrambled eggs and pancakes.

"Mornin.' What's got you up early humming

while you cook? You Betty Crocker or somebody," teased Francesca.

Detria jumped and turned sideward at the sound of Francesca's voice then replied, "I'm just happy, that's all." Detria immediately smiled when she saw Francesca stationed at the kitchen door and already dressed like she'd been up a while too.

Francesca walked into the kitchen and stood next to Detria. "You have it smelling so good up in here, I thought I was on one of those commercials about the best part of waking up is . . . Detria's homemade cakes." Francesca free-styled while Detria laughed loudly and raised a high-five in the air. "You are some crazy sister-in-law," joked Francesca. "You want some help?"

"Does it smell like I need help? And aren't you the one who asked me to make you some homemade pancakes?"

"Eww, are you in a great mood or what?" Francesca threw her head back slightly and eyed Detria in amazement.

"Go, relax over there in the dining area if you want to, unless you want to sit at the island and talk to me while I finish up breakfast," Detria suggested.

"Cool, I'll hang in here with my favorite sister-in-law."

"You can say that 'cause I'm your only sister-in-law." The two of them joked back and forth. "I guess you'll say the same thing when your little niece or nephew enters the world."

"Huh?" Francesca looked at Detria with curiosity. "You're having a baby?"

"I believe so. I took a home pregnancy test, and the result came out positive. I still need to go to the doctor to make sure."

Francesca hugged Detria. "Oh, my gosh, that's great news. I'm going to be an aunt."

"That's right. Get ready to put on your babysitting hat," Detria teased.

"You got it. Any idea when the baby is due?"

"I'm not quite sure. Like I said, I still have to go to the doctor. And we haven't said anything to Pastor. So don't let on that you know anything, not even to Stiles. I want to be certain about my pregnancy first."

"Understood and congratulations. Where's Stiles anyway?" Francesca asked while Detria placed a second pile of pancakes on a heated plate.

"He's upstairs in the study doing his morning meditation," Detria answered. She turned over bacon and sausages respectively on the breakfast grill. Like an expert chef, Detria poured almost perfect circles of batter on the grill. "He'll be down shortly. Do you know if Pastor is awake?

"No, I don't know. I haven't heard him this morning. You want me to go check on him?" Francesca offered and proceeded to turn toward the door.

"No, no. There's no need to do that." Detria shook her head. "Believe me, Pastor will smell this food and get up. It works just about every time. If he hasn't come in here by the time Stiles comes downstairs, then Stiles will check on him," Detria said then changed the subject. "Tell me, what's been going on with you since you turned a year older yourself not too long ago?"

"Like what?" replied Francesca.

"Like what's been going on with you?" responded Detria again.

"Nothing. Just trying to live the life God has for me."

"Long as you're trying under your own strength, you'll never be successful. You've got to let God do it in you and through you," Detria told Francesca without missing a beat preparing breakfast. She had pulled plates, silverware, and glassware from the see-through white cabinets.

Francesca responded, "I understand what you're saying, and that's what I mean. But truth is, I'm still tempted and bothered by my past, you know?" Francesca walked to the island and propped herself on one of the stools. "And what trips me out is that I hate to admit it, but I still miss my past—well, some of it, that is."

"God understands your struggles. Knowing that is enough to make me sing—should be enough for you, too."

"But I just want to be right. I don't want to keep battling with the same old sins. I haven't carried any of my past deeds out anymore, but God says if we think on it long enough, then we've sinned."

Detria began setting everything on the table. Francesca picked up plates and accessories without being asked. "I hear you, but God also says as far as the east is from the west, that's how far He's moved our sins from us," Detria quickly responded.

Francesca may have been the daughter of a preacher and the sister of a preacher, but Detria was confident about the scriptures. She had been captivated by the Word of God since she was a young child. She loved reading the Bible, and had done so in its entirety in more than one translation. It was probably one of the reasons Detria made a great first lady. She understood God's Word. Detria was more than Holy Rock's first lady. She was a child of God, and that was something very few doubted.

Detria and Francesca completed setting the table while they talked. When they finished, Detria stopped and grabbed hold of Francesca's hand. "You are doing fine. God has you. He loves you, Francesca."

Francesca embraced her sister-in-law. "Thank you," De—"

"Y'all started without us?" asked Stiles, who entered the kitchen with Pastor. "Pastor, do you see how they do us?" Stiles turned and looked at his father with both of his arms folded inside each other.

"Umph, umph, umph." Pastor shook his head. "I don't know, son. I guess we'll have to eat the leftovers."

"Y'all are so pitiful," Francesca said. "Get on in here so we can pray and eat this food my sister-in-law cooked," Francesca instructed joyously.

The men did as they were told, like they were two toddlers. They prayed, and then dove into the food before them.

Twenty minutes later, Stiles stood from the

table and patted his tummy while he leaned over to his wife and hugged her. "Honey, that was so good. Ooh wee." Detria smiled. The news about the pregnancy test had Stiles and Detria on a spiritual high.

"Yes, it was," Pastor piggybacked off his son's compliment. "Detria, I think you know a few ways to a man's heart."

Everyone giggled. "I plead the fifth," Detria said.

"Okay, okay. Be like that," Stiles interjected with a trace of laughter in his voice.

"Y'all can keep on talking, but I'm going to get my things so Stiles can get me home. I'm sure y'all have things to do today. I know I do." Francesca looked at her father. "Pastor, are you riding with us?"

"No, I think he's going to stay here with Detria," Stiles answered.

Detria whisked around and glanced at her husband like she was in possession of power that no one else knew about. She giggled and said, "Stiles, you know that I'm going with you, so don't play."

"Oh," he said. Stiles looked funny, but he wasn't about to pressure Detria. She was pregnant with his child. It was not the time to make her upset, and Stiles sure didn't want a repeat of the same scene he experienced the other night. "Well, Pastor, you might as well ride along with us too."

"Yeah, Pastor. That would be great. You can finally see where I live. That is, if you feel up to it," Francesca said with pleasure.

"Okay, looks like we're going on a road trip,"

Pastor replied. He stood up and wobbled, and would have fallen had Stiles not reacted so quickly.

"You, okay, Pastor? Is this what fifty-eight did to you last night? You partied too much?"

"I'm fine. I just stood up too quickly. I told y'all that I'm still a young man. If your mother was still here, she'd tell you that." His smile broadened. "I'll be back in a few minutes. I'm going to get out of my pajamas and put something else on."

"Okay, we'll be waiting," said Stiles.

Pastor returned fifteen minutes later dressed in slacks, a pullover, and a polo jacket. "Ready?" Pastor looked at Stiles, Francesca, and Detria, who were still in the kitchen laughing and talking.

Francesca reached down beside her chair and picked up her cane from off the floor. "Ready," she said.

"Let's go then," said Stiles.

The drive to Francesca's house proved to be another positive step for the family. Pastor received a tour of Francesca's 1,100-square-foot living space. She introduced him to her huge tomcat, Jabez. Pastor, Stiles, Detria, and Francesca talked until the phone rang an hour or so after they arrived. Francesca answered it and chatted with the other person on the line for a few minutes before she returned to engage in conversation with her family.

"Got plans?" Stiles asked when she returned and sat down on the sofa.

"That was one of my church members. He invited me to come over later on, that's all.

Nothing special."

"Well, don't let us hold you up," Pastor spoke up. "We should probably be getting back on the road anyway, don't you think, son?"

"I agree, Pastor," Detria answered instead of Stiles. "Tomorrow is Sunday, and we've had a full weekend—a fun weekend, but still a full one."

"Okay." Stiles got up and reached out his hand toward Detria, "Looks like I'm outnumbered here, sis."

"You sure are because as bad as I hate to see y'all leave, I understand that it's not a hop, skip, and a jump from here back to Memphis. So if you plan on getting home in time to at least get some rest and preparation for tomorrow, I suggest you get on the road." They each stood up, and Francesca walked them to the door. They all exchanged hugs and kisses while Jabez rubbed against Francesca's leg.

"I'm proud of you, daughter." Pastor turned one last time before he walked out of the door. "Be good, and I'll talk to you soon."

"Okay, Pastor. Bye, Stiles. Buh-bye, Detria. Be careful on the highway," she said to Stiles. She stood at the door and watched as they all got in the car.

Stiles pulled off. He shifted his head slightly so he could see Francesca in his side mirror. As he drove out of the gated apartment complex, Stiles watched her frame linger in her doorway. He smiled slightly.

7

*"Love is not blind; it simply enables one to see
things others fail to see."* Unknown

Detria followed her husband's advice, not
that she had a choice. She was just as eager to
find out more about her pregnancy. First thing
Monday morning she called Brooke's OB/GYN.
The scheduling nurse gave her an appointment
for the following Thursday morning. When she
called Stiles at church she could hear the
elation in his voice.

"Do you want me to bring you home
anything, dear? Name it, and I promise I'll
follow your nutritious instructions," he said.
He often bucked at the strict regimen of
healthy foods Detria insisted the three of them
eat. But no more. His wife was pregnant, and
he wanted to be the best husband and father
ever."

"Stiles, you know what? That sounds good.
All I want to do when I get home this afternoon
is go for a walk, take a hot bath, and crash. It's
been a busy day. I'm anxious to see my baby
daddy," Detria crooned into the phone.

"Oh, now that sounds like a subject that
might require some one-on-one pastoral
counseling," he shot back quickly, his mellow
baritone voice oozing seduction and control.

"I think you're right. Is there any way you
can fit me in, Pastor Graham? The sooner the

better." They exchanged more sensual banter before they ended with, "I love you," and "I love you more."

Detria's office phone rang as soon as she hung up with her sexy husband. "Hello, Mrs. Graham speaking. May I help you?"

"You got me so whipped that I forgot to ask you what you want me to bring home for dinner," Stiles asked a surprised Detria.

"Ditto, sweetie. Let's see." Detria held the phone in her hand, and then leaned back in her office chair. She placed one hand on her tummy, something she found herself doing more and more. "Umm, why not stop by The Diet Café and get three grilled portabella half sandwiches. Better yet, get a whole sandwich and two orders of grilled vegetables for me. That should satisfy the three of us."

"Three of us as in you, me, and Pastor? Have you forgotten that you're eating for two now, Mrs. Graham? I think you meant, 'the four of us,'" said Stiles in a voice bathed with warmth and concern for his wife and child.

"The four of us . . . I stand corrected." Detria giggled into the phone. "Now, will you let me get back to work so I can get out of here on time?"

"You got it. I love you. Buh-bye," Stiles said.

Detria whirled around in her chair until she faced the picture window in her office. She scanned the various shapes, colors, and sizes of the buildings that made up the heart of Midtown. She thanked God again in her thoughts, and then proceeded with the rest of the day's responsibilities.

Later that evening after they had dinner, Stiles and Detria retreated upstairs to the media room and popped in a DVD.

"You seem tired," Stiles commented when Detria yawned for the third time during the movie. "All of that yawning. You need to get plenty of rest, you know."

"I get enough rest. I just had a long day, that's all."

"I think you need to stop working out every morning before you go to work. You're pregnant, and I don't want anything to put you or our baby in harm's way."

"Stiles, we don't know for sure that I'm pregnant. Those store-bought pregnancy tests can be unreliable."

"But you haven't had your cycle. What other reason could it be?"

"I don't know," Detria answered and snuggled closer next to Stiles on the couch.

"Well, you still need to stop working out so much. You act like you're obsessed sometimes. You already look good, and you're in perfect shape."

Detria eased up and turned to look at Stiles. "I'm in shape because I work out," she said. "You know you could stand to come to the gym with me. It'll help relieve stress, and you and I both know you're under a lot of that. And working out is a hobby for me."

"Still, I don't want you working out anymore until after the baby is born."

"Why do you have to ruin a perfect evening?" Detria asked. Her tone of voice was unpleasant.

Stiles stared at her. "What are you talking about?"

"I'm talking about you trying to order me to stop working out. I know how to take care of my body, Stiles. And if it turns out that I am pregnant, that is still no excuse for me to stop working out. Uggg. Sometimes there is no pleasing you."

"Where is all the attitude coming from? I made a suggestion, and now you're huffing and puffing like I just committed the cardinal sin or something."

"I'm tired," Detria hollered and then jumped up off of the couch. "You want to make a big deal out of it, fine. But just leave me alone. I'm going to bed."

Detria sprinted from the media room and disappeared.

Stiles was left sitting on the couch with his mouth gaping open. This was the second time in a matter of days that his wife had flown off the handle over little of nothing. What he considered to be a simple discussion between husband and wife had resulted in her storming off, and he wasn't pleased. Couldn't she understand that he was concerned about her and the baby she might be carrying? He picked up the remote and turned off the movie. No use in trying to watch it now. I guess that's what pregnancy does to a woman.

When Thursday morning arrived, Stiles and Detria couldn't contain their excitement. They prayed beside their bed before they started to get ready for Detria's doctor's appointment. Stiles' voice was strong, yet he prayed in a tone that resonated honor and respect for the God he and his wife served. Grasping hold of Detria's trembling hand, Stiles lifted their intertwined hands toward the sky. He prayed for favor, for God's mercy and grace. When he finished, he embraced Detria tightly, and then gently led her to stand. He kissed her with passion, and for a few moments they stood next to their bed and embraced like their magnetism for each other was irresistibly potent.

They arrived at the doctor's office located inside the Professional Building next to Baptist Women's Hospital. Detria heard Stiles release a long sigh when he turned into the medical building parking garage. "What's that all about?" she asked, knowing that he was probably just as nervous as she was.

"I was just thinking, that's all."

"About what?" she asked. Stiles whirled into a parking space that was right next to the elevator. "Thank you, Lord, for favor," he said out loud. He got out of the car, and then ran around the front and over to the passenger's side. He opened the door for Detria and answered her question while he reached for her hand. "I was thinking of God's favor. I mean, your doctor is right next to the hospital where we're having our baby. And look at how we got a parking space next to the entrance. Now we're about to go inside and find out when we can expect our child into this world." Stiles closed the door behind Detria and wrapped his arm around her waist.

"I agree. God is awesome, that's for sure,"

Detria added. They read the directory immediately next to the elevator and found where the doctor's office was located. Once they arrived at the doctor's office, they were instructed to sign in and were given several pages of medical and insurance forms to complete. Detria was thankful that she had top health insurance, especially since the health insurance the church paid for Stiles wasn't as good as hers. Another blessing.

It wasn't long before Detria's name was called. The couple stood and followed the nurse's assistant to a small room tastefully decorated in a mixture that made it easily comfortable for parents and children alike. She took Detria's vitals and afterward informed them that the doctor would be in shortly before she closed the door and left.

Detria sat on the exam table, and Stiles squirmed in the chair that was in the cramped exam room. He got up and paced in the small room.

"Stiles, will you be still? You're making me nervous," Detria complained. Finally a tap on the door calmed Stiles down. The knob turned in slow motion, and a mocha-skinned woman who appeared to be over six feet tall sauntered inside dressed in a fashionable pantsuit that gave her the appearance of a runway model rather than a doctor. Stiles probably wouldn't have believed the woman was an M.D. had it not been stitched in a perfect font on the white coat she wore over her outfit.

"Good morning, Mrs. Graham?" The doctor glanced at the chart before she looked up and directly into Detria's eyes.

"Yes, that's me," Detria answered.

"I'm Dr. Henderson." The doctor smiled and extended her hand toward Detria, who met it with her own dampened hand. She turned in the direction of Stiles. "Mr. Graham, may I assume?" she asked rather than stated and extended her hand to him next.

"Yes, nice to meet you," Stiles said.

"It's nice to meet you as well," Dr. Henderson told him, and the two shook hands. "Mrs. Graham, so you're Brooke Smith's sister."

"Yes, and I have to tell you that she really sings your praises. From the look of my handsome nephews, I know why."

"Yes, I delivered both Jayce and Jayden." Dr. Henderson shifted her gaze for a second. "Mr. Graham, I know you're nervous." Dr. Henderson must have noticed that he continued to shift from one leg to the other. "Please, have a seat. I'll talk to you both about the examination that I'm going to perform. Mrs. Graham, first let me tell you that it's up to you if you want your husband to remain. If you do not, then I will have a female assistant come inside the room with me during your examination. We want you to be comfortable."

Detria looked at Stiles. He lifted his hands in the air. "It's entirely up to you. Either way, I'm here for you. So whatever makes you the most comfortable," Stiles told Detria.

Detria looked back at Dr. Henderson. "I'd like my husband to stay. I want him to be part of everything," she said.

Stiles jumped up. "Excuse me, doctor." He leaned over and cupped his wife's face between his hands and kissed her lips. "I love you," he whispered low and throaty before he moved back and returned to his seat.

They listened as the doctor explained the pelvic examination and blood tests, and asked detailed questions about each of them and their family histories. When she finished, she asked if they had any questions, but at the time neither Detria nor Stiles had anything to ask. Dr. Henderson was thorough, and Detria already felt glad that Brooke referred her. Dr. Henderson told them they would be moved to another examination room.

The exam proved uncomfortable for Detria, but she was willing to go to the ends of the earth to find out for sure if she was carrying a child. She wanted to hear the words come from a doctor and not some over-the-counter pregnancy kit. For Detria, it wouldn't be real until Dr. Henderson deemed it so.

After the hour-long examination and tests were done, Detria and Stiles were ushered into Dr. Henderson's office by the same nursing assistant as before. But it was well worth the wait when Dr. Henderson returned to give them the verdict. "I'm happy to confirm that you are pregnant," she said as she walked behind her desk and sat down across from the beaming couple.

"Yes," Stiles yelled and raised a balled fist in the air. "How far along?" he asked anxiously.

"Your wife is in her first trimester. She's six weeks pregnant. You should expect your bundle of joy to make a grand entrance sometime in mid-July." The doctor's voice sounded congratulatory.

Detria's hand flew up against her mouth and tears rushed forth like a bursting dam.

Stiles' eyes sparkled. He and Detria stood almost simultaneously and quickly hugged each other, and now both of them were crying. "Oh, God, thank you," Stiles said as he rocked his wife in his arms. "Thank you, so much," he looked up fully into her eyes. Tears flowed.

Detria's eyes were clouded with tears of happiness too. Dr. Henderson remained seated and allowed the couple to take in the joyous news. When they began to settle down, she patiently talked to them about some of the things Detria could experience during her pregnancy. She also discussed the importance of taking prenatal vitamins, low stress level, maintaining a healthy diet, and keeping her doctor's appointments.

Stiles and Detria walked with arms interlocked out of the clinic and to their car. Once they got inside the car, Stiles leaned over, gently placed his hand behind Detria's head, and nudged her toward him until their lips met. When he pulled away, the two of them looked at each other. Stiles kept his hand in place and massaged Detria's neck.

"The joy of being able to conceive, to actually form another human being, and knowing that tiny human being is growing inside of the woman that I love with my life is beyond comprehension." Stiles' eyes began to shine like glass. He rubbed his face against

Detria's. Their tears meshed. "For us to be blessed like this is a good gift, a perfect gift."

Detria agreed. "Yes, it is. I couldn't be happier than at this moment."

Stiles removed his hand from behind Detria's neck and leaned back enough to touch her burgeoning belly, and this time he tilted his head backward and chuckled.

"Don't you think we need to stop making out and get going?" Detria suggested and smiled while she spoke.

"I think so," Stiles said. He drove out of the parking garage. On the way home, they chatted about the various instructions the doctor had given them. Stiles made a stop at the nearby pharmacy to drop off the prenatal prescription. While they sat in the drive-thru lane, Detria pulled out her phone and tapped a key.

"Mom, it's me," Detria said and giggled in the phone. Stiles couldn't help but shake his head. "Mom, we're pregnant," she screamed into the phone. "Stiles and I are pregnant."

"Good afternoon," the voice courteously said through the microphone. "How may I help you?"

Detria whispered into the phone while Stiles handled the business at the pharmacy window, but her excitement was still evident as she wiggled in her seat. Stiles answered the clerk and placed the prescription in the chute, and within minutes they continued their drive home.

"Okay, Mom, I'll see you later. Bye now." Detria leaned her head against the headrest, exhaled, and then smiled again. "Sweetheart, my life is absolutely ideal. I can't wait to get home," she chattered. "Now that it's official I have a list of people I want to call and share the news with."

Stiles grabbed her hand and kneaded it. "Well, there goes our time together."

"Oh, now don't be like that. You know you're my sweetie," Detria crooned as she leaned over and nipped Stiles on the earlobe.

"Don't you start nuthin'" His eyes roved over his wife and the mother-to-be before he focused back on his driving. The smile on their faces appeared like a forever photo.

When they arrived home, they told Pastor the news. He was ecstatic to know he would be a grandfather.

"I sure wish that your mother was here for this. As soon as she heard the news, she would be out of that door and getting her shop on for her new grandchild," Pastor remarked.

"I believe that," Detria answered.

"Congratulations to the both of you," said Pastor. "Son." He focused his pinkish eyes on Stiles. "God is more than good, isn't He?"

Stiles answered in what could only be described as a Spirit-filled voice. "Pastor, He is; God is an awesome God. I'm going to be a poppa." Stiles jumped up and down in place like he was on fire. "Oh, thank you, Lord."

8

"Other things may change us, but we start and end with family." Anthony Brandt

Detria enjoyed all the attention from home, and family. Co-workers often remarked about her flawless, glowing complexion that before pregnancy was subject to acne breakouts. Stiles miraculously still managed both of his ministries, as he called them—full-time pastor and college professor. And he waited on his wife hand and foot without missing a beat.

Detria was blessed not to experience some of the signs of pregnancy such as nausea and weirded-out cravings. She changed her routine at the insistence of her husband. He did not want Detria working full time, then spending time at home cooking meals for him and Pastor. Detria used Fridays after work to prepare a week's worth of her delicious meals. She carefully transferred them into freezer and microwaveable containers that she labeled to show which meal was inside and the date she prepared it.

"Thank God, it's Friday," a fellow nutritionist, Jill, remarked to Detria while the two of them completed their weekly share of paperwork, reports, and folder notes.

"I know that's right. I'm going to go home and chill tonight."

"Oh, you mean after you stop off at the gym," Jill said in a teasing tone, "and after cooking your meals for the week? That's something you'll probably never stop doing."

"You'd be surprised," replied Detria.

"What do you mean? Pastor Graham must have finally laid down the law. Did he use that scripture in the Bible about wives submitting to their husbands?" The rail thin, petite brunette opened her green eyes wide, cocked her head, then laughed and pointed at Detria.

"Girl, noooo," Detria replied and smiled. "I incorporated a detour, if you can believe it. I left a pot roast slow-cooking in the crock pot. All I have to do is add steamed vegetables to it. Stiles can pop a potato in the microwave if he wants one, and so can Pastor. They'll eat on that two or three days, girl. They're not picky at all because they know I'm not standing for them eating junk food. They couldn't care less whether I cooked meals for a week or a meal every day, they just know they're going to get a meal."

"Girl, that's so funny," Jill said and then giggled.

"And guess what else is going to amaze you?"

Jill stood still as a bronzed statue. She looked at Detria and half-smiled. "Do I even dare say yes?"

"That's up to you because I'm going to tell you anyway." Detria's mouth turned upward. "I'm not going to work out today, but believe me I do plan on getting up early in the morning and going to the gym. It's actually good for me and the baby as long as I don't bench press or do any ab crunches."

"Lucky you. I cook every day except Sunday. The hubby takes me and the kids out to dinner after church. My workout consists of walking six miles a day, which I'm addicted to doing."

"I don't know what you mean by lucky me because we both do the same thing, except you choose to prepare a meal a day, and, until now, I found it better for me to cook enough meals on one evening for a week. To be honest, you and I both know that cooking at home is better than going out all the time to buy fast food that clogs our arteries and hearts."

Detria returned her focus to the last piece of paperwork, which lay in front of her. She proceeded to complete it. After she added a stack of papers and folders to her outbox for her administrative assistant, Detria gathered her personal belongings in preparation of going home. Detria pushed back from the desk and stood. She noticed for the umpteenth time how much her belly had grown, and she patted it lightly.

"Yep, that baby is going to be huge. Are you sure you're only coming up on ten weeks? You look like you just blew up overnight. And I'm not saying that to be mean," Jill said as her eyes shifted to Detria's pouch.

"It's the truth. I'm amazed myself at how big I'm getting, and I'm not quite three months."

"Well, I'm right behind you."

Detria jerked her head. "What? You're pregnant again?"

"What? Nooo. Are you crazy? I was talking about going home right behind you. Four kids are definitely enough for me, but if it was up to that husband of mine, I'd be like the woman on television who has almost two dozen kids. Can you imagine that?" Jill commented like she'd just stumbled upon a remarkable discovery.

Detria giggled then picked up her laptop and purse. "Have a good weekend."

"You too." Jill placed a folder in her outbox. "See you Monday."

"Okay," replied Detria.

Detria hummed almost all the way home. When she arrived, she sat outside in her car for a few minutes and praised God. She was overjoyed each time she thought of the blessed life she lived. She finally got out of the car. She turned the key to the front door and stepped inside.

"Pastor," she called. "I'm home. That pot roast smells so good, umph," Detria continued. "Pastor? Are you here?" Detria shrugged her shoulders and started toward Pastor's wing. As she walked down the hall she stopped in her tracks when she thought she heard something. She called Pastor's name again, but this time she moved more cautiously. She heard it again. It sounded like someone groaning in pain. She rushed farther down the hall until she arrived at the open door of Pastor's bedroom. She scanned the room in seconds. When she didn't see him, she rushed to his bathroom. Her hand flew up to her mouth when she saw Pastor lying on the ceramic tiled floor.

"Oh, my gosh." She rushed to his side and went down to her knees. A small pool of blood was next to the left side of his head. "Pastor, Pastor," she called. She used all of her strength to try to help him up, but failed. "Oh, my God. What happened to you?" she asked.

"I... fe...ll." He forced out the words. His eyes closed.

Detria reached inside her purse, which she hadn't bothered to lay down. She pulled out her phone and called 911. She was instructed to remain on the line until paramedics arrived. She lifted Pastor's head and immediately her hand turned red from the blood that poured from an open head wound.

"Pastor, the ambulance is on its way." He appeared to be losing consciousness. She wanted to keep him conscious until help arrived, so she pleaded with him to hang on. "I've got you. Just hold on. Please."

Detria heard the blare of the ambulance and ended the call. She could tell from the sound that it was about to turn on her street. Within seconds, they were outside the house. "Pastor, I've got to let them in. I'll be right back. Just hold on," she said again and sprung up off her knees and bolted to the door.

The paramedics hurried inside the house and examined Pastor's injuries. They exchanged conversation with one another while Detria retrieved the phone and called Stiles.

"They're placing him on the stretcher now," she said into the phone. She felt a wave of nausea, and her mouth grew unusually moist when she saw the bloody bandage wrapped around Pastor's head. His eyes were closed, and she heard him mumbling incoherently. Her head began to spin, and between the sight of Pastor and hearing the frightened voice of her husband on the phone, Detria almost lost control. She closed her eyes and sucked in a deep breath. "Stiles, I'm going to the hospital with Pastor. I'll meet you there," she told him.

Stiles told her to stay home, and he would meet the ambulance at the hospital. Detria wanted to be with Pastor and Stiles, but she was far too nervous and shaken so she agreed to remain at home. Stiles promised that he would call her when he arrived at the hospital.

"Fine, but I've got to hang up. They're taking Pastor outside to the ambulance," she said.

Detria informed the paramedics which hospital to transport him to, then stood in the doorway and watched them until they closed the ambulance doors and drove off with the siren blaring.

Stiles remained true to his word. He called Detria outside the hospital soon after he was told that Pastor was being examined. "Are you all right?" he asked Detria.

"I'm good," Detria answered barely above a whisper.

His voice unsteady, Stiles responded, "Baby, I need to get back inside. If you can, will you call Deacon Jones for me and tell him what's going on?"

"You know I will. Now get back inside so you won't miss seeing the doctor. And call me back as soon as you can. I love you, and I'm praying for Pastor."

"I love you too." Stiles ended the call and dashed back inside the hospital emergency room. An hour-plus later, he heard his name being called and looked up to see Pastor's doctor walking toward him. Stiles hopped up. In three long strides, he was next to the doctor. "How is he, doctor? How is my father?"

The gray-haired doctor's thick, gray eyebrows drew together. He wrapped his arms one inside the other. "Reverend Graham had another stroke. This isn't good because it's the third one in, what, less than three years?"

"Yeah, that's right." Stiles looked nervous. "Why does he keep having these strokes?"

"Tests revealed that he has cerebrovascular disease, or what we call CVD. It's one of the reasons for the multiple strokes in addition to his hypertension."

Stiles stared, speechless.

"In order to maintain brain function," the doctor explained, "it is necessary to have an uninterrupted blood supply. Because of his history of high blood pressure, he was at an increased risk of developing CVD. The head injury he sustained resulted in a mild concussion. At the time the stroke occurred, I surmise that he lost his balance, fell, and then hit his head."

"Is he going to be all right? Is he conscious? What can you do about this CVD?"

"I have him on a blood clotting medication for now as a precaution until I can perform an MRI on him."

Stiles extended his hand toward the doctor,

who reciprocated, and they shook hands. "Thank you, doctor. Can I see him?" asked Stiles.

"Because of the concussion, he hasn't regained full consciousness, but he is stable for now. You can see him shortly. I'll have the nurse take you to the critical care unit waiting room. You can wait there until they give you the okay to see him. But when you see him, please don't try to talk to him. He needs to rest for now. We're going to keep a watch on him for the next twenty-four hours. I'm sure I don't have to tell you that it's not good for him to have had so many strokes in such a short span of time. Strokes can be extremely debilitating, especially to someone like your father who has already had multiple strokes. We'll have to wait and see how much this one affects him. Now, if you'll excuse me, I've got to leave. But I won't be far away if your father needs me."

"Thank you," Stiles told the doctor again, his mouth tight and grim. He rubbed his hand over his head, and then sat down to wait for the nurse.

Stiles followed the nurse to CCU, a place he'd spent many days and some nights far too many times. He'd been inside these walls with his mother, with Pastor, and with numerous members of Holy Rock. There were times when it drained Stiles, but he had learned long ago from watching Pastor visit sick people, witness to the lost, counsel people, and bury the dead that all of it was part of the call on his life. Stiles had no doubt that God had called and anointed him to do the same and more. That meant there was no turning back.

A short while later, the nurse told him he could enter Pastor's room. He positioned his frame next to Pastor's bed. For a few moments, he stared at Pastor's lightly wrinkled face, watching him sleep. The machines that surrounded Pastor's bed, the needles that penetrated his skin, the brace around his neck, the white bandage with blood as red as an apple forming on his forehead—they all pushed Stiles into prayer. Without thinking, he laid his hand on Pastor's chest, and the presence of the Holy Spirit filled the room. Stiles cried out to the God that the man lying on the bed had introduced him to when he was a child.

He remained with his father until he heard someone walk up behind him and rest a hand on his shoulder. Stiles turned slightly and saw his friend, Deacon Jones. They embraced.

"How is he?" Deacon Jones asked.

"He's stable. But the doctor said he had another stroke. And he injured his head after apparently falling, so he has a concussion. But God is in the healing business. Pastor has been through some storms, but he has remained steadfast."

"You got that right. God's favor is evident. Why don't we step outside for a minute or two? The nurse told me I was allowed only a few minutes because I'm not immediate family," Deacon Jones said. Stiles replied by turning fully around until he faced the door. "How are you?" Deacon Jones asked as soon as they stepped into the corridor.

"Me? I'm fine. Just worried about Detria. I hate to leave her alone. I mean, my woman is pregnant. And I know she's worried about Pastor too. I don't want her to be home alone."

"Did you say pregnant?" Jones patted Stiles on the back.

"Yeah, you heard me right." Stiles smiled, temporarily dismissing the emotional pain he was in.

"When were you planning on telling me?"

"I actually planned on telling you about it today, but all of this happened." Stiles did his signature head rub.

"Man, you know I got you," Deacon Jones said in a tone that clearly defined Stiles as not only his pastor, but also his homeboy. "Crystal and the baby are with Detria. When I told her what happened, she started getting the baby's bag ready and told me she was going to go and sit with Detria. She said that she knew you would be worried sick about her. She was right."

"Man, that's a relief. Crystal knows she's a blessing. You found a good wife in her, you know."

"Believe me, I know that for sure. She's my boo. And my little Angel, having her in our lives is simply remarkable," he exclaimed with intense pleasure. "But you and Detria will experience it firsthand. I tell you there's nothing like being a parent. Look, is there anything I can get you?" Deacon Jones asked.

"Naw, I'm fine. Tired, but I'm still blessed." Stiles leaned against the wall.

"Some of the sisters and brothers from the sick and shut-in ministry should be here soon, so don't even think about spending the night at this hospital. You already know that no one at Holy Rock will stand for that. They're going to camp out in the CCU waiting room. They've already worked out shifts so that there will always be someone here representing the family. That means after you talk to the doctor and see Pastor again, I'm ordering you to go home to your wife. Someone will call if anything changes."

"I'm not going to fight you on this, Jones. I've got to learn to accept God's blessings and favor. I do need to be with Detria. I know Pastor wouldn't want it any other way. Plus, I know he's in good hands." Stiles looked upward.

When the first shift arrived at CCU, Stiles went back to see Pastor again and checked with the nurse to make sure they had his phone numbers in case they needed to reach him. The nurse assured him that Pastor's condition had not changed, but she promised to call him immediately if it did. Stiles told her that members from his church were in the waiting area and would be all night.

Stiles walked out the door and went back to the CCU waiting room. He lingered for only moments to tell the members who had arrived how grateful he was for their loyalty. Deacon Jones followed him, and they walked slowly along the hospital corridor.

"I called Crystal," Jones told Stiles. "Did you remember there was a phone in the waiting room?"

"Yeah, but there was someone on it every time I was in there."

"Well, I caught it at the right time then."

"What'd she say Detria was doing?" Stiles asked with concern.

"Lying down resting. Crystal said Detria ate, played with Angel for a while, and then Crystal ordered the mother of your child to take a nap. I told Crystal you were with Pastor again but that you would be home just as soon as you stepped on this side of the door." Deacon Jones' voice was firm and final.

Stiles cocked his head. "Hold up. Don't forget I'm the one—" Stiles pointed to himself— "who used to beat your butt way back when."

"Man, please. In your dreams. You betta be glad you're in pastor mode rather than friend." Deacon Jones laughed with a wave of his hand. "For real, go on home and get you some rest."

Stiles stepped up to Deacon Jones and gave him dap. "God bless you, man. But I'll still give you a workout that'll make you go home crying to Crystal. Now, I'm out of here. Call me if you hear anything."

"You know I will."

On his way home, Stiles prayed silently for several minutes for Pastor. After praying, he pushed the cell phone button on the steering wheel. He heard the home phone ringing. Detria answered.

"Hi, sweetheart. I was expecting Crystal to answer. She told Jones that you were lying down resting."

"I was . . . I am," Detria said in a dull voice. "When Crystal told me you would be home shortly, I told her she could leave. Angel was beginning to get fussy. I think she wanted to be at home in her own familiar space."

"Makes sense. Well, I'm on my way. You need anything while I'm out?"

"No, honey. Thanks for asking. I told Crystal about our baby news. She's thrilled. I had a good time with her and Angel. I got some practice being a mother by feeding and changing Angel. It was fun." Detria's voice rose slightly.

"When Deacon Jones told me Crystal volunteered to keep you company, I knew you would love that. How do you feel? You sure you don't need me to stop to bring you something? Do you have any weird cravings?" Stiles laughed.

Detria laughed into the phone. "No cravings yet, but it's sweet of you to ask. I'm fine. All I want is you. Okay?"

"Umm, I like the sound of that."

"Bad boy," Detria said. "How is Pastor doing?"

"I'll tell you when I get there. I'll see you in a few minutes." Stiles made a kissing sound into the phone. "I love you, girl."

"Me too," Detria said and ended the call.

9

"Children are the hands by which we take hold of heaven." Henry Ward Beecher

Pastor remained in the hospital for eight days. His head bandage had been replaced with a small dressing that covered the five staples in the back of his head. He was weak and required the use of a wheelchair. Much like the first stroke, this one left him with paralysis in his left leg and limited use of his right hand. His speech was unintelligible. It would more than likely be a long way to recuperation, and it wasn't known how much mobility and speech he would regain.

Detria arrived home from work, and once inside she went to Pastor's bedroom. He was propped up by two memory foam pillows. The television was tuned to TBN, and Pastor's head was turned away from her when she entered into the room.

"Pastor," Detria called quietly as she walked to the other side of the bed so she could see his face. His eyes were closed. Detria walked back around and pulled the cover up to Pastor's chest. She kissed him on his cheek and walked out of the room.

She went upstairs and saw Stiles lying across their bed. He was also asleep. She smiled, then proceeded to get out of her work clothes. The rustling in the bedroom must have been what caused Stiles to turn over slowly and open his eyes.

"You're home. How was your day?" Stiles said with slurred speech, having just woken up.

"It was good." Detria hung up her pantsuit. Clad in her underwear, she walked over to the side of the bed, and Stiles pulled her down next to him. He leaned in to kiss Detria.

"Yummy," he said and kissed her again. He massaged her tummy in a circular motion.

"That feels good. I'm sure the baby loves it. And you can't stop there. One of the rules of pregnancy is that husband-slash-father must massage baby and mommy every day." Detria kissed Stiles this time.

"Is that right? Well, I think that's something that can be easily arranged," he said without so much as putting up a rebuttal. "You sound tired. Do you think you need to be working full-time? And then you're still going to the gym every morning. That's one of the things I don't like about your job—having an on-site fitness center. I know there are some women who have to be on bed rest during their pregnancies." Stiles' voice rang with genuine concern for Detria and their unborn child.

"I am tired, but I don't need to be on bed rest. And exercise will not hurt the baby, Stiles, so there's no need to worry about that. I'm fine. There's a lot going on inside my body. I have a little one growing inside me. I'm not going to be ready to do a cheerleading routine every day, and even when I wasn't pregnant, there were days I'd come home exhausted," she said with light sarcasm.

"I know. Listen, I can arrange for someone from the sick and shut-in ministry to come and sit with Pastor tonight since I have the preacher's meeting. I already made dinner, so I don't want you to think about doing anything but resting."

"I told you, I'm fine. I'll see to Pastor. There's no need to call anyone. And thank you for cooking dinner. You're such a good husband, and you're going to be an even better father."

"Thank you, honey. I'm sure going to try. With God's help, we're both going to be good parents."

Detria and Stiles ate dinner together. Afterward, he left for church. He kissed Detria good-bye. "I'll see you later," he said.

After Stiles left, Detria began to feel a gnawing emptiness. The house was eerily quiet and being alone with Pastor was no longer the same. She missed the long conversations the two of them used to have. Now all she could do was sit and talk to him, or read to him as Pastor laid in his bed with gaping eyes like he was longing to speak. Tonight, while Stiles was at his meeting, Detria pulled out Pastor's favorite Bible, one that he said had been in his possession since he was thirteen years old. She laid the Bible on the bed and began to flip through its well-worn pages. She started to read when she came to the first chapter of Psalm.

"Blessed is the man that walketh not in the counsel of the ungodly, nor standeth in the way of sinners, nor sitteth in the seat of the scornful . . . oomph." Detria grabbed the lower part of her back and leaned forward in the bedroom chair where she sat next to Pastor's bed. A sharp, unfamiliar pain almost cut off her breath. "Whew." She released a concentrated breath. Detria prayed for the intense pain in her back to stop. "Ewww. Have mercy, Lord." A tear rolled down her cheek and landed on her shirt.

Pastor's eyes bulged, almost like they were about to pop out of their sockets.

"Everything's fine, Pastor." Detria patted his hand to reassure him. She breathed in and out, then straightened up, focused back on the Bible, and started reading the remaining words of the chapter. Detria rubbed her belly in a circular motion, something that had become routine for her. Only this time, she felt a rush of momentary fear run through her mind. The negative thoughts dissipated the more she read. ". . . But his delight is in the law of the Lord; and in His law doth he meditate day and night."

Detria called Pastor's name, but he didn't budge. She heard his labored breathing and was relieved that he had fallen asleep. She left the Bible open on the bed. When she stood, she felt another sharp pain, one that wasn't as bad as the first, but it stunned her to stillness. "Lord, what's wrong?" she asked out loud as she dashed from Pastor's room. She went to the kitchen, poured a glass of cold grape juice, and took off upstairs to her room to lie down. Detria thought that perhaps she was beginning to feel all the aches, pains, morning sickness, night sickness, and numerous other things most pregnant women experience. She pulled off her clothes and changed into her jammies. No sexy nightie tonight. She wanted to dive in the bed and pass out.

The phone rang. Detria fastened the last button on her jammie top, glanced at the caller ID, and answered the phone in a tone that sounded somewhat edgy. "Hey, sis."

"Ew wee. Don't you sound like one pregnant chick? What are you doing?" asked Brooke.

"About to go to bed. I've been nauseated, my back is killing me, and now I'm cramping like I'm on my cycle, only it's a thousand times worse," Detria complained. She took a swallow from her glass of juice, then sat it on a coaster on top of her bedside table. She followed up by turning the cover back, propping up her pillow, and easing down on the bed.

"Is Stiles at home?" asked Brooke.

"No, it's just me and Pastor. I just finished reading the Bible to him. It was while I was reading to him that the back pain started. Maybe I sat in the same position too long. I don't know. But Stiles ought to be here shortly."

"You haven't been spotting or anything, have you?" asked Brooke.

"No, nothing like that. I keep thinking about seeing all of that blood pouring from Pastor and the way it smelled. Ugh. Every time I think about it too long, it seems like I get nauseated."

"Oh, yeah, that's definitely the preggies,"

Brooke replied, giggling into the phone.

"You are one crazy woman," Detria said. She was glad to be talking to Brooke. It took her mind off worrying about her baby. The pain had calmed down tremendously.

The sisters talked until Brooke succumbed to the cries of her children, whom Detria heard continually making a ruckus in the background. "You go on and take care of your brood. I'll talk to you tomorrow."

"Okay, but promise me if you're still feeling bad when Stiles gets home that you'll tell him. This is not the time to keep anything about your pregnancy a secret. You might need to call Dr. Henderson in the morning and tell her what's going on too."

"Okay, okay. I will. Buh-bye."

"Bye," Brooke replied, and they ended the call. Detria pulled one layer of bedcovering up to her waist and eased down into the bed. The feel of the memory-foam mattress and pillow soothed her. She closed her eyes and prayed a short prayer out loud. " . . . Amen," she said.

Detria was awakened by the feel of Stiles lying next to her. His warm breath against her ear caused her to stir, and she turned over and melted in his embrace.

"Go back to sleep," he whispered into her ear and followed it up with a kiss on her ear lobe.

"What time is it? Is Pastor still asleep?" Detria was slightly confused.

"It's almost ten, and Pastor is asleep. I checked on him when I came in."

"Did you eat?" Detria asked.

"Remember, I ate before I left for church."

"But you didn't eat much," she said groggily. "There's still some food left."

"Will you stop worrying about me? I'm fine," Stiles repeated. "I'm the one who needs to be asking you how you are."

Before Detria could respond, a sharp cramp hit her like a jack hammer. She screamed out loud and dug her fingers into Stiles' shoulder, almost breaking skin. Stiles jumped up.

"Detria, what is it?" Detria tried to sit up, but another sharp pain knocked her back flat on the bed. "I'm calling 911," he said and grabbed the phone.

"No, I'll be fine. I've been having these cramps on and off for the past few hours. I was going to tell you. I'll call Dr. Henderson in the morning."

"No, I don't think so." He threw down the phone. "I'm taking you to the hospital right now. I don't think this is normal. Look at you." He returned to the bed and sat down. You're sweating, and your face is flushed." He scanned her body with his worried eyes. "Oh, no," he said as he witnessed the blood stains on the sheets.

Detria followed his eyes. She screamed in hysteria when she saw the fresh blood. She felt between her legs, and her hand returned bloody. Stiles ran to the bathroom, got a towel and placed it between her legs. Next, he searched frantically for Detria's jacket, put it on her, and scooped her up in his arms. He hurried down the stairs and out to the car. He didn't think about Pastor or anything else. His mind was on his wife and unborn child.

"Pastor," Detria said as Stiles sped down the street.

"Don't worry about Pastor. I'll call the Stewarts; they have an emergency key to the house, remember? I'll ask them to come over and check on him."

"O. . . kay." Detria was petrified. She couldn't lose this baby. She cried as another cutting pain hit her. She bit her lip and held the towel between her legs. The car came to a screeching halt, and before she realized that Stiles had arrived at the hospital, he had made it to her side of the car, opened the door, and lifted her out. He dashed off into the entrance to the emergency room and was met by several medical attendants. He hurriedly told them what was going on. A stretcher appeared from nowhere, and someone removed Detria from Stiles' arms and placed her on it. They took her back to one of the rooms with Stiles in tow.

"Sir, please," a nurse stopped Stiles just as he was about to go inside the room with Detria. "Please wait in the waiting area. We need to examine your wife."

Stiles was alarmed, but he followed the nurse's instructions. When he made it to the waiting room, he immediately gathered his composure long enough to find his neighbors' phone number in his cell phone. He needed them to go to his house and stay with Pastor. He used the wall phone in the waiting room to call and tell them what was going on and that they should be able to get inside because he'd failed to let down the garage door nor had he locked the entry door to the house in his haste. The neighbor readily agreed to go to the house to check on Pastor. Next, he called Deacon Jones, who told him that he was on his way to the hospital.

"No, don't come. I'll call you back and let you know how she's doing. I just wanted you to know what was going on. Pray, man. Please, pray for Detria and our baby," Stiles pleaded with Deacon Jones.

"Man, you know you don't have to ask. That's already done."

"Thank you, man. Look, I've got to go. I need to see what's going on with my wife." Stiles hung up the phone, and then nervously paced the glossy floor of the ER room that was surprisingly almost empty of patients. He didn't have to wait too long before the same nurse who'd escorted him to the waiting room returned and retrieved him.

"How is my wife?" he immediately asked.

"Your wife is fine, sir." The nurse stopped walking. "Dr. Henderson was called, and she should be coming to talk to you in just a few minutes. But for now, I want you to have a seat in this area." The nurse guided him to a small room that had a sign that said WAITING ROOM on it.

"The doctor will be here shortly," the nurse said again before she left. Stiles went in and sat down alone, anxious to hear what Dr. Henderson had to say.

"Oh, thank you, God," Stiles said and lifted his head up toward the ceiling with both hands clasping his face. "Thank you, Lord." This time tears trickled down his face. He was still crying with joy when Dr. Henderson walked in and closed the door behind her.

Stiles bounced up from the cloth waiting room chair. "How is she? I want to see Detria," he exclaimed to Dr. Henderson.

"Hold on. You'll see her, but I need to talk to you first. Please, sit back down, Mr. Graham."

Stiles obeyed. "Mrs. Graham is going to be fine. She's resting right now. But, unfortunately, she lost the baby."

Stiles broke down in tears. His body shook as emotional pain wracked his body. Dr. Henderson reached over and patted him on his back. "I'm so sorry, Mr. Graham." She passed him several tissues that were in a box on the table next to him.

"What happened?" Stiles sniffed, wiped his nose, and focused his red eyes on Dr. Henderson. "Are you saying something was wrong with our child?"

"What I'm saying is that something wasn't right with the baby's chromosomes. It could be that the miscarriage was caused by a defective sperm cell or egg. Sometimes abnormal stress can contribute to it as well, but the good news is that your wife is going to recover quickly, and I don't see why the two of you can't work on having another child." The doctor's voice was sympathetic and full of concern.

"Does Detria know?"

"Yes. We had to tell her because she had to have a procedure called a dilation and curettage. In laymen's terms, a D and C. It means we opened her cervix and removed remaining tissue to prevent infection and excessive bleeding. She'll probably continue to have some bleeding for a few days and maybe light abdominal cramps. And I'm sure I don't have to tell you that she's distraught. I'm so sorry for the both of you."

His expression serious, his eyes dark with sadness, Stiles spoke rather softly. "Dr. Henderson, I'm praying for God to give me the strength to hold up after I see her. She . . . we wanted this baby so badly. But God is able. I know He doesn't place more on us than we can bear."

"Do you need a few minutes alone? Or are you ready to see your wife?"

"I need to see my wife." Stiles stood up just as Dr. Henderson opened the door.

"Follow me. She's in exam room seven. They walked the short distance and paused before they entered the room.

Stiles walked inside the room, and Detria looked at him with swollen, water-filled eyes. Her hair was frazzled. Her beautiful smile was gone, only to be replaced with sadness. He walked over to her, and she reached for him. Stiles gathered her into his arms, and the two of them cried over their loss. He rubbed Detria's hair over and over again, mouthing words of comfort to her.

"I'm sorry, Stiles. I'm sorry that I lost our baby. Oh, God, I'm so sorry. It's all my fault."

"Shhh. It's not your fault. Don't even think such a thing. We never know why things happen, Detria. But we do know that God is still in control. And it's going to be all right."

He regained some of his composure so he could help his wife and give her the support she needed. "It wasn't your fault, okay? Please believe that."

Dr. Henderson chose that moment to step up and talk to the couple. "Detria, your husband is right. The loss of your baby is not your fault. It's not your husband's fault. It's not anyone's fault. Like I explained to Mr. Graham, it had to do with chromosomal abnormality. It happens in fifteen to twenty percent of women in their twenties like you. We don't know why, but it does. But the important thing is that you're going to be fine, and I know this is a terrible loss, but remember there is no reason why you and your husband can't get pregnant again."

Detria acted aloof, like she didn't hear anything Dr. Henderson said. Instead, she looked in the eyes of her husband pleadingly. "I want to go home. Can you just take me home?" she asked him.

Stiles shifted his eyes toward Dr. Henderson.

"Detria, I'd like you to stay here for observation for a couple more hours. I want to make sure you don't experience any complications. You need to empty your bladder before you'll be allowed to be discharged. Are you still in pain?"

"A little," Detria mumbled.

"I'll get the nurse to give you something for your pain, and I'll write a prescription for something too. If there isn't anything else for now, I'll leave the two of you alone. I'm sure you want to spend some quiet time together. And please know how sorry I am." Dr. Henderson touched Detria's arm and rubbed it lightly. "I want to see you in my office in four weeks."

Dr. Henderson focused on Stiles. "Will you please make sure you call the office and make a follow-up appointment? But if she continues to bleed, have severe pains, anything that you aren't sure about, please call me right away and get into the office to see me. Understood?" Dr. Henderson asked.

"Thank you, doctor. I'll make sure she's taken care of. I'll call tomorrow and schedule that appointment," Stiles said in a shaky voice.

"Good." Dr. Henderson left the room, leaving the couple to start their journey through grief.

10

"Love me when I least deserve it, because that's when I really need it." Swedish Proverb

Stiles couldn't shake the odd feelings he had started to develop toward Detria. It had been more than a month since her miscarriage. The empathy he had toward Detria had disappeared, and the scary thing for Stiles was he didn't know why. He wasn't a dummy by any means. He understood the medical reasons Dr. Henderson gave them for losing the baby, but the more he thought about it, the more his frustration grew. He tried to fight against it through prayer, yet he couldn't shake his mounting disdain toward his wife.

Losing a child, even though it was fairly early in the pregnancy, still had a horrific effect on Stiles. He talked with Deacon Jones about his reservations. Detria had taken on too much after her pregnancy had been confirmed. Stiles tried to get her to slow down some, but she'd refused. She was adamant about maintaining her daily routine as much as possible. He admitted that she had reduced the time she spent working out, but she still had a busy, full-time job, which she followed by coming home to look after Pastor and keeping up with the 101 other things she had on her daily agenda. Maybe she hadn't wanted a baby as badly as she said she did. If she had, why didn't she take better care of herself? The more Stiles thought about the loss, the more he felt distant from his wife. He hadn't touched her intimately since the miscarriage, and he had no desire to do so.

Stiles found his thoughts drifting toward his relationship with his ex-wife. Rena had betrayed him, and it was hard for him to forgive her. In fact, it was so hard that he was driven to divorce her. The issues between him and Detria were a far cry from the problems in his marriage to Rena, but there was still a feeling of betrayal that tried to settle in Stiles' heart. Why couldn't Detria have taken better care of herself? She didn't have to work out almost every day. He'd told her to be careful because of her pregnancy. But no, she insisted that she was not bringing harm to their child. But there was some reason for her losing the baby, and he could not swallow Dr. Henderson's explanation.

Stiles shifted nervously in his chair and used his shoulder to hold the phone to his ear. Jones was on the other end. "You know something, Jones. This is killing me, man. Detria hasn't said anything about losing the baby or anything. She's acting like everything is kosher when I'm dying inside."

"Look, Stiles. Women are different creatures. You know that. She may be walking around acting like everything is hunky dory, but inside she's probably hurting more than you can imagine. The thing is, man, you have to be there for her. Both of you need each other for support."

"I hear what you're saying." Stiles reached to the side of his desk and pulled the string to the wood plantation blinds until they opened slightly. He watched the pall of smoke that trailed behind the city bus as it passed by the church. "Thanks for listening, Jones. I guess it's going to take time for things to get normal again."

"Time and prayer. Crystal and I are going to intercede for you and Detria. You're going to overcome this. But you're grieving—both of you are. People handle grief in different ways," Deacon Jones said.

"Yeah. Well, look. I've got to go. I have a class this evening. We'll talk later," Stiles told Jones.

"Sure. Take care of yourself. And, Stiles, remember it's not Detria's fault. It's no one's fault that y'all lost the baby. God is sovereign, and He knows exactly what He's doing."

"You're right. I gotta go."

After his evening class, Stiles hung around his office at school and read some of the essays the students submitted. He made it home around nine-thirty. When he walked inside the house, it was eerily quiet. He went to Pastor's room. Pastor was lying back on his hospital bed with his head turned toward the television screen.

"Pastor, you awake?" Stiles asked as he walked around to see Pastor's face.

Pastor's sunken eyes had dark circles around them. He was frail. This stroke had done some major damage. Pastor was once a distinguished-looking man. Now, he looked like a badly preserved fifty-eight-year-old man with arms that looked like they'd been squeezed from a toothpaste tube. He hated to see his father like this. "Hello, Pastor," Stiles said when he saw his father's eyes open. "How are you doing?"

"Ugh," Pastor moaned. Stiles grasped his thin hand. He felt Pastor's gentle squeeze.

"Is there anything you need?" Stiles asked his father. He further examined him by pulling the covers back to make sure Pastor's bedding was fresh and clean. He had no doubt that it would be because Detria took excellent care of Pastor. It was Detria who practically saved his life. Who knows what would have happened had she not been home when Pastor had his stroke. Stiles checked Pastor's legs and feet, and then slowly pulled the cover back up over him. He made conversation with Pastor, and Pastor's eyes seemed to focus intently on Stiles as he spoke.

"Good evening," Detria said as she walked in the room. Her arms were folded against her rib cage.

"Hi. How are you?" Stiles asked like he was a schoolboy who'd accidentally bumped into the most popular girl at school.

"Good. Is everything all right with Pastor?" she asked Stiles and walked further into the room.

Stiles answered, "Yeah, I think he's okay. I just got here and came to check on him before I headed upstairs."

Detria moved closer. Pastor's eyes locked

with hers as she stood at the foot of his bed. He groaned like he was in pain. "Pastor, what's wrong?" Stiles asked. "Are you uncomfortable? Let me see what I can do to get you settled in a little better. Stiles began to straighten the bed sheets underneath Pastor. Pastor didn't take his eyes off Detria. "You want Detria to do this?" Stiles inquired when he noticed Pastor's piercing stare. Stiles looked over his shoulder at his wife. "Looks like you've got him spoiled. I don't think he wants me to do this. He keeps looking at you." Stiles smiled.

"Let me see." Detria walked past Stiles and finished what he'd started. Pastor groaned several more times while Detria tugged on the sheets and gently eased Pastor onto his side to make sure he was dry. Incontinence and basically a loss of bowel control was another result of the stroke. "How is that?" Detria asked and moved out of the way.

Pastor's eyes seemed to relax somewhat, and Stiles moved next to him. He patted his father on the shoulder, and then leaned his long body down to kiss Pastor on his forehead.

"It's about time for your night meds," Detria said. Stiles watched her as she walked into Pastor's bathroom. When she returned, she held a blue pill holder in her hand and a paper cup filled with water. She passed it to Stiles.

Stiles lifted his father's head, removed the pills, and placed them in Pastor's opened mouth. Detria passed the cup of water to Stiles next. Stiles proceeded to hold the cup so that Pastor could drink from it. "Try to drink all of it, Pastor," Stiles told him. Pastor did.

He squeezed the paper cup in his hand. "Would you like me and Detria to pray with you before we go upstairs?"

Pastor nodded. Stiles reached for his wife's soft hand. A flicker of desire surged through him. He was glad. He didn't want to neglect Detria. She was a good woman, and she proved it every day by the way she took care of his father. It was good to have help during the hours both of them were away at work, but Detria had stepped in and provided Pastor's care from the time she came home from work until bedtime. The strength of heart she displayed toward him and his father was one that he didn't want to take for granted.

Stiles bowed his head and prayed for God's healing power to shower down upon his bedridden father. He prayed until he felt his spirit growing full like he'd inhaled a mighty rush of wind. He squeezed Detria's hand as he prayed harder and harder. When he finished, his eyes were teary, and he sounded exhausted. Stiles looked at Pastor, whose eyes were also shining from the mist of tears that had formed in the corners of his eyes. Stiles let go of Detria's hand, which felt like it was trembling. He reached for a tissue next to Pastor's bed, and then proceeded to wipe the tears from Pastor's eyes.

"I love you, Pastor," he said. "Rest well." Stiles took hold of Detria's hand again.

"G'night, Pastor," Detria said. "I have the monitor on, so if you need something, anything, all you have to do is make a sound, and Stiles or I will be here, like always."

Stiles led the way and Detria turned off the light switch. They left Pastor's room.

"You want something to eat?" she asked Stiles as they neared the kitchen.

"I think I'll have a glass of juice and a sandwich. But you go on upstairs. I know you're tired too. It's not easy working a full-time job and then coming home every evening to take care of your ailing father-in-law. I can't tell you how grateful I am for you," Stiles said.

This time Detria took the lead. She walked in the kitchen with Stiles still holding on to her hand. "Sit down," she ordered. "It won't take me but a minute to make you a sandwich."

Stiles released her hand and did as he was told. How could he not be enthralled by such a wonderful woman? What was his problem? He was baffled. He watched her as she prepared one of his favorite sandwiches—roast turkey and ham with all the fixings. She poured him an eight ounce glass of grape juice, placed the sandwich on a plate along with some potato chips, and sat it before him.

"Aren't you going to have something?" he asked, then took a bite of his sandwich.

"No, I ate leftovers, and you know it's too late for me." Detria sat in the chair across from Stiles. "What's happening?" she asked.

Stiles stopped chewing. He focused on Detria. She looked at him with something fragile in her eyes. "What are you talking about?"

"I'm talking about us, Stiles. You—" she pointed at him—"and me." Detria pointed at herself. "Since I lost the baby, you've barely held a full conversation with me. And God knows that you haven't touched me, held me. Need I go on?"

Stiles was momentarily speechless. He searched the recesses of his mind. He wanted to tell her that he believed she could have done something, though what that something was, he didn't know.

"Look, things have been tough for both of us. I mean, losing a child is something neither of us has experienced before. I—" Stiles rubbed his forehead back and forth. "I think about my mother's death, and now Pastor is in there suffering, and on top of all of that, for you to—"

"For me to what?" Detria's tone registered a subtle change. "For me to have a miscarriage? Are you blaming me for losing the baby?" She suddenly bounced up from the chair. "That's what this is all about, isn't it?" she cried out.

"I didn't say that. You said that. So don't make this out to be about me," he snapped back. He balled up his napkin and threw it on top of his half-eaten sandwich and chips. "I'm done." He got up, bolted out of the kitchen, and bounded up the stairs.

Detria hung her head, and tears rushed from her eyes and dropped on the table like giant pellets of rain. She rocked herself like a baby. "It's all your fault," she cried. "It's your fault."

Suddenly, she heard Pastor groaning rather loudly. Immediately, Detria raced to his room. Stiles was at her side by the time she turned on Pastor's bedroom light.

"What's wrong? Pastor, are you all right?"

113

asked Stiles.

Detria shooed Stiles away. "Go back to doing whatever it was you were doing. I'll take care of Pastor," Detria said. She rolled her eyes at Stiles. He turned and practically stormed out of the room. Detria remained still until she heard his footsteps fade and the door to their bedroom close.

In two quick steps she was stationed by Pastor's side. She watched the whites of his eyes flash in warranted fear. She turned off the monitor, and then yanked the cover off of him. With a tightly balled fist she punched him with full force on the side of his thigh.

"If I hadn't been trying to help you, I wouldn't have lost my baby," she said to him. Her voice dripped with venomous hatred toward Pastor. "I convinced your son to take you into our home. I took care of you and your wife before she died. And this is how you repay me? You repay me by causing me to lose my baby? Trying to pick you up, to save your life. And what do I get out of it?" She punched him again.

Pastor's mouth opened, his face was reduced to a bevy of frowns. His eyes loomed large and fierce with pain. Detria placed her hand over his mouth and leaned in so close to Pastor's face that there was barely an inch between them. "Don't you dare try to call out to your precious son. Did you know that he blames me for the loss of my child? Me," she mumbled with so much force her face turned a shade darker. "I hate you for what you've done," she mouthed and punched him again.

She pulled away from him and saw tears streaming down the side of his face. With one hand she wiped them away forcefully, and then jerked the covers back up around his neck. She pinched her lower lip with her perfect, even teeth. "Sleep on that." She whirled around and walked out of the room.

Detria slammed their bedroom door as she walked in and jarred Stiles from his sleep. He twisted around in the bed and propped his body on one elbow. The sight of his bare chest snapped Detria's attention from the pain that nestled in her heart.

"Sorry," she said.

"How is Pastor?"

Short of patience, she responded, "He's fine."

Detria despised the act she'd committed against Pastor, a man who had been nothing but kind and loving toward her. The first time she struck him had been a week after she lost the baby. The quickness with which it had occurred shocked her to the core. It started when Pastor lost control of his bowel. It frustrated Detria because she had just come inside the house and said good-bye to the home health aide who sat with Pastor during the day. She went into Pastor's room and, as usual, spoke to him and sat beside his bed to tell him all about her day. He seemed to enjoy it, and Detria believed that she detected a sparkle in his eyes whenever she spent time with him. Within minutes of telling Pastor about something that went on at the office, she smelled a foul odor, and there was no mistaking what had happened.

"Why didn't you point to the bedpan, Pastor? It's right next to you." Detria got up and went to Pastor's chest of drawers to get a clean Depend pad and bed covering. The stench was so overbearing when she opened the adult pamper that she had to step back. "This is ridiculous, Pastor. I know you can't talk, but you can use your hand to point. My goodness, this is too much to have to do." The more she tried to wash his soiled body, the more Detria's anger mounted. She finally got him cleaned up, only to have him lose control again. A look of disbelief, mixed with rage and frustration consumed her to the point where she began to yell and scream at Pastor. She jerked his body and used as much force as she could when she cleaned him for the second time. Before she pulled the cover up, she punched him on his thigh. "Next time, point to the bedpan," she yelled. "You're no baby. Remember, you made me lose mine, and I'll be darned if I treat you like one."

Detria was physically and emotionally ill after that first time. She'd heard about elderly abuse, but she reasoned that wasn't what happened with Pastor. She'd merely lost her temper. It was hard to change mess off a full-grown man. Added to that was the fact that Stiles had been totally acting weird. He had dismissed her advances toward him, and they hadn't made love even though Dr. Henderson had given Detria the go-ahead to do so. Stiles managed to either be asleep by the time she went to bed or in his study. There were other times when he came home later than he normally did, and the sweet kisses of love and affection, and the whatnots had disappeared. How could life change at the drop of a dime? How could her once picture-perfect dream life be turning into a nightmare of sorts? How had she changed from a God-fearing woman to a person who abused a helpless, defenseless human being?

"What are you just standing there for?" Stiles asked, which caused Detria to snap back to reality.

"Nothing. I was just thinking about something." She proceeded to pull off her robe and climb in the bed next to her husband. She pulled up the covers, and then leaned over to kiss Stiles. This time he didn't move, but Detria believed it was only because she kissed him on his cheek.

"G'night," he said and turned on his side with his back toward her.

"I love you," Detria told him.

"Me too," he answered.

Detria massaged her sore knuckles. It was a cruel reminder of the person she tried so hard not to be.

11

"We come to love not by finding a perfect person, but by learning to see an imperfect person perfectly." Sam Keen

Stiles lay in the bed. Normally, before he went to sleep, he and Detria would spend time talking, cuddling, and basking in their love for each other. The kiss she'd given him made him feel somewhat guilty. He turned away from her and silently prayed.

Lord, I need your strength to help me to make things right. I ask that you help me to love my wife the way a husband ought to. I need you to deliver me from the grip of grief that has me neglecting what I am to do toward her.

Stiles turned toward Detria and began to caress her hair. "Detria, I love you," he told her. Detria remained flat on her back. No words escaped her, and Stiles continued to verbalize what God had placed in his heart to share. "I'm sorry for not being here for you. Losing our baby was hard for me, but what I failed to see is that it was probably even harder for you. I've been behaving like a fool."

He eased closer to Detria. She turned her head toward Stiles and their eyes met. When his warm lips touched hers, a light sound of passion rose from her, and Stiles allowed his love to resurface. "I'm sorry, so sorry," he whispered into her ear. His hands roamed over her softness. "Please forgive me," he pleaded.

"There's nothing to forgive. It was all my fault," she said.

"Don't think like that."

"I can't help it. I didn't want to lose our baby." She began crying. "I wanted our baby so badly."

"Shhh, I know you did. And none of this is your fault. I'm going to be here for you like I should have been in the beginning." Before Detria could say anything, Stiles' lips seized hers once more, and he began to really kiss her. There was no turning back. He was where he needed to be, and where he wanted to be. The sensation of her body took Stiles to new heights as it answered his in return.

"I've missed you. I've missed you so much," Detria said as they lay in each other's arms, spent from their lovemaking.

"I've missed you too," Stiles responded. He continued to hold on to her and plant light kisses over her body. They fell asleep in each other's embrace.

The following morning, Detria and Stiles got up at their usual time. Stiles spent part of his time getting ready for the day ahead by continuing his affection toward Detria. They dressed and went downstairs. The sun hadn't quite come up all the way.

Detria darted to Pastor's room. Guilt ate away at her like acid on skin. "Good morning, Pastor," she said and turned on the light in his room. She stood next to his bed and looked at him. His eyes opened, and Detria saw fear and pain. "Why did you make me do that last night? You know I wouldn't hurt you for anything in the world, but you just seem to do everything you can to make me angry."

Pastor groaned, but his eyes did not leave Detria's face.

"You don't have to worry. I promise not to hurt you again. Stiles has actually forgiven me. And don't worry, I didn't tell him that it was your fault that I lost our child. You should be grateful for that." Detria walked away and returned with a washbowl filled with warm, soapy water. She washed Pastor's face with soft strokes. "It's hard taking care of you every day, Pastor, knowing you caused my miscarriage. But I'm trying. I want to be a good daughter-in-law, and you've made it difficult for me, but don't worry, I'm going to keep praying for God to help me."

Pastor opened his mouth like he was trying to speak, but only the familiar groans escaped.

Stiles walked in the room. "Good morning, Pastor." Following his routine, he walked over, took hold of Pastor's hand and squeezed it lightly as he leaned forward to kiss him on his forehead. "You know, today is rather special. Not only is it a day that the Lord has made, but it's the first day of your therapy. Two occupational therapists are coming today. They'll be here two hours for three days a week. And if you're thinking about the home health aide, there's no need to. She'll still be here every day. Stiles stood erect. "I think you like her." Stiles chuckled. He turned to Detria. "Honey, what do you have to say about Pastor and what's the aide's name again?"

"Ms. Tammy is the one I think Pastor's a tad bit sweet on," Detria continued, joking where Stiles had left off. "The other one is Ms. Edna. I think she's a little too timid for Pastor." This time round, Detria giggled.

Stiles wrapped his arm around her waist. The doorbell rang. "That should be Ms. Tammy, so we're going to get out of here, Pastor."

"Honey, I'll get the door. Buh-bye, Pastor."

Stiles said a morning prayer for his father. When he finished, he turned to leave the room and saw Ms. Tammy standing in the doorway lifting her bowed head. She must have come while Stiles was praying.

"Good morning, Ms. Tammy."

"Morning, Pastor Stiles. How's my favorite patient doing this morning?" she asked as she and Stiles shook hands.

"I think he's better now." Stiles turned and winked at Pastor. "Oh, Ms. Tammy, I told Pastor that the occupational therapist will be starting today." Stiles looked down at his watch. "I believe they'll be here around ten o'clock. They might call before they come."

Ms. Tammy waved her hand. "The office already called and told me. Ten is right. You have a good day, Rev. Graham."

"You too, Ms. Tammy. Bye, Pastor." Stiles met Detria in the kitchen. She was sitting at the table with a bagel and a glass of orange juice. She had a banana, a bagel, and a cup of hot green tea ready and waiting for Stiles.

For Detria, last night had been the answer to her prayers. Stiles had forgiven her. The past weeks had been unbearable. And Pastor hadn't made it any better. There was just no getting around the fact that he'd been responsible for her loss and for Stiles' lack of attention. But after spending last night in the arms of her husband, she had her desires met, and she fulfilled his needs. The next thing on Detria's prayer list was to correct the wrong she'd done by convincing Stiles to allow Pastor to move in with them. It had been the worst decision of her life, and now she was living to regret it every day. There was no getting around it. In the beginning of their marriage, Detria couldn't have been happier, but progressively things had gotten worse, and she had to find a way to fix it.

Fixing it meant getting Pastor into a long-term care facility where he could have round-the-clock care and be out of her hair. She'd played the Good Samaritan for far too long. Furthermore, she hadn't banked on Pastor having another stroke. For goodness' sake, he was young on the age scale, and here he was having a third stroke. No way was she planning on spending her life wiping some grown man's butt. Cooking for him and checking on him was one thing, but she had bitten off more than she cared to chew.

"Stiles, I'm on my way to the gym, and then I'm headed to the office, so if you need me you can reach me on my cell."

Stiles took a couple of sips of the piping hot green tea. "Ahhh," he said. "Okay, baby, have a good workout—not that you need to work out."

"I really don't, especially after last night. I

122

think we both had a good workout," she said. Her lips turned upward, and she swayed seductively before she pulled his blue and white striped tie and kissed him. "I should be home no later than four-thirty today."

"I'll meet you here. We can go to Bible study together. That is, if you plan on going."

Detria had missed several Bible studies since the miscarriage. She wanted to avoid the pity stares and comments she was sure to get from Holy Rock. She'd already been bombarded with cards and phone calls. She loved the attention, but she didn't like the reason for it. Now that Stiles had come alive again, Detria felt that maybe her life could finally get back on track.

"Yes, I think I'll go tonight, so will you let Ms. Tammy know that we'll need someone to sit with Pastor this evening."

"Sure thing. Have a good day, baby. I love you," Stiles told her and walked her to the door.

"Me too," she answered.

With his cup in one hand, Stiles hugged Detria with the other and watched until she got in the car, opened the garage, and drove out of sight. Stiles remained in the entryway for a few seconds with an indelible smile plastered across his handsome face. "Thank you, God, for answered prayer."

He returned to the kitchen and completed his breakfast. Before he left the house, he returned upstairs to his study and spent a half hour meditating on the Word of God.

12

"Be who you are and say what you feel because those who mind don't matter and those who matter don't mind." Dr. Seuss

"How are things on the home front?" Brooke asked Detria. The sisters had talked earlier that morning and decided to meet for lunch. They sat at a table at the East End Grill. Detria picked over a garden salad while Brooke devoured her order of chicken wings and loaded baked potato.

"Actually, you have perfect timing," Detria replied.

"Perfect timing? Tell me about it," responded Brooke.

"Well, Stiles and I, we sort of. . . ." Detria couldn't stop grinning.

"Come on, tell me."

"We made up last night." Detria wiggled around in her chair.

"See, I told you that the two of you would be all right. Detria, that man loves you. And you have to understand that he was not the only one who suffered a loss. We all did. Now, maybe you think it wasn't the same magnitude as your grief and pain, but the truth of the matter is, we were all sorry about your miscarriage. And the good news is that now that things seem to be turning around for you and Stiles, this will strengthen your marriage.

Anytime you go through a trial or hardship as a couple and come out on the other side still together, sis, I'm telling you, it is a blessing. Do you know how many couples split over something not even as major as this?"

"Yeah, I know. And I'm so thankful that we made it. I love that man so much, Brooke. But I have come to one conclusion," Detria said.

"And? It is?"

"Pastor needs to be in a long-term care facility. I can't do it anymore, Brooke. I won't do it anymore. I mean, he needs round-the-clock care, and at first I thought I could do it, but that was before the miscarriage. If it wasn't for him, I would still be pregnant."

"What? Hold up, girl. How did you arrive at that conclusion?" Brooke placed a forkful of the baked potato in her mouth.

"I didn't tell Stiles or anyone about this before because there was too much going on. But I tried to lift Pastor when he had his stroke. You know I found him in the bathroom with his head busted, and so without thinking my first instinct was to try to get him up. I felt a strain in my belly and a sharp pain in my lower back, so that's when I had to give up and leave him on the floor until paramedics arrived. If it wasn't for him—" Detria felt a knot form in the base of her throat.

"Detria," Brooke saw the serious look on her sister's face. She reached across the table and embraced her hand. "Sis, don't do this to yourself or Pastor. I'm sure if you talk to Dr. Henderson, she'll tell you that this miscarriage was not your fault or Pastor's. It takes more than trying to lift someone off the floor, especially someone as lightweight as Pastor is, to cause a miscarriage. Please, don't carry around that weight."

"I keep telling myself that. But every time I look at that man now, I can't help but think about it. You know, what if?"

"Detria, you've got to pray. And I'm going to be praying for you too. The idea of putting Pastor in a long-term home might not be such a bad idea. I know he's only fifty-eight, but his body isn't fifty-eight. The man has been through a lot over a short period of time. And the type of care he needs should be done by professionals. So I agree with you on that."

Detria sighed and then placed some salad into her mouth. While chewing she said, "You are my favorite sister, you know that?"

"Yeah, rah, rah, rah." They both started laughing.

Later that evening, Stiles and Detria went to Bible study. Stiles preached from the book of St. John, chapter fourteen. "'Let not your heart be troubled.' . . . People, we have to learn how to lean and depend on Jesus. I know there are some difficult days for many of you. That's life. As soon as you get over one trial, there's another one waiting for you. As soon as you think everything is about to be good, something else bad comes along. But this life is not one that is free from trouble, people. We are not promised days of ease, without problems and situations. On the contrary, God says that we will endure various trials, but we are to be of good cheer because He has overcome the world. We have no reason to walk around with our heads hung low and our hearts heavy. When we find ourselves in a trying situation, that's the time to pick up the Word and begin to encourage yourself."

Bible study ended on a good note. Detria had always enjoyed the manner in which Stiles so easily broke down the Word of God. He had a knack for making it sound so simple. Detria closed her Bible, and began to mix and mingle with some of those in attendance who couldn't wait to give her a hug, ask how she was doing, and tell her how much they had been praying for her.

It was almost eight-thirty by the time they arrived home. Detria had made up in her mind that since things were better between her and Stiles, it was time to talk to him about Pastor. The time was even more perfect when they walked inside the house and met Ms. Edna retreating from the laundry room. She looked at both of them and shook her head.

"I don't know how to do nothing but come out and say it." Ms. Edna started talking nonstop. Every now and then her arms glided through the air like she was about to take off from a runway. "That man needs to be in one of those assisted living places. I'm telling you, the care he's getting here isn't enough. I been gone a week; had to take some time off work for myself, and I come back to this. Ms. Edna was much older than Pastor. Her thin frame was no match for her booming voice. She pushed back strands of gray hair that kept falling in her face with each word she spoke.

Something just ain't right—and I'm not about to get the blame for nothing. I don't know why no one else saw this. Must not been cleaning him up properly or something for them to miss it. But I tell y'all, you betta do something and do something now. This poor man ain't been looked after properly. I'm telling you—"

"Hold on, Ms. Edna." Detria swallowed hard. "I don't understand."

"What's going on? What brought on this outburst? Stiles asked the aide.

"Didn't you hear a word I said, young man?" Ms. Edna said.

"Yes, ma'am, but—" "But nothing," she interjected. "I'll tell you what brought this what you call outburst. I just had to change your father's soiled clothing three times. And I'm not talking about just urine. And come here, let me show you what I'm really worried about." She used her forefinger as a leader, and they followed her. "Look at this. I tell you, it's a crying shame," she said. "Some folks need to get a taste of their own medicine. Going around taking advantage of the sick. It ain't right." She pulled the cover back from Pastor.

Stiles' hand flew up to his forehead. He bent over like he'd been sucker punched in the stomach. "What happened to him? Did he fall? Why didn't you call 911?"

"Hold up. See, that's exactly what I'm talking about. I'm not going to be the one to get blamed for this. You and your wife know I just came back on duty today." Ms. Edna peered at Detria. Detria had turned a shade darker and looked like she was in shock. "I've already written up my report," said Ms. Edna, "and I've called my supervisor and left a message on his answering machine."

Stiles and Detria stood and looked at the large, black and purplish bruises on Pastor's thigh. It was so bad the skin was almost broken.

"I suggest you get him to a doctor right away. If he didn't fall, then I'm afraid to think that somebody did this on purpose."

"No, how could this have happened without any of knowing about it, or seeing it?" Stiles said. "Did you call Ms. Tammy and ask her about this?" asked Stiles.

Ms. Edna looked at him with eyes ablaze. "That woman wouldn't hurt a fly. And yes, I did call her. She don't know nothing about it. She said she must have been on the opposite side of the bruise when she changed him. I believe her, but then again, something happened to this poor soul," Ms. Edna ranted and shook her head from side to side. "Lord, have mercy."

Detria remained still and speechless. When she finally spoke up, her voice was calm and steady. "Pastor probably fell out of the bed. I know I've caught him trying to get up by himself when he knows he can't," she said in a less-than-tender voice. "Pastor, you're going to have to behave yourself. You don't want to be strapped down to the bed, do you?" she asked him.

Pastor groaned.

"There'll be no such thing, Pastor." Stiles slightly recoiled. "Pastor, did you fall?"

Pastor's eyes seemed to shift away from his

son's. "Did one of the aides do this to you? The therapists? My God, tell me what happened to you," Stiles yelled.

"Well, I'm getting out of here. And I'm going to be truthful with you," the nurse said. "I won't come back. I can't afford to be part of this kind of thing. Much as I love working here, I won't put myself in the midst of wrong. My supervisor should be calling y'all in the morning. They're probably going to want to do a full-scale investigation on this. Good night."

Detria walked the woman to the door. "I am so sorry about this," Detria told her. "But I'm glad you told my husband that he should consider a nursing facility."

"He should. Honey, that man has a long recovery ahead of him. And with bruises like that on his leg, I'm afraid to tell you what I think has been happening to him. But I know I've seen abuse of elderly people too many times. Now I know he isn't considered old, but he might as well be because he can't talk. He can barely move, and he sure can't care for himself. Honey, you're going to wear yourself down if you try to do what a full-time staff needs to be doing. I stand behind my suggestion that he be placed where he'll have access to help twenty-four hours a day, seven days a week."

Detria opened the front door. "Thank you, Ms. Edna. Maybe my husband will take heed to what you said." Detria placed her forehead in her hand. "I hate to see my father-in-law like that. He just lost his wife less than two years ago, and that really took something out of him.

I thought if he came and lived with us, things would get better, but then he had the stroke. This is his third one."

"Child, you're a good one. I know you want to please your husband. But ain't nothing but tension and division coming in this home if that poor man has to stay here. You can't do it alone, and neither can your husband. And he's the pastor of a church too. Come on, that's like having two or three jobs."

"You really do understand, don't you?" Detria said.

"Yes, I sure do. I've been in this line of work for seventeen years, and I've seen it all. Well, I need to get home. I wish y'all luck. Good night, Mrs. Graham."

"Good night, Ms. Edna. Be careful," Detria said, and then closed the door. After she locked the door, she returned to Pastor's room where Stiles had remained. She walked up behind him, wrapped her arms around his waist, and laid her head against his back.

Stiles remained silent for several moments. "How could this have happened?" He rested his head inside his hands. His strained voice was a dead giveaway that he was crying. "Who would want to do such a terrible thing to another human being?" Stiles reached over and grabbed hold of Pastor's trembling hand. "Pastor, I'm so sorry this happened."

Detria moved around next to Stiles. "Honey, we don't know what happened yet. Wait until he sees his doctor. I'll call first thing tomorrow morning and see about getting him in, even if they have to work us in. But I think Pastor has been trying to get out of bed by himself and probably fell as a result. I don't believe anyone would intentionally hurt him, let alone strike him."

Stiles looked at her with dazed eyes. "There is no way Pastor tried to get out of the bed, fell, and then manage to pull himself up and get back in the bed. He'd have even worse injuries than he has already, and they wouldn't be concentrated in one area of his body. These bruises are in a place we wouldn't normally see when he has on his clothing. I mean, other than the aides who come in here, you're the only one who cleans and changes his soiled clothing." Stiles shook his head and bit his bottom lip. "I swear, and Lord forgive me for swearing, but I'm not going to rest until I find out what happened to you, Pastor." Stiles' voice rang with tenderness as he looked down on his father. He turned swiftly, and in a pained voice he directed his question toward Detria. "Which one of them is so evil and sick-minded that they've been beating my father?"

Detria tried to conceal her nervousness. Was she evil? Sick is what Stiles called the person. Lord, maybe he's right. Maybe I am evil. But then again, what about how this man ruined my life? I lost my child because of Pastor. "Is there anything I can get you? Some cocoa, tea, anything?" Detria asked in an effort to redirect Stiles' thoughts, if only for a moment. "Honey," she rubbed him up and down along his back. "We'll get to the bottom of this. I know we will."

The following morning, Stiles' suspicions

had been confirmed. Pastor's doctor was highly concerned after he examined and x-rayed Pastor. He didn't hesitate to share his displeasure with Stiles and Detria.

"I don't like this at all. His injuries are definitely not from a fall," the doctor explained. "First of all, Pastor Graham doesn't have the strength to get up out of his bed without substantial assistance. And if he did, I believe he more than likely would have sustained more serious, multiple injuries rather than a concentrated injury. The X-ray showed heavy bruising. Nothing is broken. But the bruises on his thigh should have been reported by whoever takes care of him. Seeing that nothing has been done until now to help him, it's my professional opinion that someone has been abusing your father." The doctor raised both hands and shrugged. "It's sad, but it's true."

Stiles stood abruptly and rubbed his hand back and forth over his head of black hair. "Doctor, how is he doing? Is the injury bad?" Stiles asked. Detria remained seated and quiet.

"He'll be all right, if that's what you're asking. But he's been taking some hard licks, that's for sure. Some of the bruising looks like it happened weeks ago. There's another area that's a fresh bruise. I think I'd like to admit him to the hospital just to keep watch over him for the next twenty-four hours. I'm going to start him on some intravenous antibiotics to ward off infection plus some pain medication. He can barely move that left leg now because of the pain and stiffness. This doesn't help his condition at all."

"My Lord," Stiles said. "I don't know what to say."

The doctor remained quiet, but peeked over his glasses at Stiles and then toward Detria.

"I'm stunned," Detria remarked.

"Mr. and Mrs. Graham, it's my duty to report this to Adult Protective Services. I also need the name and contact information of the home health agency that provides services for your father. They need to be made aware of this as well. I'm sure they'll want to do an investigation."

"Sure. No problem," Stiles said. "Detria, do you have the name and number with you?"

"Yes. It's in my cell phone." Detria retrieved her phone from her purse and began to scroll through it. "Do you have something I can write the information on?" she questioned the doctor.

"Yes." He pulled a notepad and a pen from his white jacket. Stiles reached for it and passed it to her.

"Thank you." Detria walked over to the small table in the examination room and began to write. When she finished, she passed everything to the doctor.

The doctor focused his attention back on Pastor. "Pastor Graham, we're going to send you to the hospital. Just for overnight observation, okay?" Pastor nodded his head slightly. "Can you tell me if someone's been hitting on you?"

Pastor didn't budge. Stiles walked over to the examination table. "Pastor, tell me. Who did this to you?" he pleaded.

Pastor groaned, but no intelligible words came forth.

Detria walked up. "Pastor, you have to tell us what happened. Can you write it down for us?"

Pastor stared at her; then he looked at Stiles.

"Look, don't worry about it right now. The hospital ambulance will be here any minute to transport you. I'll stop by later tonight to see you," the doctor told him. "Mr. Graham, we'll be in touch. And I think you need to act on this pretty quickly to find out what's going on. Unfortunately, elderly abuse is rising. It makes for a sad day when I see this kind of maltreatment against another human being."

"No doubt. Thank you again, doctor." Stiles and the doctor shook hands. Detria remained still and quiet.

The ambulance transported Pastor to the hospital, and Stiles and Detria trailed behind.

"Detria, you haven't noticed those bruises on Pastor?"

Detria sighed heavily. "No, well, I mean, I may have seen them, but I didn't think it was from someone beating on him, for goodness's sakes. He took a pretty bad fall when he had the stroke. He was banged up pretty badly then, so I thought they were residuals of his fall."

"Detria, that was two months ago." Stiles hit his hand on the steering wheel. It was seldom that Detria saw Stiles angry. "You should have said something."

"Oh, so now this is my fault? Is that what

you're saying? Look, I know you're upset. I am too, but do not make this out to be my fault. I hate that he's bruised and battered just as much as you do. I can't take this much more."

Stiles jerked his head and looked over at Detria. She appeared to be almost hugging the passenger door. "Take what?" he yelled. "I ask you a simple question, and you get all worked up. My father has been beaten. Do you understand that? It had to be one of the caregivers who did this to him. He can't talk, so I'm going to talk for him. If you have a problem with that, then tough."

Detria folded her arms and turned away from Stiles' glare. "You need to watch where you're going before you hit somebody," she told him as she looked out the window.

"Don't worry about that. I've got this. What I don't get is your sudden attitude."

"I don't have an attitude. I just don't like the fact that you're insinuating that I should have seen the bruises on Pastor and immediately known what happened. I'm a nutritionist, not a nurse or doctor," she snapped.

Stiles turned into the hospital parking garage. His BlackBerry rang while he was driving around the garage in search of an available parking space. "Hello," he said. He remained quiet for several moments. "Hold on, please. I need to write this down." He pulled into a parking space and turned off his ignition. He reached for a piece of paper in his console and an ink pen, then began to write down what the person on the other end told him. "Thank you, so much. I'll be there as soon as I can."

"I'm going to check on my father, and then I have to head to Dyersburg Regional Medical Center. That was one of the members from Francesca's church," he said to Detria.

Detria opened the door and got out of the car. "What's going on? Something wrong with Francesca?"

"She was rushed to the hospital earlier today."

"What happened?"

"The man on the phone said she had been complaining about flu-like symptoms for the past few days. He went to her apartment to take her something to eat. He said when he got there, she was still complaining about feeling weak and feverish. While he was there, she fainted, and that's when he called 911. She was admitted to the hospital."

Stiles walked toward the hospital entrance, and Detria tried to keep up with his fast pace.

"Hold up, will you?" she told him.

Stiles stopped and waited for her to catch up. "Look, I don't mean to sound like I'm blaming you for anything. It's just that this thing with Pastor is getting to me. Now my sister is in intensive care? Lord." Stiles looked up toward the ever-darkening sky. "We need you, Father. We need you." He placed his arm around Detria's shoulder, and they walked inside the hospital. They stopped at the information desk and asked the receptionist to look up the number of the room where Pastor would be taken.

Stiles and Detria remained at Pastor's

bedside for the next half hour while nurses moved in and out of his hospital room. Once Stiles was assured that everything was being done to make Pastor comfortable, he prepared to leave the hospital and drive to Dyersburg.

"Pastor, I'll be back first thing tomorrow morning," Stiles told him. "Everything will be fine. I'll see to that. I'm going to find out who's been doing this to you? Do you hear me?"

Pastor didn't open his eyes nor did he respond. The pain medication the nurse gave him must have taken its effect quickly. Stiles heard Pastor's labored breathing when he leaned down to kiss him on his forehead. He gently rubbed his father's arm.

"Come on," he turned around and said to Detria, who was seated in one of the chairs in Pastor's room. "I need to get you back to the house," he whispered.

Detria stood and silently followed Stiles. When they were in the hallway, Detria remarked, "I'm going with you to see about Francesca."

"No, I need to go alone. There's no telling how long I'm going to be there because I don't know what's going on. It'll be better if one of us remained in Memphis to be here for Pastor."

Detria sighed. "I guess you raise a valid point. I hope Francesca is all right."

"Me too, Detria. Me too." He grabbed hold of Detria's hands, and they walked to the car.

The drive home was relatively quiet except for the sound of gospel music playing on the radio.

When Stiles pulled up in front of their

house, he leaned over and kissed Detria. "I'll call you as soon as I know something," he told her and pushed the remote to open the garage.

"You aren't going to come inside to at least get a sandwich and something to drink? It's been a long day."

"I know, but I'll be fine. I'll stop somewhere and grab a burger or something. I really need to get up there, so I don't want to waste any more time."

"Okay, have it your way. But call me, Stiles. Don't have me sitting here worried about you too," she emphasized.

"Don't worry. I'll call. G'night, baby. Try to get some rest. You have work tomorrow too, so I know you need to get a good night's sleep."

"Yeah, well, let me get inside." She got out of the car and disappeared behind the entryway to their home. Once behind the closed door and the safety of her home, Detria broke down. She leaned trembling against the door and slid down to the floor as she covered her face with her hands and sobbed. "What am I going to do? Oh, God, somebody help me, please."

13

"In time of sickness the soul collects itself anew." Latin Proverb

A forecasted thunderstorm slowed Stiles' road trip to Dyersburg Regional Medical Center. Giant pellets of rain and nickel-sized balls of hail pounded the car while lightening skipped across the sky. The sound of thunder reverberated through the air like a mortar round. Stiles drove through Ripley, Tennessee. The streets were almost vacant of other vehicles. The paved highway glistened like black diamonds, and the absence of lights on the road made the dark skies more pronounced.

Stiles tried to remain focused on the road, but the fierce thunderstorm and now the sound of his cell phone ringing, provided an unwanted distraction.

He pressed the talk button on his steering wheel. "Hello," Stiles said. The caller on the other end was Jones.

"Hey, why didn't you tell me what was going on, man? Detria called Crystal and told her about Pastor and Francesca. You know I would have made that trip with you."

"Yeah, I know it, man. But everything happened so quickly," Stiles said. "Now I'm in the middle of a bad thunderstorm. I'm about thirty minutes outside of Dyersburg, but with it storming as bad as it is, it's probably going to be closer to forty-five minutes, maybe even an hour, before I make it to the hospital."

"Do you know what's wrong with Francesca?" asked Jones.

"No, only that she fainted earlier today. When she was taken to the hospital, they admitted her." Stiles had never revealed to Jones that Francesca was HIV-positive. As far as Stiles knew, there weren't many people who did know. Another clap of thunder and a zigzagging flash of lightening rocked the car. "Whoa," Stiles yelled as he watched the bright display. "Look, just keep a check on Detria for me. I'll call you when I can. This storm isn't playing. I need to let you go, man. I need to concentrate."

"Okay. We'll be praying for you, Pastor Graham," said Jones as he switched to Stiles' pastoral tag.

"Thank you, I appreciate that. See ya." Stiles ended the call and put his full focus back on the highway.

At the Graham house, Detria had decided to call and tell Crystal about Pastor and Francesca both being admitted to the hospital. Crystal expressed her sorrow and offered to sit with her to keep her company, but Detria turned down the offer. She was far too jittery about the day's events. She finished her conversation with Crystal, and after taking a bath, she laid out her clothes for work the next morning. She wanted to call Stiles, especially when she saw the severe weather warning ticker scrolling across the bottom of the flat screen television. But after thinking about it for a moment, she decided against it. Her dilemma was serious. Stiles seemed really angry with her when she told him that she didn't know the seriousness of Pastor's bruises. How could she have been so stupid? What was she thinking? She lay across their bed and rested her head in the folds of her arms. Not only had she lost their child because of Pastor, now she felt like she stood on the verge of losing her husband if he ever found out that she was the reason Pastor was laying up in a hospital bed. She was an abuser. How could her life have changed so drastically and suddenly?

Detria jerked her head upward and spoke in an accusatory voice. "God, how can I be blamed for what happened to Pastor when he did what he did to me? He doesn't deserve to be alive when my baby is dead. I hate him for what he's done. It's all his fault." She flipped over on to her back. "If Stiles finds out, then I'll lose everything," she cried out. "And you—" she pointed a finger toward the sky—"you are the one who allowed this to happen." Like a child having a temper tantrum, Detria started screaming and punching the bed. "I can't take this. I have to do something. You have to do something," she continued to bellow.

She cried until her eyes puffed up and her throat ached. When the phone rang, she wanted to ignore it, but then she sat up and looked at the caller ID. It was Brooke. She reached for a tissue to wipe her snotty nose and tear-streaked face.

She swallowed hard and hoped she would sound like nothing was wrong. "Hey, what's up?"

"Nothing. I was waiting for you to call and let me know how your father-in-law was doing. I talked to Momma and Pops, and they said they hadn't heard anything either. How is he?"

"The doctor admitted him to the hospital, just for overnight. They gave him some intravenous antibiotics. He should be ready to come home some time tomorrow." Detria didn't know if she should disclose what the doctor said to Brooke or not. She chose not to go into detail.

"Well, how are you? You sound kinda out of it." Brooke almost always detected when something was wrong with Detria. Tonight was no different.

"There's nothing wrong. I guess I'm just a little worried about Stiles."

"What's wrong with Stiles?" asked Brooke.

"Oh," Detria placed her hand on her forehead. "Brooke, today has been one of those days. Stiles got a call from somebody in Newbern. Francesca was admitted to the hospital in Dyersburg. He's on his way up there."

"What happened to her?"

"I don't know. Whoever called didn't say, and if he did Stiles didn't tell me. I'm tired, Brooke. I'm really tired."

"Tired of what? Are you sick too?" The change in Brooke's voice registered concern for her sister.

"Nooo, it's nothing like that. I'm fine health-wise. It's just that I believe I'm getting too overwhelmed. Working, taking care of Stiles' father when I get home, and trying to be the perfect wife—all of it is overwhelming." Detria held back the tears. She tried to maintain the even flow of her voice so Brooke wouldn't be able to tell she was all choked up inside.

"The past few months have been hard. Extremely hard. You're trying to do all of these things, but you have to take some time for you, Detria. If you want to be a good wife, you have to be good to yourself. You already have a huge responsibility by being the first lady. That in itself is mind-boggling to me. I'm so inspired by your courage and tenacity. As for Pastor Graham, you can't do it all. You're not Mother Teresa, Detria. You need to talk to Stiles and tell him that Pastor is going to need round-the-clock care from professionals. You cannot do it any longer."

"Brooke, I know, but I promised before Stiles and I got married that I would help take care of Pastor the same way I helped them out when Mother Audrey was alive."

"The key words are helped out, Detria. You're doing more than helping out with his father. You're taking care of him by yourself from the time you get off work until the next morning when the aides return. I mean, Stiles is either at church or teaching his class at the university. I can't say I blame you for being a little overwhelmed. And then I hate to mention this, but I have to."

"What?" A knot formed in Detria's throat.

"You've lost a child, Detria. You haven't
allowed yourself to grieve. At least that's my
opinion. You don't talk about it to anyone. You
don't want anyone to talk about it with you.
Instead, you returned to work and went right
back to living like nothing happened. When is
the last time you and I have hung out? When
is the last time you've visited Momma and
Pops?"

Detria couldn't control herself this time.
She began to cry again. Tears dripped onto the
phone receiver. She used the crinkled piece of
tissue to wipe her running nose. "What does
hanging out with you and visiting Momma and
Pops have to do with any of this? And why
bring up the death of my baby—my precious
baby who I didn't have the chance to hold, not
one time?" Detria wailed into the phone. Her
chest heaved.

"Detria, let it out. You need to cry. You've
always tried to be strong. And you are. But
being strong doesn't mean that you cut off
your feelings and act like nothing bothers you.
Stress and holding things inside can lead to all
sorts of maladies. Sis, I love you," Brooke said.
"I want to see you happy. I want to see you and
Stiles happy like me and John. We've had our
ups and downs during our marriage, but I
know that I can count on him, and he knows
he can count on me. But the truth remains,
I'm not going to be able to say yes to everybody
all the time. You have to learn how to do the
same thing. Regardless of what you might
think, you are not a superwoman. Suffering in
silence will only hurt you and lead you to do

something you might regret."

Detria sniffled and wiped her nose again. "Yeah, I hear you, but it's so hard. And . . . and," she stuttered slightly, "I feel like Stiles blames me for his father's injury."

"Why would he blame you? You've been nothing but good and kind to his daddy. Girl, don't make me get riled up over here. I'll be like Tyler Perry—don't make a black woman take off her earrings."

Detria released a giggle through her sobs. "That's one of the reasons I love you. You're so crazy."

"I mean it. There's no way he can make this out to be your fault. And I know you better not be sitting over there believing that."

"You're right. And he's not. I guess I'm just in a sorrowful state right now, but I'll be okay."

"Promise?"

"I promise," Detria replied.

"Good. Call me again if you need to talk. Oh, and keep me posted about Francesca," said Brooke.

"I will. I'll talk to you tomorrow." Detria perched the phone back on its charger. "God," she said, "forgive me. Don't hold my actions against me. I'm sorry for yelling at you. I'm sorry for the pain and injury I've caused Pastor Graham." Slowly she picked up the remote from the night table, turned on the television, and balled up in a knot on the comfy bed. She surfed through the channels speedily until she saw one of her favorite fitness shows. She fixed her eyes on the woman exercising and talking. After fifteen minutes or so, her eyes grew heavy, and she could no longer fight the call of sleep.

14

*"It is not good for all our wishes to be filled;
through sickness we recognize the value of
health; through evil, the value of good; through
hunger, the value of food; through exertion, the
value of rest."* Dorothy Canfield

Stiles parked and grabbed an umbrella from the floor of the backseat. The rain hadn't let up at all. If anything, the storm had grown fiercer. He opened the car door and the umbrella, then ran until he made it to the covered hospital entrance. Shaking the water off the red and black, wide-brimmed umbrella, he closed it, shook his body like a wet dog, and proceeded to patient information. He was given directions to ICU.

Once Stiles arrived in the ICU area, he wasted no time inquiring about his sister. A nurse talked to him briefly and updated him on Francesca's health after seeing Stiles' name listed in Francesca's privacy file. Stiles listened carefully.

"Ms. Graham is resting comfortably. Her doctor will not be returning tonight, but she's in good hands," the nurse said.

"What's going on with her? Why is she in ICU?" asked Stiles as he stood with his arms wrapped like a pretzel.

"Your sister is having complications primarily due to her HIV diagnosis. Her immune system is severely damaged," the nurse practitioner continued to explain. "HIV has mutated and is more pathogenic."

"What does that mean in regard to my sister's overall health?"

"The doctor can explain it in more detail when you see him, but what I can tell you is that her T cells are being destroyed at a faster rate, so her body can't keep up with replacing the cells. I'm afraid she's been diagnosed with full-blown AIDS."

Stiles placed his hand over his mouth and let out a deep, long sigh. He leaned his head back. "God, no," he said. "How can this happen? There are people walking around every day with HIV who've yet to succumb to full-blown AIDS. Couldn't something have been done to prevent this?"

"Over time, Mr. Graham, it can happen. We are more knowledgeable about HIV and AIDS, but unfortunately there is nothing we can do to stop a person from acquiring AIDS. What your sister has is called an opportunistic infection. Opportunistic infections vary, but the one your sister has is called PCP. She's probably been feeling pretty bad for a while but may not have told anyone, including her doctor."

"Obviously, it's serious or she wouldn't be in ICU, but is it treatable?"

"It is. But it usually strikes children with HIV. It's treated with Septra or Bactrim. In Ms. Graham's case, her CD4 cell count is extremely low, and now that she has developed AIDS, the infection can be life-threatening."

"Is she conscious? Can I go in and see her?"

asked Stiles. He was visibly shaken but determined to pull himself together for the sake of his sister. It was bad enough that Pastor was lying in a hospital bed in Memphis, but to also have his sister in the grip of death was stifling for Stiles. He followed the nurse practitioner into the ICU area and on to a room filled with sterile clothing. She gave Stiles a mask, paper-made scrubs, and disposable shoe covers to put on before she allowed him to enter the patient area.

"Your sister doesn't need anything that can lead to more infections. She is quite vulnerable now. The practitioner outfitted herself as well, and they walked out of the ICU dressing area. She stopped in front of a door marked ICU3. The small window allowed Stiles to see inside the room before they entered. He saw the white sheets and the steel bed rails.

He walked inside the cold room. The force of the storm prevailed outside, and the ventilator made similar sounds inside. Stiles prayed within for God to give him strength to withstand seeing his sister in such a terrible condition.

"She may be asleep. We've kept her pretty sedated so she'll be able to rest and hopefully get some relief." The nurse's voice was low and calm. "She's on a ventilator to help with her breathing."

Stiles approached the bed. Francesca's eyes were closed. Seeing the tubes going down her throat, the IV needle planted in her arm, and the tubes leading from her nose almost made Stiles break down and cry. He used his godly resolve to remain steady.

"Hey there, sis." Francesca remained still except for the ventilator, which caused her chest cavity to go up and down. He took hold of her cold hand and gently massaged it. "You're giving me a scare, you know that? Is this your way of getting me to come up here to see you?" He said it in a joking manner, yet Francesca remained still. She looked like she was sleeping peacefully.

Stiles turned and looked at the nurse. "She probably doesn't hear you right now. If she did, she would probably open her eyes, but like I said, she's heavily sedated. I'll leave you alone with her. Since you're from out of town, you can stay with her a little longer, but then you'll be asked to leave until the next scheduled visiting hours.

"Thank you, uh—" Stiles looked at the name badge pinned on her chest—"Nurse Wilcox. You've been kind and patient. May God bless you."

"You're welcome. I'll be close by if you have further questions." She left the room.

Stiles planted his exhausted body in a chair parked next to Francesca's bed. He continued to hold her hand.

"Francesca, I love you. Everything is going to be all right. You're going to be all right." He kneaded her hand ever so tenderly. "Father, heal my sister. Do what people say is impossible, Father God. You said if we come to you believing we have already received what we ask for, it shall be done. I believe, Father. Do it, Lord Jesus."

Stiles bowed his head and sucked in his breath. The mask covering his nose and mouth took some getting used to, but he managed to talk to Francesca with greater ease as he became accustomed to the protective measures put in place for his sister. For the next twenty minutes, he sat beside her. He prayed out loud, talked out loud, and then prayed to himself.

The sound of the booming thunder reminded him of the awesome power of God. Stiles allowed his tears to fall, believing that God saw everyone and gathered every tear shed. His mind began to race, and soon he was transformed into a grieving man. He thought about the loss of his mother, the loss of his baby, and pastor's battle with sickness. He reflected on Detria and their marriage. Feelings of loneliness and despair fought to overpower him.

"Francesca, I'm going to step outside for a while so you can rest, okay? I'll be back at the next visitation." Stiles went into the ICU waiting room. He saw a familiar face. He recognized him as was one of the men who had come to Memphis with Francesca's group a few weeks prior. The slender, black-haired white man approached Stiles and immediately stretched his hand toward him.

"Hello, Pastor Graham. I'm Tim Swift. Everyone calls me Brother Tim. We met when our church group came to Memphis."

Stiles nodded in recognition. "Yes, I recall. Are you the one who called to tell me about my sister?"

"Yes, sir. I am."

"I want to thank you for doing that."

"How is she?" asked Brother Tim. "They won't let anyone in to see her unless they're with the immediate family." A riffle of wrinkles on his face marked his concern.

"She's heavily sedated and on a ventilator. They say she has some type of infection. It's pretty serious," explained Stiles. "Has she been complaining about not feeling well?"

"Not really, but I spend a lot of time with Francesca, and for the past couple of weeks she hasn't been herself. She tries to play things off, like she's invincible, but I'm learning how to see through her."

Stiles noticed the change in Brother Tim's facial expression when he spoke about Francesca. Stiles recognized the look of affection that replaced Tim's stress frowns.

"My sister is a pretty tough cookie." Stiles laughed.

"Yes. That she is," agreed Brother Tim. He changed the subject and began talking about other members of Francesca's church who were deeply concerned about her health and well-being. "Francesca is loved by everybody. Our pastor and several other members were here not long before you brought the storm in with you." This time it was Brother Tim who led in laughter.

"No, I can't take credit for that," replied Stiles.

"I know that's right. Anyway, our pastor prayed for Francesca's healing. She's really a special woman to me."

Stiles spoke up. "God knows what He's doing. I have to remind myself of that from time to time, especially during difficult circumstances like this. We don't always know the reasons God allows certain situations to occur in our lives, but one thing is for sure, whatever He allows He will eventually work out for our good. I mean, I could be angry and puffed up right now because both my sister and my father are in the hospital. On top of that, I don't know if Francesca told any of you, but my wife and I lost our first child through miscarriage not long ago. So much has been happening, but I try to remain strong in the Word and stay on my knees."

"I hear you. Prayer definitely changes things," added Brother Tim. And I had no idea about your father. I hope it's nothing serious," he added.

"Thank you for your concern," expressed Stiles.

Brother Tim stroked his goatee. "I don't' recall Francesca mentioning that her father was ill."

"That's because he was being admitting into the hospital around the same time you called about Francesca. I didn't have time to tell her."

"I understand."

"I hope you don't mind my frankness, and if you don't want to answer this question it's fine, but are you and my sister involved with each other?" Stiles wanted to know for his own sake. He didn't know whether Brother Tim was aware of Francesca's sexual orientation, but it was far too apparent that he had deep feelings for Francesca.

"We're friends. That's what she tells me, but she's well aware that I'd much rather take our friendship to another level. I've heard her testimony, so I know her life hasn't been a bed of roses. Neither has mine. God had to allow some unpleasant things to take place in my life before I recognized that He is the only one who could clean me up and make me a new creature. Since I turned my life over to God, I feel like I've been given a second chance. God has restored time for me and given me so much more than I've lost. I love Francesca, and I'm praying that if she's the woman for me, God will open her eyes to receive me as her mate one day."

"Whoa, I didn't know it was like that." Stiles smiled so big that all his front teeth showed. "Praise God, brother. I'll be in prayer about it."

"I appreciate that."

"How much longer are you going to hang around?" asked Stiles.

"I'm not on a time table. I want to make sure Francesca's out of the woods before I leave for the night," remarked Brother Tim. "I live in Dyersburg, so it's no problem for me if I have to be here all night. I can easily run to the house in time to get ready for work in the morning."

"I can't tell you how much I appreciate you, man. It's good to know that Francesca has someone in her life who is genuinely concerned about her and who loves her. She's a lucky woman."

"I'll be a blessed man if God grants me the

desire of my heart. That woman in there—" Brother Tim pointed toward the ICU area— "has a giant slice of my heart."

"I hear you. Well, if you don't mind, I'm going to go downstairs and make a few phone calls, one being to my better half. I want to give her an update on Francesca. I'll be back as soon as I can."

"Go ahead. I'll be here. If you'd let the nursing staff know that I'm in here on her behalf, I'd appreciate it."

"Sure. I'll tell them," Stiles said. He walked out of the waiting room and delivered the message to the nursing station about Brother Tim.

Stiles retrieved his BlackBerry from his side. He hit the number two on the phone, and it readily called his home phone.

"How is she?" asked Detria as soon as she picked up the phone.

"They say she has what is called an opportunistic infection, and she has AIDS now too. She's on a ventilator because the infection has caused serious problems with her lungs. They have her sedated, hoping that will allow her to rest and give her lungs time to heal."

"Oh, Stiles, I'm sorry to hear that."

"Me too. Have you checked on Pastor?"

Detria stuttered. "No, but I will when I finish talking to you. I've been resting, and then I talked to Brooke. I was going to call, but then you called. I'm sure he's fine. What time will you be heading home?"

"I don't know. I'm thinking that I might spend the night. I want to be sure she's out of the woods before I leave."

Detria sighed into the phone. "Are you sure that's all there is to it?"

Stiles' mouth curved downward and a deep crease formed between his eyes. "Detria, not now. My sister is in ICU, it's storming like crazy outside, my dad is in the hospital, and you still want to make this all about you? Please."

Detria couldn't seem to maintain her mild tone. "Look," she yelled into the phone. "I'm not making this about me. I was just asking you a simple question, but I guess you just answered it. Honestly, Stiles, you are a real piece of work, you know that?"

"I don't have time to argue with you, Detria. I thought I would call to give you an update on my sister and hopefully find out how my father is doing. But it seems like that wasn't such a good idea. I'll call you back if I decide to make the drive home later tonight.

Stiles didn't quite understand why Detria was aggravated so easily. The last couple of months had been tough on both of them. Well, at least they had been for him. If he had to give his two cents' worth, he would say that Detria didn't act like a woman who had miscarried her first child. Lately, she didn't act like his wife half the time because she was always so busy doing her thing. The gym had practically become her life. She refused to discuss the miscarriage with him and how it affected both of them. And when it came to Pastor, it was like she was perturbed by his presence in the house. She rarely read to him like she used to, and the only time Stiles noticed her going into Pastor's bedroom was when she had prepared food for him or needed to clean him up. Things around the house felt different. Where was the concerned, kind, giving woman he had married, the one Pastor adored? Stiles allowed his mind to drift to a place where he didn't want it to go. Could she have—? No, don't be ridiculous. He forced the dreadful thought out of his mind just as quickly as it had come.

15

"Affection is responsible for nine-tenths of whatever solid and durable happiness there is in our lives." C. S. Lewis

The week passed by swiftly for Stiles. Pastor was discharged from the hospital and admitted to Health South Rehabilitation Center for inpatient occupational and speech therapy. He was fortunate enough to have some of the same therapists who had worked with him after his previous two strokes, including the speech therapist. His health began to slowly improve, and there were few signs remaining of the physical abuse he had experienced.

Stiles talked to Detria about whether or not he should tell Pastor about Francesca. They both agreed that now was not the time. Stiles prayed that Francesca would continue to show signs of improvement before he broke the news to Pastor. Either way, Francesca's AIDS diagnosis was going to be tough for Pastor to hear.

Detria left work and struck out to the gym to start her rigorous, two-hour workout regimen. Her figure revealed a woman with not only curves, but also well-defined muscles. For Detria, working out was her stress reliever. She didn't want to tell Stiles, but not having Pastor to come home to every day had improved matters. She was able to let go of some of the rage that had built up inside of her. The guilt she felt for abusing Pastor was not rearing its ugly head as often. Her strained marital relationship seemed to be improving too. Detria rode with Stiles to visit Francesca once. The site of Francesca was almost too much for Detria to bear. Francesca had dropped a significant amount of weight in a small span of time, which caused her to look weak, thin, and sickly. She drifted in and out of sleep most of the time Detria and Stiles were there.

Detria thought Brother Tim was exactly as Stiles had described him—humorous, God-fearing, and one who did not hide his feelings for Francesca.

Detria was glad someone was interested in Stiles' sister. It wasn't every day that a person could look on another individual with love and not contempt, especially one with Francesca's past. Detria didn't condemn Francesca because of her sexual orientation and her past criminal history of petty thefts and assault; she was pulling for Francesca to turn her life around.

Detria moved from one piece of exercise equipment to the next. She laughed and talked with some of the other regular patrons. After an hour of strenuous workouts, she went to the lap pool and followed it with a stint in the steam room. She came out feeling the results of her daily regimen. Now she could go home and prepare a healthy meal for herself and Stiles—that is, if he was coming home in time for dinner.

Before she left the gym parking lot, Detria sat in her car and called Stiles to see what his agenda was for the remainder of the evening. After reaching his voice mail twice, she sent him a text message. She waited several minutes but received no reply. Detria shrugged her shoulders, started the car, and drove out of the parking lot at a faster speed than was legally allowed. She understood that at times Stiles would be unavailable because of his pastoral duties, but knowing that didn't keep her from getting frustrated. She felt isolated and alone. It was hard to know who she could trust outside of her family.

If First Lady Audrey were still alive, Detria believed things would be far better. First of all, Pastor wouldn't be living with them, and Audrey would make sure Stiles was putting in the time he should with his wife. But Audrey wasn't there with her, and now she had no one she felt understood the emotional turmoil going on inside of her when it came to her marriage. Brooke was always willing to listen, but Detria didn't want to sit her baggage of troubles on her sister's front porch. She had to learn how to fend for herself. Somehow she had to find a way to get her life and her marriage back on track.

She was Stiles' helpmeet, and she loved him with all her heart. But more and more, it seemed that Stiles' time and attention were focused on the church, his students, and his family, with her needs excluded altogether.

Detria opened the garage door. No car. No Stiles. She went inside and didn't stop until she entered their bedroom. Her mind had totally disregarded her plans to prepare dinner. She stepped out of her clothes, and then detoured to the luxurious master bathroom. Detria loved the smell of scented candles. It was another source of relaxation for her. She lit the candles that lined the rim of the Jacuzzi bathtub, and then proceeded to the closet to retrieve bubble bath. She turned on the faucets full force, poured in some of the bubble bath, and watched as hundreds of bubbles formed.

She lay back in the hot tub of water, her head resting against the rim. With her eyes closed, Detria prayed out loud. "Lord, forgive me for all the wrong I've done. Forgive me if I've been selfish. I want to be a good wife. I want to be a good friend to my husband. I want to be a great supporter to him, Lord. Forgive me for what I did to Pastor. I need your help. I need a word from you, Father."

Detria's eyes remained closed, which kept back the tears that wanted to escape. She remained silent and breathed in the aroma of the candles. She lay in the tub until she heard Stiles' familiar footsteps bounding up the stairs.

"Detria," he called out.

"I'm in here," Detria answered.

Stiles walked into the bathroom and stood at the entrance. "Hi there," he said.

"Hi."

"Sorry I didn't call you back. I was in a staff meeting at the university, so my phone was off. I see you're doing one of the things you love."

Stiles smiled at her.

Detria's heart pounded. She loved Stiles so much. Seeing him standing in the door made her excited. His explanation of why he hadn't returned her call or text was the farthest thing from her mind.

"No problem. I just got in from the gym. I was calling you to see if you were going to be home in time for dinner."

"I'm here." Stiles walked toward the tub. "I'm all yours." He began to peel off layers of clothing. "Mind if I have my dessert now?"

Detria smiled. She reached out her soapy hand and welcomed Stiles as he removed his last item of clothing and stepped inside the tub.

"I've missed you so much," she said after Stiles kissed her deeply. His hands expertly caressed her. He seemed to know every nook and cranny of her body. These were the times Detria missed. For the next hour, she wallowed in the comfort of her husband's arms. If only for now, everything seemed right in her world. She wasn't going to waste any more time thinking about the past, about the loss, or about when Pastor would be coming back. All she wanted was happening right now, and that was perfect for Detria.

16

*"Consider it all joy, my brethren, when you
encounter various trials, knowing that the
testing of your faith produces endurance. And
let endurance have its perfect result, so that you
may be perfect and complete, lacking in
nothing."* James 1:2-4, NASB

Rena had come to love each day in Andover
more than the day before. With a boyfriend like
Robert Becton and his children in her life, a
satisfying career, a home close to her parents,
and the pain of the past finally behind her, she
felt revitalized and renewed. Her focus was on
her life, and the happiness God blessed her to
have showed in her upbeat personality. She
was more involved than ever before in her
career, and it felt absolutely wonderful. The
Association for Library and Information
Science Education was going to honor her for
her work introducing youth to new media
studies by incorporating it into the high school
curriculum. Robert's kids adored her. She had
a church home she loved. Life couldn't be
better.

"What time did you say your flight leaves
tomorrow?" Robert asked.

Rena smiled. "Three." She picked over her
salad before gathering a few green veggies on
her fork and placing it in her mouth. "I think
I've told you that, oh, about ten times since I

planned this trip."

They finished eating their lunch, something that had become a routine for them since they officially became a couple. They remained professional at school, but it was still no secret that Dr. Robert Becton and librarian Rena Graham were an item.

"I wish I could accompany you," Robert said.

"I know, but you have to get your students prepared for the annual science exposition next week. And that's no problem, Robert. I'm a big girl. Plus, Momma is going with me."

"Well, make sure she takes plenty of pictures and records the event. I want to see you when you accept the Youth Services Award. ALISE is a prominent, well-known organization, and they're lucky to have you as one of their members," Robert complimented.

"Of course you would say that." Rena giggled. "Even if it is true."

"You are so full of yourself, aren't you?" Robert quipped.

"I can't help it. I got it from you." Rena walked a smidgen ahead of Robert. "Aren't you, Dr. Becton, the one who's always telling me how wonderful and beautiful I am?"

Robert displayed a sheepish, boy-like grin. "True," he answered.

"Okay then." She spread both hands. "I decided to stop fighting you and begin agreeing with you." Rena gave him a huge smile. "Especially since it's all true." She used the back of her hand to stifle her bubbly outburst.

They dumped their food trays in the proper

area, then walked toward the door facing the science building, which curved gracefully around the immaculately landscaped courtyard. Few students enjoyed or probably even recognized the serenity and peace the courtyard offered. The sun was bright, the skies clear. The weather was absolutely gorgeous. Days like this were what Rena enjoyed.

The needs of teenagers seemed so simple to Rena. Teenage boys would much rather stroll the hall casually between classes and eyeball the girls huddled next to their lockers. Girls enjoyed focusing more on the latest fashionista or cute guy.

Near the end of their stroll to their assigned work areas, Robert and Rena exchanged a light kiss and departed. Rena arrived back at the library ready to finish out the remainder of her work day. She sorted through several new books that had arrived, answered her e-mails, followed by entertaining a group of upper class students enrolled in her new media production video class. Toward the end of the day, she heard her cell phone ringing. It was her mother.

"Hi, Mom. What's up?"

"How's your day going, honey?" her mother asked.

"Great. I'll be out of here in about an hour."

"I didn't want anything in particular. I just wanted to tell you that I just finished talking to Ellen Hunt in Memphis."

"Ellen Hunt? Do I know her?"

"I thought you did. She was in my Sunday

School class when I was at Holy Rock."

"Okay. I don't remember her, though her name does sound slightly familiar. What were the two of you talking about?"

"She calls every now and then," Rena's mother answered. "But she told me that Pastor Graham had another stroke. I believe this is his third one. She said he had been in the hospital too."

"Is he all right?" Rena asked.

"She said he just got out of the hospital, but he's in a rehab hospital now. Like his first stroke, it affected his speech."

"I am so sorry to hear that. And he's not an old man either. That's the sad part."

"Honey, a stroke can affect just about anybody. We have to keep him lifted up in our prayers. But that's not all she told me."

"Wait a minute, Momma." Rena laid down her cell phone and assisted a student who approached her desk. "Okay, I'm back. Now, what were you saying?"

"I was about to say that Ellen told me Francesca is seriously ill and in ICU."

"What happened?" Rena asked. She leaned back in her office chair, and suddenly sweat formed on her brow and she felt her hands lightly tremble.

"She said that she had some type of lung infection. They had her on a ventilator. She doesn't know how long she's been sick, but she said they announced it at church last Sunday. Of course, they asked for everybody to pray for the family. The Grahams have been going through so much. I feel sorry for Stiles, even though he did you wrong."

"Momma, let's not go there. Stiles and I are in the past. It's over. I refuse to reflect on yesterday."

Rena understood that her mother's intentions weren't to be vindictive against Stiles, but she knew that Meryl Jackson hadn't taken it well when Stiles decided he wanted a divorce. Rena had finally come to understand that God does have a way of making the most evil things work out for the good of His children. She wouldn't be where she was today if it had not been for the tests and trials of her past. But hearing that Francesca was ill did shake Rena up. What if it was related to her HIV? What if Frankie had AIDS? Rena wiped the fraction of sweat from her forehead with a tissue she found in her side desk drawer.

"Ellen said that Stiles didn't preach Sunday. He was in Dyersburg with Francesca. That's where she's in the hospital. She also told me that Stiles' wife had a miscarriage."

"Sister Ellen knows everything, at least it sounds like she does," Rena commented. "I am really sorry to hear all of this. I'm going to try to get in touch with Stiles. I need to find out how Francesca is doing, and Pastor Graham too, of course."

"Look, I didn't call to tell you this so you'd get yourself involved with them again. I thought you'd want to know, that's all."

"I know that, Momma. And I'm glad you told me. Anyway, I need to get off the phone. It's almost time for me to get out of here, and I still have a few things to wrap up before I leave. I won't be back in the office until Friday."

"Yeah, I know. I guess I'll finish packing too. Call me later after you get settled."

"I will. And if you hear anything else about Francesca and Pastor Graham before we leave tomorrow, call me. If not, then I'll check with you later on."

"Okay, baby. Bye."

"Bye, Ma."

Rena ended the call. She didn't have much time to focus on what her mother shared with her because several students and her volunteer library assistant bombarded her with questions about a number of subjects.

Rena ended the day by tidying up her desk and office to make it easier for the library assistant. She searched around her office to make sure she wasn't leaving anything she planned to take on her trip. She spotted her jump drive, picked it up, and plopped it inside one of the side pockets in her laptop bag. Before she turned off the light, she glanced around one more time.

At home, Rena thought about what her mother had told her about the Grahams. She went online almost zombie-like and started a search for Dyersburg Hospital. She found the listing and called patient information. She was given the room number and phone number for Francesca. Rena sighed with a bit of relief. If Francesca was in ICU and on a ventilator like Mrs. Hunt told Rena's mother, then Francesca must be doing better since she had a room number and phone.

Rena looked at the number she'd written

down on the pink Post-it note. Should I call? Or do I need to let the past stay in the past? Rena's concern for Francesca won. She sat on the couch, picked up her landline, and dialed the number. She was greeted by a busy signal but continued to clasp the phone in one hand until the noise finally jarred her from the daze she'd fallen into. She hit the end button and began to pray for Francesca's health and well-being.

Rena called and talked to Robert and the kids while she prepared a light meal of mixed vegetables and baked cod. Robert was a great guy. Rena loved his sensitivity and kindness. He was a man who had experienced his own share of setbacks in life. He didn't judge her because of her past; in fact, it endeared Rena to him even more. To be able to look at the dirt of someone's past, know their faults and the messes they'd made at times in their life, and still love that person was nothing short of the mercy of God. Maybe one day she would love Robert just as much, if not more, than he loved her. There was no mistaking that she loved him, but there were times when Rena's mind reflected on her sour marriage to Stiles.

He had been her first love, and she wanted it to last forever. But life was not so simple. Things happened that she hated to think about, but the things she had done also helped to shape and mold her into the woman she now was. It was her past that brought her to her present. Frankie was part of her past; so was Stiles and the entire Graham clan. But Frankie had been her dearest and closest friend too. That was something she could never forget. No matter what happened between them, Francesca had been by her side through some tough times and vice versa. Rena dialed the hospital number again. This time after a second or two of silence, the phone began to ring.

Rena wasn't expecting to hear the voice on the other end. It wasn't Francesca's, that was for sure. "Hello," the light male voice said.

"Uh, hello. I'm calling for Francesca Graham. Is this the right room?"

"Oh, yes it is," the man replied. "Francesca is sleeping right now. I can take a message and let her know you called," he said politely.

"Oh, okay. That will be fine. My name is Rena. Rena Graham. I'm a friend of Francesca's. I heard she was in the hospital."

"Rena Graham?" the man repeated her name into the phone.

"Yes, that's right." Rena didn't bother explaining to the man that she was Stiles' ex-wife. She didn't want to go into her personal business with a stranger on the phone. "How is she doing?"

"She's doing much better. Will she know who you are?"

"Yes, she will. We were best friends for years. I used to live in Memphis, but I'm now in Massachusetts."

"Okay," the man sounded as if his memory had just returned. "You were married to Francesca's brother, right?"

"Yes." Rena did not want to get into a question-and-answer session about her relationship with the Grahams. All she wanted to know was if Frankie was going to be all right.

"I'm Tim. I'm a friend of Francesca's. We attend the same church," he explained.

"I heard that she was in ICU and on a ventilator," Rena told him.

"She was, but God is a good God. She was taken off the ventilator earlier today. They moved her to a private room. She's still drifting in and out of consciousness, but that's mostly because of the medication."

"I see. Is any of her family there, by chance?"

"No. Her brother left around noon going back to Memphis. He's supposed to be back some time tomorrow. But, like I told him, I live close by and Francesca is special to me, so I'll be here as much as I'm needed. And there's always someone calling or coming by from our church to sit and pray with her. God has her in His hands."

Rena felt herself calming down the more she listened to Brother Tim. His voice soothed her, and somehow she believed that Francesca was in good hands.

"Thank you for letting me know how Francesca is doing. Will you take down my phone number and tell her that I called?"

"I'd be glad to. I'm sure she'll be excited to know that you called."

Rena wondered if that would be true. Would Francesca be glad to hear that she had called? They hadn't spoken since Audrey's repast. And Rena hadn't returned the last call Francesca made to her. She'd forgiven Francesca so many times throughout their friendship, but she didn't want to re-open ongoing communication with her. She wanted her life to be just the way it was. But hearing that Francesca was seriously ill changed Rena's perspective of everything. Her love for Francesca was still kept tucked away in her heart. She and Francesca had been through it all, and there was no way Rena was going to ignore her during her time of sickness.

"Thank you again, Tim. I'll call to check on her again soon."

"You're welcome. God bless you."

"God bless you too," Rena replied. "Good-bye."

Rena refocused on preparing for her trip to Boston the next day. She felt honored to be recognized for her work by ALISE. It was more evidence of God's favor on her life. She sat down on her bed and paused for a few moments after she placed the last item inside her carry-on luggage. So much good was happening in her life. She had a man who simply loved and adored her, and wanted to marry her.

Rena tilted her head and rested her hands in her lap. She replayed several instances when Robert had proposed to her. She always had a reason why she couldn't marry him. She loved him deeply, or so she believed. But if that was the case, why couldn't she tell him yes? Why couldn't she accept the fact that Robert loved her and that her past didn't determine the future he longed to have with her.

Rena shifted her thoughts to Stiles. He was happily married to a wonderful woman. He had moved on with his life. The fact that his wife had a miscarriage was unfortunate, but Rena viewed it as a sure sign that Stiles and Detria were moving forward with establishing a family. If he could manage to wipe the slate clean and start anew, what was holding her back? She got up and went to her cozy home office. She pulled up her acceptance speech for the upcoming function and printed it out. Reading over the speech helped her think about something other than marriage.

The phone rang. Rena shifted around in the swivel office chair and went into her bedroom. "Hello," she answered.

"Hi. What are you doing?"

"Well, right now I'm talking to you."

"All right, smarty pants," Robert said.

"It's the truth." Rena giggled. She liked joking around with Robert.

"Okay, what were you doing before you started talking to me?"

"I just finished packing, and I printed off my acceptance speech. I was reading over it when you called. What are you doing?" Rena asked.

"Talking to you," Robert answered.

"Okay, okay. You got me back," Rena told him.

"I was thinking. . ."

"What were you thinking, Mr. Becton?"

"I was thinking that when you come back home Thursday morning, I'd meet you and your mother for breakfast."

"You mean you would miss a day of school

to meet me for breakfast? To what do I owe such an offer?" Rena walked slowly across the bedroom floor. A smile stretched wide across her face.

"Oh, what was I thinking? Let's make that dinner."

"You are so full of it," she answered him.

"Yeah, full of love for you," he said.

"That was corny, Robert. Is that all you've got?" They continued to exchange friendly banter. Rena indulged in her conversations with Robert. He had a way of bringing out the best in her.

"Since I have you laughing, let me ask you something? When are you going to marry me and the kids?"

"Robert, don't put the kids in this. You know I'm a softie when it comes to them."

"Hey, I have to use what I have. If the kids are what it's going to take for you to become Mrs. Becton, then that's what I'll have to use."

"You are so mean. You're using your own kids to get me to marry you? I think I'll have to report you to the Bureau of People Who Use Kids to Get Other People to Marry Them."

"And you're talking about me being corny. That was terrible." Robert laughed into the receiver. "Seriously, you know I want you to be my wife more than anything, Rena."

"I know that, Robert. And believe me, I want to be your wife, but I'm just not ready. I still need some time to get me together. I want to be the best wife I can be. You deserve nothing less."

"Do you love me?" he sounded serious.

"Of course I love you. What kind of question is that?" Rena sat down in her bedroom chaise. "I just need more time. I've made far too many mistakes in my life, and I don't plan on bringing you or the kids in on all of my hang-ups."

"Hang-ups? You're never going to be perfect, Rena. No one is. Shucks, you've got to let go of the past. It's time to move on with your life—with our life. It's hard seeing you every day and not being able to hold you and make love to you. It's hard for me to come to your place and then leave at the end of the night. I want you lying beside me for the rest of my life."

Rena listened with the same intensity she always did when Robert brought up the M-word.

"Are you still there?" Robert asked.

"Yes, I'm here. I was listening to you. And I want to be with you too. Believe me, I do. But something is keeping me stagnated. I don't want to ruin your life. I don't want to be a disappointment to you and the kids. You deserve someone who can give you all of themselves, and I don't know if I can do that."

"Rena, please. Please, think about it. Pray about it. I want you. The kids want you. We need you."

"I think about it all the time. I love you. Please don't doubt that. Just give me a little more time, Robert."

Rena heard him sigh on the phone. "Sure," he answered. "I guess I'll let you get back to rehearsing your speech. I'm going to go in and check on the kids. I'll see you tomorrow before you leave."

"Okay. G'night."

"G'night, Rena. I love you."

"I love you too, Robert."

Rena leaned back in the chair. What was it? Why couldn't she just marry Robert? What was she so afraid of? She realized that Robert wouldn't wait forever. He was a good man, and somewhere out there, if she didn't step up to the plate, another woman would be more than willing to love him. She wanted to be his wife and not just his woman. She wanted their relationship to be consummated in every way, but that meant commitment. Could she commit herself to him? Because of her herpes, she didn't know if she could give him children, or if she would transmit the disease to him. There were so many bits and pieces of the puzzle of her life that still needed to be put together. Now that she'd learned Francesca was ill, she worried even more. Was Francesca's illness due to her HIV or herpes?

Could HIV be lying dormant in her body, waiting to rear its vile head if she chose to marry Robert? She didn't want to jeopardize Robert's health. He had children who depended on him. He'd already been through enough with his past wife. Rena didn't want to be the one to bring along a trunk full of baggage that held all of the junk of her past. Robert was right: she needed to petition God. Only He could help her make the right decision.

She put the phone down and grabbed a novel she had been reading from the table next to her. Rena flipped aimlessly through the pages, unable to concentrate on the book.

The phone rang. "Who could this be?" she said out loud. She looked at the phone, but the call read RESTRICTED. Rena decided not to answer. She didn't want to be bothered with a telemarketer. All she wanted to do was read and then go to bed. When she attempted to return to her book, the phone disturbed her again. Again, it was a restricted call with no number showing. This time she answered.

"Hello," Rena answered in a voice any caller would identify as frustrated.

"May I speak to Rena?" the man asked.

A lump formed in the base of Rena's throat when she recognized that the voice on the other end belonged to Stiles. There was no mistaking his one-of-a-kind, magnetic voice.

"Stiles, this is Rena."

"Hi. How are you? You sound like you're teed off about something? Did I catch you at a bad time?"

"No. I was just reading. The ID says restricted. I usually don't answer restricted calls because most of the time it's a telemarketer. Then you called right back, so I guess you could say that I was rather perturbed." She repositioned her body more comfortably.

"Brother Tim told me you called the hospital to check on Francesca. He gave me your phone number. I wanted to thank you for calling."

"Of course. No problem. One of your church members talks to my mother from time to time. She called and told her about Pastor and Francesca. I am so sorry to hear about their illnesses." Rena did not mention that the woman also told her mother about him and Detria losing their baby.

"News does get around fast, doesn't it? Anyway, it's good to know you still care."

"Why wouldn't I?"

Rena was baffled as to why he would question her concern. It wasn't like she hated any of them. She just couldn't be friends with Francesca anymore. As for Pastor, he had always been near and dear to her. She sometimes felt she was to blame for his health problems. A flash of memories quickly flooded her mind. It was like reliving the whole incident of Pastor's first stroke. The harsh argument between her and Francesca that awful day close to three years ago was the catalyst that brought on Pastor's first stroke. At least, that's what Rena believed. Bouts of guilt over the incident attacked her from time to time—another reason she didn't feel she should be marrying Robert. She had too many pieces of the past clinging on to her for dear life. Until she could let go and let God totally heal her, there was no way she could give her all to another man. Maybe if she explained it to Robert like that, he would cut her some slack.

"I don't see why you wouldn't. It's just a surprise to me, that's all," Stiles replied, which yanked Rena from her daydreaming.

"I'm sorry. What did you say?" she asked him.

"Nothing really. Anyway, I thought I'd call you back. I spoke to Francesca's doctor. She's doing better. She's not in ICU anymore. They moved her to a private room, and she's being weaned off the coma-inducing meds. Pastor is in Health South Rehab Center getting occupational and speech therapy. The doctor believes he's going to be fine. He's getting stronger and better every day."

"Oh, Stiles. That's good news. Thank you, God," Rena screamed lightly into the phone. "What's wrong with Francesca though?"

"She has an opportunistic infection that has a major effect on the lungs. It's a secondary infection that people with HIV can acquire. It's usually found in children with HIV, but it's not limited to children, which is obvious. Unfortunately, it's life-threatening, and on top of everything else, it's usually seen in individuals who have AIDS."

Rena's right hand involuntarily landed over her heart. "AIDS. Oh, my God. No, Stiles. Please, tell me that Frankie doesn't have AIDS."

"I wish I could. God knows I wish I could tell you anything but that."

Rena felt like her heart was about to explode. She heaved. Each breath she took caused her to get that much more upset. Tears gushed from her eyes. Sobs poured from her throat.

"Rena, please don't cry. Please, don't cry," Stiles begged. "Francesca is going to pull through this. She's already doing better. Today an AIDS diagnosis doesn't have to be a death sentence. We have to believe God."

Rena couldn't help herself. There was no way she could hear Stiles when she was in this frame of mind. She would be next. She just knew she would. It wasn't over. She and Francesca were being punished by God for their unnatural, sinful acts. "Oh, no," she screamed into the phone. "Oh, God, don't let this be happening. Please," she continued to scream and sob into the phone. "What if I have HIV? Or, worse, AIDS?"

"Rena, listen to me. Don't do this to yourself. Now I wish I hadn't told you. I don't know what I was thinking," Stiles said. His voice trembled. "I'm so sorry, sweetheart. I'm so sorry."

"Stiles, I have to hang up. I can't talk anymore. I . . . I'll talk to you some other time."

"Wait, Rena. Don't hang up. Don't shut me out. Let me call you later on or tomorrow. I'm going to the hospital first thing tomorrow morning. I'll call you then."

"No, I can't talk to you right now. I can't talk tomorrow either. I just need some time to digest this. I'll call you. What's your cell phone number?"

"It's—"

"Hold on," she said between sobs. "I've got to get something to write on." She stood and stumbled her way to her office. She searched through watery, blood-shot eyes until she saw the pen and Post-its on the computer desk. " 'K . . . what is it?"

Stiles gave her the number and said, "Rena, are you going to be all right? Is there anyone I can call to come over there with you?" He asked question after question. "Is your friend with you?"

"I'll be fine." Rena sniffed on her way to the bathroom. She tore some toilet tissue off the roll and used it to blow her nose and wipe her tears. "I've got to go now. I'll call you."

Rena hung up the phone, rushed to her queen bed, and fell down on it. She bawled until her eyes were practically swollen shut.

17

"One of the hardest things in life is watching the person you love, love someone else." Unknown

Detria stood with her back against the office door and listened to Stiles on the phone. She couldn't believe what she was hearing. Stiles was talking to Rena. He practically begged her to let him call her again. Calling Rena sweetheart? She had never been the jealous type, but this was a little too much for her to keep calm about. She stood out of his view until he finished talking.

"So," she said. "That was Rena you were talking to?"

Stiles jerked around from his desk and appeared startled. "Yes. I called to check on Francesca earlier, and Brother Tim told me Rena had called the hospital to check on Francesca. Seems that one of our church members called Rena's mother, Mrs. Jackson, and told her about Francesca and Pastor."

"Oh, I see." Detria's arms were folded, and she walked further inside Stiles' home office. Look, Stiles, I know in your ministry you have to talk to a lot of people. I know you talk to a lot of women too, and I've never had a problem with that. But what I do have a problem with is hearing you call another woman sweetheart. And what I also have a problem with is that the woman happens to be your ex." Detria rolled her eyes in anger. "We already have enough problems as it is."

Stiles squinted and cocked his head back. "What? I don't know what you're talking about."

"I heard you calling your ex-wife sweetheart. That's what I'm talking about. Don't even try to deny it, Stiles. Then you tell her that you want to call her again. For what? She has nothing to do with this family anymore. Okay, wait. Let me back up a minute. I can understand that she would want to know how Francesca is doing, but what I don't understand is the way you were communicating with her. She is not your wife. I am."

"I know that. And if I called her sweetheart, I didn't mean anything by it. She was crying on the phone," Stiles defended. "Obviously, she's upset. I was talking to her, trying to calm her down like I would anyone else who just received bad news."

"As far as I know, I don't believe you go around calling women you counsel sweetheart—unless I'm missing something."

Stiles got up from his chair. "Detria, let's not do this tonight. Honey, I love you. Nobody but you. I'm sorry. I didn't mean anything by it, I promise. Rena was upset, and I was merely trying to tell her that I would be here for her if she needed to talk. She was devastated to hear about my sister."

"I bet," Detria said.

"Don't act like this," he said. He walked up to her and pulled her into his arms. He kissed her on her neck, and then followed up with kisses along her cheek until his lips found hers. "Don't you know I would never do or say anything to jeopardize our marriage? I love you."

Detria accepted his kisses and apology. "I love you too," she whispered. "I love you so much. I'm just so worried about us, Stiles," she told him between kisses. "I don't want anything or anyone to come between us. Not ever."

Stiles leaned back, lifted Detria's chin up, and gazed into her eyes. "You don't have to worry your pretty little head about anything like that. Come here," he said and reached for her hand. He returned to his office chair and pulled Detria down on his lap. "I know things have been strained between us lately. We haven't really talked much about anything that's been going on in our lives. I mean, from losing the baby to all of this with Pastor and Francesca. I know it's been hard on you, one thing after another. Added to it all, I'm not around much. But none of this is your fault. We have to be here for each other, baby," Stiles explained.

Detria seemed intent on listening to her husband. She returned his gaze with her own and rubbed the side of his face as she listened.

"We've been through a lot in the short time we've been married. I believe we're going to come out stronger for it too. God has something great planned for us, Detria. We're going to have that family we both want so badly. We're going to hear the pitter-patter of little feet running around here one day. We're going to see Francesca healed and Pastor restored to health. Just wait and see. Watch what God does."

This time Detria took the initiative and kissed her husband. Her passion mounted, as did his. They eagerly embraced and allowed themselves to be swept away in the moment.

Stiles took hold of her hand again and led her upstairs to their bedroom.

Detria rested in Stiles' arms. It felt good to be cuddled against her husband. She missed his touch so much. He was right about everything he had said. They had to be there for each other through the good times and the not-so-good times. She couldn't keep blaming Pastor for the death of her baby. She had to forgive him in the same way she had asked God to forgive her. As for being jealous, she wouldn't allow herself to believe that there was anything between her husband and his ex. Stiles was not a cheater. No one would ever be able to make her believe otherwise. It was time for her to get her act together.

Detria listened to Stiles' labored breathing. She used her free hand to caress his sweaty, still body. She loved everything about this man. She refused to give in to anything that could come between them, including her own actions. Her thoughts jumped to her resentment toward Pastor. He was improving each day. For that, Detria was thankful to God. No matter how angry she was at him, she understood that Pastor was a good man—a man who loved God and his family.

She glanced over at Stiles again, and a tiny tear drop slid down her face and onto his chest. How could she have been so evil and mean toward another human being? It was not in her character or nature, or so she thought. She didn't know what Pastor's intentions would be once he was able to speak clearly again. Would he tell Stiles that she was the one who abused him? Maybe she should tell Stiles herself. Detria eased away from her sleeping husband and sat up in their bed. She placed both hands against her face. Rampant thoughts ran through her mind like a Zippin Pippin. She thought of something her mother used to always tell her and Brooke—it's better to suffer the consequences of telling the truth than to suffer the consequences of telling a lie. Detria had to make a decision.

Detria looked over at Stiles again. He was snoring lightly. She got out of the bed and went into the bathroom. Standing before the mirror, she analyzed her life. Since her miscarriage, she had changed drastically, and not for the good either. She was living a double life. There was one part of her that appeared compassionate, kind, and loving. There was another part of her that had no regard for others. She proved it when she beat on an ill, innocent, and defenseless man who had shown her nothing but love, gratitude, and acceptance. It was time for her to confront Pastor. She had to beg him to forgive her even though he had every right not to. As for Stiles, she had no idea what she was going to do. Right now, she couldn't see herself confessing to him that she was the one who had hurt his father.

Detria decided that as soon as Pastor was doing better, she was going to go visit him. It was time for her to get her life back in order and move on toward her future. She hoped that would include settling things between her and Pastor so Stiles would not discover what she'd done.

The home health agency had cleared all of their staff from any wrongdoing. There was not enough evidence to place the blame on any one person. Stiles remained unconvinced and dismissed the agency from working with Pastor in the future. Detria felt lucky that Stiles hadn't blamed her even once for what happened to Pastor. She mouthed a prayer and asked God to be with her when it came time for her to talk to Pastor. It would probably be difficult, and she wouldn't blame Pastor if he didn't want to see her. But she knew she had to try. If she was going to save her marriage, she had to ask Pastor to forgive her and convince him to keep quiet. She was determined not to become Stiles' next ex-wife.

18

"There is no revenge so complete as forgiveness." Josh Billings

In the ensuing days, Pastor showed marked improvement. He was now able to get up and walk around the therapy room. He still had significant weakness on one side of his body, but he was no longer bedridden and suffering in silence. His physical wounds had healed as well. In the short time he'd been at rehab, his speech pattern had improved dramatically. Most of his words, if one listened closely, were intelligible. Stiles was in total amazement at how God was proving again just how powerful He is.

Not only had Pastor's health picked up, but Francesca was expected to be discharged from the hospital soon. She wouldn't be leaving with a clean bill of health, but the good news was that Francesca had pulled through a life-threatening illness.

It was Saturday morning. The day was already gorgeous, with the temperature hovering around seventy degrees. The clear blue sky was radiant. Stiles had gotten up at the first sign of sunlight and left for Dyersburg.

Detria left the house not long after Stiles and went to work out. Afterward, she called Brooke and asked her to meet her at a nearby deli for lunch. Brooke agreed.

"Hey, sis. How's it going?" Brooke asked as she took a seat inside the booth with Detria.

"That's why I called you. I need someone to talk to. I can't keep what I've been hiding inside any longer. If I do, I'm afraid I'll end up like Pastor—stroked out."

Brooke wrinkled her mouth and flapped one hand. "Girl, puhleeze. What are you talking about? You know you have a tendency to make a mountain out of a molehill."

"Are you ladies ready to place your order?" the waitress asked.

"Yes," Brooke answered right away. "I'll have the special please."

"What kind of soup, and do you want the half ham or turkey sandwich?"

"I'll have the tortilla soup with the turkey sandwich half."

The waitress turned and looked at Detria. "And you, ma'am?"

"I'll have the same, please. And may I have a glass of water with lemon?"

"Sure," the waitress replied before she turned and left.

"Now, tell me what's going on with you," Brooke urged.

"I don't know how to tell you. It's so terrible. I'm afraid you'll hate me."

"Hate you? Now you're really bugging out. How can I hate my own sister?"

Detria's face suddenly turned ashen.

"You really are serious, aren't you?" Brooke asked when she looked at Detria's ghastly face.

"Do you think I would be here about to have a nervous breakdown if I wasn't serious? I don't know how to start, so I'll just come out and say it. You remember when Pastor had the stroke, and then I lost my baby?"

"Yeah, and?"

"Well, you also remember that I told you I believed Pastor was the reason that I had a miscarriage?" Detria's face turned from a pale, ashen color to a bright crimson.

Brooke's eyebrows furrowed. "Yes, but I still don't think that was the cause, honey. Why do you keep thinking that?"

"I told you why. The day he had his stroke, I was the one who found him. He was laid out in the bathroom with a big gash on the back of his head. I tried to pick him up. He was so heavy, but I knew I had to get him up. I didn't think that I could be hurting my baby." Detria hurriedly wiped away the tears from her eyes with her fingers. "I got him up enough for him to sit up against the tub, and then I called 911."

"Okay, so how did that. . . . Oh, no," Brooke said as if she suddenly had an epiphany. "That's right. You had the miscarriage not too long after that happened."

"Yes," Detria answered and wiped more tears from her eyes.

"Detria, I still do not believe that caused your miscarriage. I mean, Dr. Henderson told you differently too."

"I don't care. She gave me some cockamamie story about the egg being defective or that a miscarriage means that something would have been wrong with the baby. But I don't buy that, at least not in my case. I know it was because of Pastor. Stress and strain can cause a miscarriage. That man is the reason my baby is not alive today." Detria bowed her head.

The waitress returned with their orders. Detria barely looked up when the waitress sat their orders on the table. The sisters discontinued the discussion until the waitress left.

"Did you ever tell Stiles about this?" Brooke asked.

"No, and why are you acting like this is the first time you've heard all of this? I told you that I didn't tell anyone. No one . . . nada," Detria said. Her tone sounded on the verge of anger. Neither of the women touched their food. Brooke seemed to be disturbed by what she heard. "But there's something I didn't tell you."

Brooke took a spoonful of her soup, and then returned her attention to Detria. "Come on." She reached over and took hold of Detria's hand. "Let it out. You've been holding this stuff in for far too long. I can't believe this."

"Well, it's true, and here goes the rest. And before I tell you, I'm asking you not to pass judgment on me, Brooke. I don't need you or anyone else to condemn me. I've condemned myself enough already."

"You can tell me, Detria. You should know that by now. You can tell me anything."

"I abused Pastor Graham. I was so angry. No, I was downright furious that he made me lose my child. I hated him, Brooke. I hated him so much that almost every time I went in that room to take care of him, I would hit him and hit him. I hit him on his upper thigh so it would be less noticeable. I punched him over and over again for every pain he caused me to feel over the death of my baby. My baby didn't have a chance to enter this world because of that man." Detria cried.

"Wait here," Brooke instructed Detria. "I'll be right back."

"Where are you going?" Detria asked between sobs. "I'll be right back."

Brooke returned with two carryout boxes. She hurriedly placed the food in the containers.

"What are you doing?" asked Detria.

"We're getting out of here. I paid at the register. Now let's go. You don't need to be sitting in a public place this upset. We're going to my house. John took the boys to the auto show. We have the place to ourselves for at least a few hours. Do you think you're able to drive?"

Detria used the napkin to clear her tears. "Yeah, sure."

"Come on, then. Let's get out of here." Brooke picked up the carryout, and the two of them left the restaurant.

Fifteen minutes later, both cars pulled into Brooke's covered double driveway. Once inside the house, Brooke directed Detria to go into the family room, and she went toward the kitchen.

"Do you want me to warm up your soup and sandwich?" Brooke asked Detria from the kitchen.

"No, I don't want it right now. Maybe later."

"Okay, just remember to take it when you leave. I set it in the microwave," Brooke said as she entered the family room and sat down on the couch next to her sister. "So, let me get this straight. You've been physically abusing your father-in-law?"

"Not now, but yes, I did physically abuse him. I don't know what came over me. The first time I did it, I felt so awful. I begged him to forgive me. Of course, he couldn't talk, but his eyes spoke volumes. Then it happened again and again. Every time, I thought of the pain I felt losing my baby. Oh, God, Brooke, I am a terrible, terrible person. And when Stiles finds out that I was the one who hurt his father, he's going to hate me. I know he will."

"Shh, it's going to be all right. Did anybody discover that he was being abused?"

"Yes, one of the aides first noticed it and told me and Stiles about it. She reported it to her employer. Then when he had to go back into the hospital, the admitting doctor saw the bruises. He reported it to Adult Protective Services. Of course, Stiles was furious. APS did an investigation into the home health agency that was responsible for Pastor Graham's home care, but they never could prove that the aides did anything to him. And no one suspected me. If they did, I didn't know about it. You know Pastor Graham is in rehab now. He's doing well, and his speech is returning. I know when he gets better he's going to tell Stiles what I did. Then my marriage will be ruined. My life will be over when everybody finds out that I'm an abuser. They're going to look at me like I'm demon-possessed." Detria sobbed.

Brooke got up hurriedly and left the room. She returned with a box of tissues and gave them to her sister. She eased close to her and wrapped an arm around her shoulder. "First of all, Stiles is not going to leave you. Second of all, no one is going to think that you're demon-possessed. Thirdly, you went through trauma, serious trauma, when you had that miscarriage. You tried to pretend like you were all right, but I knew you were hiding your pain. You've always been good at that. You want people to think you're invincible and that your faith in God is insurmountable. But what you've failed to realize is that your strength is made perfect in weakness, Detria. God knows you're not a mean, cruel person. You've gone through your own personal torment. Losing a child through miscarriage is major. I can see why you blamed Pastor Graham. To be honest, I probably would have to if I had been in your situation. But the thing you have to remember is that it wasn't Pastor Graham's fault. It was nobody's fault. God is in control of every single situation that occurs in our lives, Detria. You have to remember that. And God knows your weakness. He knows the pain you experienced."

"Yes, I know that, but Stiles isn't God. He won't understand. He won't forgive me."

"How do you know unless you sit down and talk to him, just like you did with me? Honey, Stiles adores you."

"I don't know. I don't know anything

anymore. I'm so messed up inside, Brooke. I feel so bad. I'm going to go and talk to Pastor Graham in a few days. I have to beg him to forgive me. I have to let him know how sorry I am. And I made up my mind that I'm going to ask him not to tell Stiles what I did."

"Detria, I don't know if that's a good idea. I think you should pray about telling Stiles the truth. How can you have a relationship built on trust if you don't trust your husband enough to tell him what you did? He's a man of God, Detria. And Stiles should understand your pain and hurt because he felt the same sense of loss as you did."

"You don't hate me?" Detria zeroed in on her sister's intense stare.

"Hate you? Why would I hate you? I love you. You're my sister." Brooke hugged Detria. Both of them cried on each other's shoulders.

Detria pulled away from Brooke and wiped her face again. "Brooke, what am I going to do?"

"Listen to me. This is fixable. I know it is. I believe what happened to you after your miscarriage was postpartum depression."

"Postpartum depression? But I thought that happened only to women who gave birth to a child. I didn't know it could happen to women who had a miscarriage."

"Well, that's where you're wrong. Your hormone levels change during pregnancy, which I'm sure you are aware of."

Detria nodded her head slightly. Brooke continued to talk.

"Just because you didn't carry your baby to

full term doesn't mean you can't experience postpartum. Postpartum depression is a serious illness, Detria. It can occur in the first few months after childbirth, but it can also happen after a miscarriage or stillbirth. I'm not trying to give you some far-fetched excuse for your actions, but what I am saying is that you are not in this alone. I wish you had come to me. I'm so sorry that you've been keeping this bottled up inside you for all of this time."

"I do feel better talking about it. I don't know what I'd do without you, sis."

"If I have anything to do with it, you won't have to do without me for a long, long time. What I want you to do now is nothing. I don't want you to think about going to see Pastor Graham or about telling Stiles anything. First, you have to see about yourself. That means you need to talk to a counselor. A psychologist would probably do you good. There are plenty of Christian psychologists to see, if you're concerned about that. And I'll go with you. No one has to know but us. Then after you talk to the psychologist, you'll be better able to make a decision about what you need to do. I'll be praying for you, and I'll pray that Pastor Graham finds it in his heart to understand what happened to you, and that he'll forgive you."

"And Stiles? What about my marriage? Brooke, I'm still scared."

"Listen, haven't you heard a thing I've said? We're going to get you through this. Stiles is going to understand. I know he will. Just try to trust in God, Detria. Don't let the devil make you give up."

Detria sniffed. "Okay."

"Do you want me to warm up your soup? Knowing you, you probably haven't been eating much. I can tell you've lost weight, and don't tell me it's because you've been working out either."

"I have been working out."

"Yeah, but you haven't been eating much I bet, now have you?" Brooke asked.

"Not really."

"I'm not going to accept no for an answer. You're at least going to eat your soup. Then I want you to lie down and take a nap. Your mind needs some rest. Don't fight me on this, Detria."

"I'm not, Brooke. I'm too tired to fight anymore."

19

"The love of a family is life's greatest blessing."
Unknown

Stiles made his way to Francesca's room. He was eager to see his sister after having been unable to drive up to Dyersburg for almost a week because of his busy schedule. Thank God Francesca was able to talk on the phone every now and again. Plus, Brother Tim had been a constant by her side. Stiles caught the elevator, got off on Francesca's floor, and made his way to her room.

"Knock. Knock." Stiles opened the door slowly upon hearing Francesca's weak voice telling him to come in.

"Hi, sis. How are you feeling?" Stiles asked. He stood by her bed and leaned down to kiss her on the cheek.

"I'm feeling fine. God is good," she said.

"Where is your beau?" Stiles asked. He smiled along with his inquiry.

"Boy, what are you talking about?" Francesca managed to put a smile on her face.

"You know who I'm talking about. Your man, Brother Tim."

This time Francesca grinned. "You are so crazy. But to answer your question, Tim just called. He'll be here later on this afternoon. He had to work overtime today."

"Oh, I see. That gives me a chance to grill you on this dude. I don't want some shyster trying to come up on my baby sister."

"I've been round the block too many times to fall for that," Francesca answered.

"Do you like him?" Stiles' voice grew serious, and the smile was no longer on his face.

Francesca paused. "I think I do. I mean, it's different, you know? Oh, I guess you don't know." She giggled, and so did Stiles. He sat down in the chair next to Francesca.

"Why didn't you tell me about him?"

"I don't know. I guess I didn't know what was going on myself. All of this is so not like me. I've never been in a relationship with a man, except for when I was on drugs and doing any and everything to get my next high. And then with Tim, things just happened. I didn't even know we were getting close to each other until one day he came over and started talking about how much he cared about me and how much he wanted to be my man. I was like, 'You have got to be kidding.'" Francesca giggled.

"I wish I could have been a fly on the wall to see and hear that," Stiles commented.

"At first, I looked at him like he was crazy. This guy knows how messed up I used to be, and he was standing in my apartment talking about his feelings. It was so out there."

"I think he's a good man, at least from the times I've talked to him. My spirit sets well with his. And I do know that he likes you. He likes you a lot."

"To be honest with you, that's what I don't

understand, Stiles. How can he like me after hearing my testimony? I mean, the people at church know the kind of life I've led. He knows my story, and yet not only Tim, but my church family also has really been good to me, especially since I've been in the hospital."

"That's nothing but God, girl. God already has people lined up along our path who will love us, direct us, and help us. He knows every move we make and every misstep we take, yet He loves us anyway. You've gone through a lot, sis. I can't say that I've always understood why you chose the things you did in your life, but I do know that God knows. And no matter what has occurred, or how bad things are, God is the one who has our backs. Maybe Brother Tim is a man God has allowed in your life to show you what love between a man and a woman can really be like. God's love is not based on conditions and circumstances. He loves us just because."

"I'm so glad He does, Stiles. I'm lying here in this hospital bed with full-blown AIDS. At times I've asked God to take me on away from here to be with Him. But for some reason, I'm still here. That tells me there is still something God needs me to do. As for Tim, I care about him. I care about him a lot. I think I might even be in love with him. Now I know that may sound crazy to you. An in-it-for-life lesbian like me is in love with a man? That's cheesy, isn't it?" Francesca grinned again. "God sure has a sense of humor."

"That He does. But God can change the heart of any man or woman, boy or girl. God has the first, middle, and last words to say. I'm glad He brought Brother Tim into your life. I don't know what the future holds for the two of you, but I believe it's going to be good, if you let it. You've got to get up out of this bed and proclaim God's goodness to people like you, who have given up hope. You have a story to tell, Francesca. I know I haven't always been the kind of brother you needed me to be, and for that I'm sorry. But I'm here for you now. Believe it or not, you've taught me a few things about love and forgiveness."

"Wow, that's heavy coming from you, bro'." Tears streamed down Francesca's face.

Stiles took his fingers and wiped them gently away. "I have to say what I mean. Your life has been a journey, but through it all God has brought you full circle. I see Him living inside of you again, Francesca. Great things are ahead for you. I know it, and I believe it."

"Thank you. I receive it too." Her voice was tender. "How is Pastor?"

"I guess it's time to tell you what's been going on."

Francesca tried to ease up in the bed. Stiles stood quickly to help her get in a more comfortable position. "What are you talking about?"

"The day I received the call about you being in the hospital is the same day Pastor was admitted to the hospital."

Francesca's face fell into a frown. "Is he all right?"

"Yes, he's going to be just fine. He had some complications from his stroke." Stiles left out the part about Pastor being abused on purpose. He didn't think it was necessary to divulge that kind of heartrending information to his sister. He didn't want her to have a setback. "He's in Health South Rehab undergoing speech therapy and occupational therapy. He's up walking around, and his speech is returning. He doesn't know that you're in the hospital. I didn't want to tell him until both of you got better."

"I'm glad you made that call. Had he known about me, it probably would have made matters worse for him. He would have been trying his best to convince you to bring him up here."

"I know it. I still don't know when I'm going to tell him."

"Don't. Just tell him that I've been asking about him, and that I'll get down there to see him as soon as I can."

"I will. He knows you love him. That's the important thing."

"But I want him to know that I haven't been ignoring the fact that he's in the hospital. I don't want him to think I've deserted him."

"I promise you that I won't let him think that. He doesn't have a phone in his room right now, so that's good. That way he doesn't have to worry about who's calling and who's not."

"Good. The doctor said I may be going home in a few days. I can call him then. I thought I might be going home today, but the doctor came in early this morning and said he wants to keep an eye on me for a little while longer before he discharges me."

"Obey the doctor, Francesca. I know how thick-headed you can be, and you do too." Stiles laughed..

"How is Detria doing? Are you all pregnant again?"

"She's doing okay. And no, we aren't pregnant again. I think she's still having a hard time dealing with the loss of the baby. Believe me, I understand what she's going through because I feel bad myself. But I also believe that God is going to restore what we have lost. No child will take the place of the one we lost, but God is going to turn our tears of sadness to tears of joy. He's going to give us a family. He's going to make sure you're an auntie and that Pastor is a grandpa."

"That's good, Stiles. That's real good."

Without warning, Francesca's eyes closed and Stiles heard her light breathing. She had fallen asleep instantly. He sat next to her and watched her as she slept. He forced his tears to stay back as he thought of losing his sister. He prayed that God would let her live and not die. There was so much more ministry for Francesca. She had someone who loved her and wanted her just the way she was. Stiles softly took hold of her hand and gently began to massage it. His memories of his mother were strong, and grief made his heart grow heavy. He thought of his child being in heaven with Audrey and smiled slightly.

His own body began to succumb to fatigue. He laid his head back against the chair, and within minutes he was asleep.

The phone rang and woke Stiles up. He

looked around like he was confused as the hospital room phone continued to ring. When he found his bearings, Stiles walked around to the other side of Francesca's bed and picked up the phone. Francesca hadn't budged an inch.

"Hello."

"Hello. Stiles, is that you?"

"Yes. Rena?"

"Hi, there. How is Francesca?"

"She's doing much better. She's sleeping right now."

"Tell that girl when she wakes up that I said to stop pretending to be asleep so she won't have to take my calls. I know that game." Stiles could hear Rena laughing on the other end. He laughed too.

"I'll be sure to tell her that. How are you doing?"

"Great. I was sitting here at home watching the Food Network, and I thought of Francesca. I hadn't heard back from you, so I thought I would call to see how things were going. Is she going to be getting out of the hospital any time soon?" Rena asked.

"I think so. She was saying that the doctor came in this morning and told her she may be going home in a few days. You know Francesca, she's a fighter. If there's any way she can get out of here, she will."

"I know that's right. How is Pastor getting along?"

"He's doing better too. Thank you for asking."

"No need to thank me. I still care about

Francesca and Pastor. I always will."

"And me?" Stiles asked.

"What about you?" Rena responded.

"Do you still care about me?"

Rena remained quiet.

"Oh, it's like that, huh?" Stiles tried to sound like he was laughing, but he really wasn't.

"No, it's not like that. Of course I care about you. I'm a child of God so I am commanded to love. You just caught me off guard, that's all. Well, I'm not going to hold you. Will you tell Francesca I called?"

Stiles acted like he didn't hear what Rena said. He followed up with questions of his own. "You still with that guy you brought to my mother's funeral? What's his name, Bob? Robert? I guess you're married to him by now, huh?"

"For your information, Robert is fine, and we are not married, but we are very much still together," Rena answered with added emphasis. "I told you when I talked to you after your marriage that I had no plans of getting remarried any time soon."

"Oh, is that right?" Stiles raised his eyebrows. He had no idea why he was giving Rena a hard time, but he was enjoying it. "I can't believe Robert has allowed you to be single for this long?"

A voice of anger penetrated through the phone. "Look, no man allows me to do anything. I am my own person. Of all people, you should know that, Stiles."

"Oooh, sounds like somebody's getting a

little testy. Anyway, tell me, Mrs. Graham, when are you two jumping the broom?" This was one of those times Stiles was glad he could reminisce a little by calling Rena by his last name. There were women who asked for the return of their maiden names when they got divorced, but not Rena. The request had never come up. Deep inside, part of Stiles was glad she still wore his last name.

"It's Ms. Graham, please. Anyway, what's with all of these personal questions?"

"We are still friends, and I'm just curious. You mean you're going to jump on me because I asked a few personal questions?"

"Don't worry, Stiles. I'm sure when that day comes, you'll find some way to hear about it. Anyway, please tell Francesca that I'm praying for her. Oh, and tell Pastor too. I really have to hang up now. Take care of yourself."

"You too, Rena. I'll check you later." Stiles looked at the phone, smiled, and put it back on its base. He walked back around the bed to reclaim his seat. He looked around Francesca's bed until he saw the television remote. He flipped through several channels until he found something of interest.

20

*"There is only one person who could ever make
you happy, and that person is you."*
David Burns

Rena tried to dismiss the questions Stiles
had asked. Why was he interested in her
personal life when he had a wife at home?
There was no reason for him to inquire about
Robert and their relationship. It irritated her,
something Stiles always seemed able to do at a
whim. Today was no different. A phone call to
check on Francesca had turned into a
question-and-answer game with her ex. The
worst part about it was that she had allowed
him to interrogate her. The fact that he had
called her Mrs. Graham further infuriated her.
"How dare he," she yelled out loud.

The doorbell rang. Rena jumped off the den
chair like an angry cat. "Robert," she mouthed.
"Wait just a minute. I'm coming," she said.

Rena opened the red front door. "Hi,
sweetie," she said and moved to the side to
allow Robert entrance.

"Hi, yourself," he answered in return and
kissed her lips.

"I thought you were going to bring the kids
with you."

"I was, but then my sister called. She
wanted to take them to a birthday party one of
her co-workers is having for her little boy at,

uuuhhh, that pizza place—"

"Chuck E. Cheese's?" Rena said.

"No, not Chuck E. Cheese's."

"Incredible Pizza?" Rena guessed again.

"Yep, that's it. Incredible Pizza. Their being gone gives us at least a couple hours of alone time. I like that," Robert said as he reached out to embrace Rena.

Rena eased out of his arms. "We don't want one thing to lead to another." As much as she wanted to indulge in lovemaking with Robert, she knew she was not going to take that step until she was his wife. She was celibate, and she planned on remaining that way until the day God saw fit for her to commit herself to a man in marriage. She hoped that man would be Robert.

"Marry me, then. I want you so badly, Rena. I don't understand what the holdup is." Robert's sense of frustration was obvious in the pleading tone of his voice.

"Robert, why do we have to talk about this now? Can't we just enjoy spending some alone time together? Hey, it's nice outside. Why don't we go take a walk in Andover Park?" Rena suggested. She turned around and headed for her room, but Robert reached out and stopped her.

"I don't want to go to the park. I want to go to a justice of the peace."

Thoughts of Stiles' interrogation minutes before returned. "Robert, do we have to do this?"

Rena didn't know how much longer she could put off marrying Robert. She had given him every excuse she could think of not to, but he was not about to give up. What was wrong with her anyway? She heard Stiles call her Mrs. Graham. Why would he mess with her head like that when he was a happily married man? A preacher at that. The nerve of him. She looked at Robert and blurted out words she wished she could take back as soon as she said them.

"If you want to get married, then fine, Robert. We'll get married."

"Are you serious?" he asked.

"What do you mean, am I serious? Of course, I'm serious. You keep hounding me about marrying you. Now that I tell you I will, you act like you're stunned."

She didn't mean to snap at him, but she was confused and mad at the same time— confused because she wasn't sure what she felt for Robert sometimes, and mad because Stiles had pushed her buttons—again. What he possibly got out of taunting her, Rena couldn't begin to guess. It wasn't like Stiles still loved her and wanted to be with her. Even if he did, there was no way that could happen. She was not about to be anybody's other woman. As for Robert, sometimes he reminded her of Stiles, especially when he was like he was today— demanding and pushing her to marry him. How many times had she told him she would marry him when the time was right? Her conversation with her ex forced her to say yes to Robert before thinking.

"Hounding you? Is that what you think of me? I love you. I don't mean to hound you." He turned her loose and walked over to the sofa and sat down. "We need to talk."

"Talk?" she said and placed one hand on her hip. "What do we need to talk about, Robert? You asked me to marry you, and I said yes. Now you don't seem satisfied with that answer. What do you want from me?" Both hands flew up in the air out of frustration. She placed one hand on her forehead and took several awkward steps around the living room.

"Hey, come on. Calm down. Please," Robert asked. "Come sit down next to me. I promise I won't try anything. Let's just relax. You seem tense."

Rena accepted his invitation. She parked herself next to him on her sofa. Robert reached around and placed his arm around her and brought her in closer to him. He was true to his word. He didn't say anything nor did he try to kiss her. Several seconds passed without an exchange of conversation.

"Do you want to talk about it?" he asked her.

"Talk about what?"

"Whatever has you in this mood."

She made the quote sign with her fingers and said, "I'm not in a mood, Robert. I just get tired of people always trying to find out what I'm thinking and trying to force me to do things that I'm not ready to do."

"I'm not people, Rena. I'm your boyfriend, fiancé, or whatever you call me. I don't know who's been pressuring you or trying to force you to do anything, but it's not me. Now, do you want to talk about it or not?"

"I'm sorry, Robert. I guess I'm just tired. I've been on the go for the past few weeks. I didn't mean to snap at you."

"Are you sure that's all it is?" he asked.

"Yeah, that's all it is. I love you, and I do want to marry you. But I want to be sure about my marriage this time, Robert. I worry about whether we'll be able to have children. I don't want to give you herpes. And what if I end up with HIV? What then? I know you say that you're okay with my past, but I'm not okay with my past, if that makes sense."

Rena looked at him intently. The last thing she wanted to do was hurt Robert. He was a good man. He treated her with the utmost respect, admiration, and love. He was a man who loved God. Most of all, he was a man who said her past did not dictate their future. But Rena wasn't so sure.

"It makes sense, but how many more times do I have to tell you that I don't care about your past? I could have walked out when Francesca called herself telling me all about you and her at Audrey's repast, and no one would have blamed me for doing so. But I stayed because I love you. As for the herpes, Rena, I plan on being with you for the rest of my life. I can't be overly concerned about something that may or may not happen. That bridge will have to be crossed if we ever get to it. The same about HIV. You've been getting tested every six months like the doctor suggested, and your test comes out negative every time. You have to believe, Rena. As for children, there's nothing that stands in the

way of you having children. I know there's a
chance that a pregnancy for you might mean
complications for a baby, but we have to stand
on the Word of God. We have to give all of our
concerns to Him, sweetheart." Robert leaned
his head against hers. "I love you, Rena. I want
to spend the rest of my life with you. I wish you
felt the same."

"I do, Robert. Just give me time."

"I don't want to sound pushy, but I guess I
am. How much more time do you need, Rena?"

"Robert, we need time to learn more about
each other. You don't even know if your
children's mother will come barging back into
your life. What are you going to do if that
happens?"

"Rena, stop making excuses already. Don't
make this about me or my ex-wife because you
know it's not about that. It's about you and
me." Robert pounded a flat hand against his
chest. His face turned a shade lighter.

"I don't want to do this right now," Rena
yelled. "Why can't we just go out and spend
some time together, just you and me?" Rena
turned and looked at Robert again. His face
appeared to be drained of color. "Robert," she
grabbed his hand. "I don't like to see you upset
with me. I want to make you smile and laugh."

"You know what? Sorry if I don't feel like
laughing right now." Robert stood and took off
in the direction of the front door. "I'm out of
here."

Rena quickly stood up and took hold of
Robert's elbow in an effort to stop him from
leaving. "Don't do this, Robert. You're acting

really petty right now."

Robert snatched his arm out of Rena's grip. "Petty? Is that what this conversation is to you? Petty? You know what, Rena? You might just be right. Maybe I'm the one taking this too seriously. But I thought loving someone, proposing to that person, and wanting to spend the rest of your life with that person was serious. Thanks for setting the record straight." Robert hurried to the front door and opened it. "I'll talk to you later."

Before Rena had time to respond, Robert had walked outside and closed the door behind him.

Rena opened the door and chased after him. "You are so full of it," she shouted.

Robert kept walking toward his car. This display of avoidance fueled her flames. "You want me to believe that you're so high and mighty, like you're rescuing some damsel in distress." Robert stopped inches from his car door. He bit down on his bottom lip. Rena could see his chest deflate like he'd taken a huge sigh.

"I've never come at you like that, Rena. I've been real since the first time we met."

"Real? Did you say real? Oh, I don't think so. You've been fake. That's what you've been. There is no way a man is told by his woman's ex-lover that they've had a longtime sexual affair, and he just waves it off like it's nothing. That's exactly what you want me to believe. And," Rena said with added force, "not to mention that the ex-lover happened to be another woman. Come on, Robert. Be for real.

You really want me to think you can overlook something like that? I don't think so. But let's not stop there, Mr. High and Mighty," she mocked.

She moved so close to him he probably could feel tiny splatters of her spit as she spoke angrily to him. "I have herpes—that, by the way, is contagious. Oh, but you know that already. I may not be able to have children. Suppose I come back home one day from having an HIV test and tell you that it came back positive? You want me to wave that off and pretend like I'm totally healthy? You want me to run off and marry you, and we're supposed to live happily ever after like some fairy tale? Well, I don't think it's that cut-and-dried, Robert Becton. I will not wake up one day and have you blame me for giving you herpes, or anything worse for that matter. I won't be the one responsible for making life for you and your kids miserable. So don't you dare—" She pointed a finger in his face. "Don't you dare come off like you're some saint and that you can see past all my faults. You're not God, Robert."

"Don't you know I know that," he screamed back and pointed his long, thick finger toward her. "I never have said I was God. I've never tried to portray this . . . this perfect man you're describing. All of this time, and you don't know a thing about me. I'm not your ex-husband. I'm not the one who told you to get out. I'm not the one who has the problem with forgiveness. He is. Stop looking at me and seeing him."

"How dare you accuse me of looking at you

and seeing him? I've never done any such thing. Yes, I'm having problems letting go of my past. I can't help that right now. Only God can deliver me from the battle I'm fighting against myself. As for you, you are just so darn self-righteous."

"Self-righteous? Isn't that something? Here I am standing before you, pleading with you to be my wife. All I'm guilty of is falling in love with a woman who happens not to be perfect and who happens to have made her share of mistakes just like me and the rest of the people in this world. But here I am getting bashed because I choose not to dwell on those mistakes, and instead would rather spend my time loving you, not making you feel bad about something that's done and over with. I'm through." Robert opened the car door and got inside. He started the engine and left Rena standing in her driveway with a look of anguish and shame on her face.

Rena watched him speed off before she dashed back inside the house. She slammed the door behind her, leaned against it, and cried. Robert was right. She avoided the subject of marriage like the bubonic plague. There was far too much fear inside her—fear of what marriage to Robert would mean. There was no way she was supposed to believe that Robert could accept her unconditionally. No way at all.

21

*"You can't undo anything you've already done,
but you can face up to it. You can tell the truth.
You can seek forgiveness. And then let God do
the rest."* Unknown

Detria left Brooke's house after she awoke
from a two-hour nap. Brooke had been right
about one thing: she was exhausted. For her to
fall asleep like that at someone else's house,
even if it was her sister, was unlike her. She
drove in the direction of home. It was time for
her to make a decision about her life. The only
problem was, she didn't know what that
decision was going to be.

Detria neared the expressway. Her car
operating like it had a mind of its own, she
found herself taking the 240 North exit toward
downtown. She had to go see Pastor. Stiles had
told her that his health was improving
considerably. If he couldn't talk, he could
listen to what she had to say.

Detria pulled into the circular driveway and
drove around the lot until she came upon an
empty parking space. Before she got out of her
car, she prayed for God to direct her words and
for Pastor to be receptive toward her.

She sucked in a deep breath, let it go, and
then proceeded into the building. Detria had
drilled herself on what she was going to say to
Pastor Graham.

Detria approached the information desk and asked the receptionist where she could locate Chauncey Graham. After receiving the room and floor numbers, she continued toward the elevators and pushed the button.

"Lord, help me get through this," Detria whispered as she studied herself in the mirror-like reflection inside the elevator.

Detria approached Pastor's room. The door was open so she cautiously walked inside the semi-private room. She nodded her head at the man in the first bed. Pastor looked up from the chair where he was seated watching one of his favorite judge shows.

Detria thought she saw a glimmer of fear in his eyes as she spoke. "Hello, Pastor. How are you feeling today?"

Pastor did look frightened. He reached toward the side of the bed like he was trying to find the button to call for a nurse.

"Pastor, don't. I'm not here to hurt you. I promise," Detria said when she saw him fumbling for the button. "I need to talk to you. Please, Pastor."

In a manner that could be described as conscientious and deliberate, he opened his mouth to reply. "He . . . hel . . . lo," he stammered until the word escaped his lips.

"My goodness, you're talking, Pastor. Praise God." Detria smiled and walked closer to him. She leaned over and gave him a light hug. "I know you're probably wondering what I'm doing here," she commented. Pastor looked at her but didn't say a word. "I've been thinking about you. Stiles has kept me informed about your progress. You look well." Detria continued to ramble, unsure how she would approach the subject with someone else in the room. She hadn't planned on Pastor having a roommate. "I had some errands to run close by, so I thought I'd stop in to see how you were getting along," she lied without reason.

Pastor remained quiet, but his eyes stayed on Detria. She began to feel somewhat uncomfortable. "Have you talked to your son today?"

Pastor shook his head.

"He hasn't called?" Detria scanned the room but did not see a telephone. She remembered suddenly that Stiles had said that Pastor didn't have a phone in his room. "Well, you know Stiles. He'll be here sometime today, I'm sure," she said. Her uneasiness mounted. For a few minutes she kept quiet and pretended like she was enjoying the judge show along with Pastor.

A commercial gave her an opportunity to speak again. "Pastor, how would you like to take a walk with me? Not far. Maybe to the recreational room I saw down the hall. Do you feel like walking? Getting a little exercise?"

"Umm."

Detria thought he was about to tell her no, but contrary to her thought, Pastor slowly reached for the walker that was propped against the wall.

"Let me help you with that," Detria offered. She grabbed the walker and released the holding mechanism until the walker opened up like an umbrella. She helped Pastor stand. "You're doing great, Pastor. I am so proud of you." Her voice was soft and smooth. She was still nervous about being at the hospital, but she did her best not to let it show. What if Stiles popped up? What would she say then? No need to worry about that. I'm here now. God is with me. I can do this.

With extra caution, Detria held on to Pastor until he placed both hands on his walker and began to take small steps.

It took them almost ten minutes to arrive at the vacant recreational room. Detria saw several round tables and chairs. She chose the table closest to the door to make it easier for Pastor and helped him sit in one of the chairs.

"I'll let your walker stay next to you. No need to fold it up. I won't keep you in here long, but I do want to talk to you, Pastor. Do you mind?"

"No," he answered.

"I don't know where to start. I thought I had what I would say all planned. I prayed on my way here because there has been so much turmoil in my life, Pastor." She reached across the table where Pastor's hands rested and laid her hands on top of his. "Pastor, I'm here to tell you how I've been feeling, to talk with you about why I did what I did. I know there is nothing that can make you understand why I treated you the way I did, but I have to try to explain my actions anyway."

Pastor struggled to speak. He finally got the words out. "Thadz fine."

"Pastor, I've been angry a long time. I've been angry at you." Detria thought Pastor's eyebrows furrowed, but she couldn't be sure.

She continued to talk. There was one thing she was glad about: Pastor, whether he could speak plainly or not, had full understanding of what she was saying. His brain and memory had not been affected from what Stiles told her the doctors said. That was a miracle and a blessing in and of itself. "I guess you're asking yourself, 'Why would she be angry with me?' You should be the one angry at me. But that's why I'm here, Pastor. You see, I believed that you were the cause of me losing my baby. The day I found you in the bathroom and tried to pick you up, I thought I did damage to my child." Detria fought back tears, but she suspected her eyes were probably shining anyway.

This time, Detria did see Pastor's eyebrows furrow. He shook his head. "No. No," he mumbled.

"Maybe you're saying no because you think I'm crazy for believing you were the blame. Or maybe you're saying no because you don't know what else to say. Whatever the reason, I'm just here to tell you how I felt. And to be honest, I still feel some anger toward you at times, but I've been praying, Pastor. I've been praying so hard," she said. "But after I lost the baby, every day I saw you, every day I spent taking care of you meant another day I was reminded of my loss."

Detria patted her chest. "You deprived your son of his first child. I hated you, Pastor." Detria waved her hands and shook her head. "Now, you might be thinking that I was wrong, and maybe I was, but again I'm just speaking the truth. That anger and rage led to my abusing you. I've never done anything like that to anyone, Pastor. You must believe me. The first time I struck you, I thought I was going to lose my mind. I hated myself for what I had done. But then, thoughts of my baby kept flooding back over and over again, and every time I saw you, I hated you more. My rage mounted, and I wanted you to hurt like you had caused me to hurt."

Pastor's eyes filled with tears. Unlike Detria, he was not able to catch them as they overflowed and cascaded down his face. Detria searched in her purse and found a package of tissues, then used one to wipe the tears from his eyes.

"Pastor, I was wrong for hurting you. I was mixed up on the inside. I think I still am in a way." The more Detria talked, the more she wanted to talk. She had a breakthrough of sorts because for the next thirty minutes or so, she poured her heart out. "I know there is nothing in the world you would intentionally do to hurt me or my unborn child. But when I lost my baby, I wasn't thinking like that. All I could think about was, if I hadn't lifted you, then I wouldn't have put the strain on my body that caused me to lose my baby. I didn't care that my doctor said losing the baby was God's way of saying something would have been wrong with my child. I didn't care if something would have been wrong. I wanted my baby regardless." Tears poured down Detria's face.

She turned slightly so Pastor couldn't see the hurt she was sure was etched across her face. "Stiles doesn't know that I was the one who abused you. He still believes it was one of the ladies from the agency. How can I tell him that his wife . . . that it's me who brought harm to his father? How do I confess it to him, Pastor? I love my husband. I love him with all of my heart. This is about to drive me insane. I don't know what to do about it. I don't blame you for not wanting to be around me. I've seen fear in your eyes when I would come in your room at home. You couldn't speak out for yourself. You had no one to tell. You took the pain that I inflicted on you. Oh, God, I am so sorry, Pastor." Detria bowed her head and allowed tears to fall. She used her hands to cup her face.

She cried until she felt a trembling hand rest on the crown of her head. Detria slowly lifted her head and looked over at Pastor. His eyes seemed full of compassion and sorrow. She was deeply moved. "Can you ever forgive me? Can you ever look at me without despising me?"

With tear-filled eyes, Pastor nodded. He paused for several seconds between each word that poured forth until he was able to say fully, "I forgive you."

Detria didn't know how to respond. She felt like her heart was about to spill over with joy. She stood up, went to Pastor, and embraced him as tears dripped on top of his full head of salt-and-pepper hair. Detria rocked him in her arms.

"Thank you, Pastor. Thank you, so much—"

"What's all of this about?"

Detria jumped when she heard her husband's voice. Standing next to him was one of the nurses.

"Mr. Graham, I told your son I saw you coming down here with a beautiful young woman hanging on to you," the nurse said with an upturned mouth.

Detria found it hard to smile. She didn't know how much Stiles had heard. "We were just talking. I was telling Pastor how good it was to see how much he's improved," Detria said with a voice that she felt was shaky.

Stiles must not have noticed anything out of the ordinary initially because he walked up, hugged his father, and then embraced Detria. "You didn't say anything about coming to see Pastor," he told her.

"I know. I had to come downtown to run a couple of errands and thought I'd stop in to check on him."

"How are you feeling today, Pastor? Looks like you've been crying? Are you in pain?" He turned around and looked with suspicion at Detria.

"Crying? Why would he be crying? He's fine," Detria responded.

"No cry. Good," Pastor managed to say with ease.

The nurse spoke up. "Are you in pain, Mr. Graham?"

"No. Feel fine," he answered the nurse.

"Well, if he keeps up like this, he'll be out of here before you know it. Won't that be great, Mr. Graham?"

Pastor nodded.

"No, let's not nod. I want you to talk every chance you get."

"Yes," Pastor said to the nurse.

"I'll leave y'all in here to visit. If you need anything, let me know," the nurse said, and then turned and exited the room.

"God is good, I tell you," Stiles said.

Detria smiled awkwardly. Her heart kept up a rapid pace, but she was beginning to feel confident that Stiles more than likely had not heard the depth of her conversation with Pastor. The three of them lingered in the recreational room, and Stiles used the opportunity to tell Pastor that Francesca had been asking about him without mentioning her sickness. There would be time for that, but this was not the time to do so.

Pastor seemed to beam with happiness when Stiles told him Francesca had asked about him.

"Francesca said her church has been praying for you. I can't wait to tell her how good you're doing. You're going to be excited to hear something about her, I bet."

"What?" Pastor asked.

"I believe your daughter has herself a boyfriend."

Pastor managed to smile. "Boyfriend?" A questioning look came across his face.

"Yep, boyfriend," Stiles repeated.

"This is the first I've heard of this myself," Detria chimed in. "You've been holding this back from me and Pastor for how long?" she asked Stiles.

"Not long. I had to hear it straight from the

horse's mouth. Hey, let me see if I can get a hold of her now."

Stiles pulled out his cell phone and scrolled through the numbers until he came across Francesca's number at the hospital. It would be a great opportunity for Pastor to hear his daughter's voice without knowing where she was. He hoped Francesca wasn't asleep. He had left her only a few hours ago, and she was napping. Tim had made it to the hospital too, so Stiles felt more assured that Francesca was awake.

The phone rang a couple of times and Francesca answered. "Hey, sis. I'm here at the hospital with Pastor. He wants to speak to you."

"He wants to talk to me?" Francesca asked. "Praise God, he can talk again," she said, though her voice still sounded faint.

"Yes, he can talk again. And he may not be able to tell you all of what he wants to say, but just so you know, I told him about your man," Stiles said. He laughed. "Hold on just a sec. Here you go, Pastor. Stiles passed the phone to Pastor.

"Fran," Pastor said. "Fran," he said again.

"Hi, Pastor. It is so good to hear your voice. God is good, isn't He?"

"God good," Pastor answered. "Boyfr—"

"Don't listen to your son, Pastor. He's going overboard. I do have a dear and close friend. You may not remember him, but he was with the group that came to Memphis a few months ago. His name is Tim, but everybody calls him Brother Tim. He's right here with me. I think you'll like him, Pastor."

"Good to you?" Pastor said almost coherently.

"Yes, he is, Pastor. You'll get a chance to meet him again soon, okay?"

"'Kay. Bye." Pastor passed the phone back to Stiles.

"Sis, how are you?" Stiles asked in a voice that sounded ordinary and unconcerned so as not to get Pastor worried.

"I'm good," she said, but Stiles could hear how weak she was.

"We'll talk later."

"Tell her that I said hello before you hang up," Detria chimed in.

"Oh, my lovely wife says hello," Stiles told Francesca.

"Tell my sister-in-law the same. Bye, bro'."

"See ya, Francesca." Stiles ended the call and placed his BlackBerry back in its case on his waist.

"Pastor, I think it's time we get you back to your room. Your roommate is probably wondering where that strange woman took you off to," Detria said.

"Come on, let's get you up," Stiles told Pastor.

Pastor returned to his room and sat on his bed.

"Pastor, I'm going to get ready to leave. It was good seeing you," Detria said as Stiles stood and focused on something playing on the television. Detria embraced Pastor and whispered in his ear. "Thank you. Thank you so much." She kissed him on his cheek. She felt his arms reach around her waist as he returned her hug. She felt absolutely wonderful. The feeling of guilt over what she had done had just about disappeared.

Detria touched her husband's shoulder to get his attention. "Are you staying here or leaving?"

"I believe I'll follow you out. I've had a long, harried day. I want to get some food in this belly." Stiles patted his stomach. "And then I need to start revising this week's sermon. Pastor, are you going to be all right?"

"Yes. Fine," Pastor said.

"Great. Then we'll check on you later. We love you, Pastor," Stiles said for both himself and Detria. "God bless you, sir," Stiles told the man in the bed next to Pastor.

On her drive home, Detria felt overjoyed. She couldn't wait to call Brooke. There was no way she would have been able to tell her the good news when she got home. With Stiles there, it would have been nearly impossible to express her gratitude to Pastor for all that had transpired during her visit. Detria dug around inside her purse until she felt the smoothness of her cell phone. She pushed the number four key and waited for the phone to connect. "Hey," she said when her sister answered.

"Hey, what's up with you?" Brooke asked.

"I called to tell you that I just came from talking to Pastor."

"You did? How did it go?"

"Better than I could ever have hoped. I told him everything. I feel so relieved. I asked him to forgive me, and he said that he would. It was indescribable. God heard my prayer. Brooke, I feel like I can move forward with my life. You just don't know how wretched I felt."

"I still think you should ask Dr. Henderson to refer you to a good psychologist. You still have some unresolved issues. And are you going to tell Stiles?"

"I don't know. We'll see, though. I want to talk to Pastor again. But maybe you're right. Maybe I do need to talk to a professional, at least a few times. I'll see."

"I'm so glad for you, Detria. John, the kids, and I are going over to Mom and Pops. Why don't you and Stiles meet us there? Momma cooked some turnip greens and a pot roast. She invited us to come over. You know she doesn't know what it means to cook only enough for herself and Pops, so there's going to be plenty."

"That actually sounds like a good idea. Let me call Momma, and then I'll call Stiles to see what he thinks before we get all the way home. But I'll come even if he decides not to."

"Good. I'll see you in a few," Brooke said and hung up the phone.

Detria's mother loved the idea of her and Stiles joining them for dinner. It had been months since her children and their families had been over at the same time. Detria called and asked Stiles if he would join them, and he agreed. Detria smiled, then turned up the radio to listen to a group singing one of her favorite songs, "Our God Saves."

"Yes, you do save, Father God," Detria said. "Yes, you do."

Stiles told Detria to meet him at home so they could go to her parents' house together. Detria agreed. The two of them freshened up when they got home and then went to her parents'.

Dinner at the Mackey's' turned out to be fun for Detria. Stiles acted like he had a great time too. If the amount of food eaten was any indication of how much of a good time he had, then Stiles would have definitely taken home a first place trophy. Detria enjoyed playing with her nephews. It reminded her of how much she wanted to have a family with Stiles. Perhaps God would smile on her again and give her another chance at being a mother. She wasn't without hope that it would happen one day.

Before they left her parents', Detria prepared a nice-sized carryout of food for herself and Stiles. The couple exchanged hugs and kisses with everyone, and then left for home.

"That was a great dinner, wasn't it?" Detria asked. She massaged Stiles' thigh while he drove.

"Yeah, I had a good time, and don't get me started on the food. I forgot what a Grade A cook my mother-in-law is." Stiles laughed. "I'm so full, but I'm still glad you brought plenty of leftovers."

"I know you are," Detria quipped. She leaned over and kissed Stiles on his cheek.

"What was that for?" he asked and looked at her with pleasure on his face.

"Because."

"Because what?" he asked.

"Because I love you. Because I'm glad we're at this point in our lives. Because I adore the man you are."

"Whoa, are you setting the stage to get a larger ring or something?" He whipped into the far right lane. "If you are," he added, "then you might be on the right track."

"Is that right? Well, you ain't seen nothing yet," she cooed into his ear and lightly bit the tip of his earlobe. "Wait until I get you home," Detria teased.

Stiles chuckled. His head went back, and then he sped up when he made a left turn on to their street. "I'm going to hold you to whatever it is you have in mind."

"Do you think you can handle it?" she continued with her flirtatious antics.

"I'll let you be the judge of that," Stiles said with a look of delight plastered on his handsome face.

"Oh, shucks." Detria pouted her lips.

Stiles pulled into the garage and turned off the car. "What's wrong?"

"I forgot that you have to work on your sermon. Oh, well, what I had in mind will just have to wait. Maybe next time."

"Oh, no. Don't think you're going to get off that easy. I already have my sermon outlined. I have to pull it up and work on a few things that God placed in my spirit. After that, I'm all yours." This time he was the one who kissed her. His lips lingered on hers and his hands expertly caressed the body he knew so well. The sounds of love that escaped from both of their lips filled the garage.

Suddenly, Detria pulled away. "The last one in the house is a rotten egg," she screamed, grabbed the containers of food, and fled out of the car, but not before Stiles beat her to the door, opened it, and rushed inside.

"Come here, my rotten egg," he said and whisked her in his arms.

22

"You are what I never knew I always wanted."
Fools Rush In movie

Two additional weeks passed before Francesca was discharged from the hospital. Brother Tim talked with Stiles and told him that he would take Francesca home, so there was no reason for Stiles to drive all the way to Dyersburg.

Francesca leaned her head back on the car's headrest. "I don't know how to thank you for all you've done for me," she told Tim on their drive to her apartment.

"How many times have I told you that there's no need to thank me. I love you, Francesca. I think you know that, don't you?"

Francesca remained quiet and looked out the window. Her mind was full of confusing thoughts. Was this real? Could she be in love with Tim? If she was, did that mean she was never a lesbian? She didn't know what to think about her sexuality, but she admitted to herself that her heart did pound faster whenever she saw Tim. He did make her laugh, and he always made her feel special. But what about her sexual orientation? What about the years she spent in the arms of other women? What about Rena? Rena? Oh, I need to call her. I can't believe she called to check on me. She must think I don't give a darn about her concern since I haven't called her back.

"Hey, you," Tim said. Francesca jerked her head around. "Have you heard anything I've said? You seem like you're in another world."

"I'm sorry. My mind just went to some other things. I was thinking about Rena."

Tim stopped at a red traffic light. He turned his head and looked at Francesca. His hand began to lightly caress her hair. "What about Rena?" He didn't act the least bit perturbed or uncomfortable with the fact that Francesca brought up her ex-lover.

"You told me she called. Stiles told me she called, and I've yet to call her back. I was just thinking that she must think I really don't give a care about her show of concern. That's all. And it's not just her. There have been so many people who've been praying for me and who sent cards and flowers." Francesca looked over her shoulder at the backseat and viewed the balloons, box of cards, flowers, and other tokens people had sent while she was in the hospital. "It makes me realize just how much God loves me, even after all the hurt I've brought into people's lives, including Rena's. I just can't believe she still cares about me."

The light changed, and Tim continued to drive. "Francesca, the main thing you have to do is stop beating up on yourself. God has forgiven you, and it sounds like Rena has too. I mean, you were more than, well, lovers," Tim sort of stumbled over the word. "The two of you were best friends forever, you know."

Francesca looked at Tim. He looked over at her. "What?" he asked.

"I love you, Timothy Swift."

Tim's face turned red. His eyes glistened. He quickly focused back on the road.

"Are you all right? Did I say something wrong?" she asked him.

"No. You just don't know how long I've wanted to hear you say those words. I've prayed and prayed. I know it wasn't easy for you to tell me that you love me. I—"

"Don't say anything. Just listen and drive," she said, and then grinned. "I don't know if my love is enough for you because I don't know how to love a man, Tim. I don't know if what my heart is feeling is the kind of love that you need and deserve. All I know is that you are extremely special to me. And if there is any chance, any chance at all, of having a relationship with you, then I want to go for it."

Tears streamed down Tim's face as he stared ahead.

"I don't know how I can be much of anything to you, especially now that I have AIDS, but I do know that I want to spend my time trying."

Tim made the final turn onto Francesca's street and pulled up to the security gate. She passed him her entrance card and the gate slowly opened. Tim parked in front of Francesca's apartment. Without saying a single word, he jumped out of the car, walked around to Francesca's side, and opened the door for her.

Francesca was still weak. He helped her into her apartment. She looked around the quiet space. "I miss him already. I didn't know how much until I walked in here," she said to Tim. "My baby probably thinks I ran off and left him. I want him to be curling around my legs like he always did whenever I came in the house," she said of her cat.

Tim gathered her in his arms. "I know you do, baby. But Jabez is in a good home. A real good home. You know the Wilkins family has always adored Jabez. I've been going by their house and checking on him. He's the boss, the top cat around that place." Tim chuckled.

Francesca managed to smile. "That's good. It's just that I wanted him home when I got here."

"You need to get settled in yourself first. I promise that I'll go pick up Jabez in a day or two. You need some time to adjust to being at home again. Okay?"

"Okay," Francesca said and touched her face like she had a nervous twitch.

"Let me go outside and bring your things in. Why don't you have a seat in your favorite old raggedy recliner?" Tim said.

Francesca laughed out loud. "Oh, no you didn't just call my beautiful, soft recliner raggedy?" She managed to pick up the fluffy pillow from the chair and used it to hit Tim on his chest.

He grabbed hold of her and kissed her. Francesca pulled her head back. She didn't know what to say or do. She'd never been kissed by a man—never desired to be kissed by one until Tim. The butterflies in her stomach fluttered.

"I'm sorry about that," he said. "I couldn't

help myself. You're so beautiful, Francesca."

Francesca leaned her head against his chest in silence. When she spoke she said, "Maybe you should get the things out of the car. I'm going to take your advice and sit down in my raggedy chair." The two of them looked at each other and smiles cascaded across both their faces.

Tim made two trips to get all of Francesca's gifts and clothes from the car. He came back inside her apartment and placed the last of the items around the apartment.

"Will you sit down, please?" Francesca asked him.

Tim obeyed and plopped down on the bright, tangerine-orange sofa nearby. "Since you've admitted your unfailing love for me, tell me something."

"Don't start nothing, Tim. I said I love you. I did not say that I was in love with you."

"Well, let's clarify that right now. Francesca Graham, are you in love with me?" Tim got down on the floor, onto his knees, and crawled over to where Francesca sat.

She laughed and petted him on the head like she would Jabez. "You are so crazy," she told him. She replaced a look of amusement with one of seriousness. Her tone of voice matched her expression. Francesca caressed the side of Tim's bearded face with the back of her hand. His face felt rough yet tender at the same time. She felt that funny feeling inside her tummy again. Her words came out slowly and with executed caution. "I am in love with you, Tim. I don't want anyone else in my life but you," she told him.

Tim rested his head on her legs. His hands moved along the contours of her body. He glanced back up at her. "I want you to be my wife. I want to spend the rest of my life on earth with you, Francesca. Will you marry me?"

Francesca took his head in her hands and tilted his face upward. She looked at the obvious love that seemed to glow in Tim's eyes. At that moment, she felt a sense of peace and total acceptance. Marriage had never entered her mind—not ever. Her life had been spent living on the streets, doing drugs, and hanging out with her lesbian lovers and get-high friends. Now, here she was, a woman living with a death sentence over her life, but who was still loveable and loved.

"Yes. Sounds like a pretty good idea," Francesca told him.

He kissed Francesca all over her face. He didn't stop until his mouth covered hers.

23

"One reason God created time was so that there would be a place to bury the failures of the past." Unknown

Pastor and Stiles watched the movers unload the last piece of Pastor's furniture into his new home. Kirby Pines Life Care Community was where Pastor decided to move after he was released from Health South Rehab.

Like Francesca, he stayed in the rehab hospital far longer than any of them expected. But the improvement Pastor experienced after working with the therapists proved to be more than worth a one-month stay.

Pastor looked forward to being on his own again. He had prayed and thought about it while he was at Health South. There was no way he could go back to living with Stiles and Detria. He couldn't put the weight of his health problems on his son and daughter-in-law. He didn't want a repeat of what had already happened.

The road had been long and definitely tough at times for him, and he prayed every day for God to not allow him to be bitter toward his daughter-in-law. God answered his prayer because Pastor felt nothing but pure compassion for Detria. He welcomed the change he was about to embark upon.

Pastor had made the final decision to move on his own while he was in rehab, and there was no turning back. He asked some of the nurses to research various assisted-living homes, and Kirby Pines impressed him the most. One of the patients at Health South lived at Kirby Pines too. It took some convincing and standing up for himself before Stiles gave in to Pastor's decision.

"Pastor, I really do like this place. I believe you're going to have a good time living here," Stiles said when they walked inside the one-bedroom apartment unit. "I tell you, at first I was dead set against you living on your own again, but I know you're not really alone. God is with you. And the staff here has been outstanding. Who knows, maybe you'll regain the use of your legs enough to drive your car again. Or we could see about getting you one of those hand controls to drive with once you're fully recuperated."

"I like the thought of driving again," Pastor said. At Kirby Pines, he would receive comprehensive health care. He could continue his occupational therapy, which had given Pastor a new lease on life. Maybe he could prepare to move forward in life without Audrey by his side.

The six hundred-plus-square-foot apartment was more than sufficient and comfortable in Pastor's eyes. When Stiles finally finished arranging the furniture, he left Pastor alone to get used to his new surroundings. Just as Pastor was about to catch the end of one of his judge shows, he heard a knock on the door.

"Who could this be? Maybe a welcome committee," Pastor joked as he ambled over to answer the door.

Much to his surprise, when he looked through the peephole, he saw his daughter-in-law on the other side and quickly opened the door to welcome her in. "My, my, my. Come on in here, Detria."

Detria stepped inside and looked around the furnished apartment. It looked totally different from when she, Pastor, and Stiles first took a tour of a model apartment at Kirby Pines.

"This is really nice, Pastor. Of course, you're going to have to let me put my feminine touches on the place," she said. She continued to walk through the apartment until she had visited each area.

"So, I guess I have your stamp of approval, huh?"

"Yes, you do. My hubby did a good job placing the furniture in the right position. I'll have to give him a pat on the back when I get home." Detria laughed.

"Sit down," he offered, and Detria did so on the brown and tan sofa.

"I see you're watching Judge Judy. I don't know if Judge Mathis will like that," she teased.

Pastor chuckled lightly and sat down in his chair across from Detria.

"So, tell me, what brings you here, child?"

"I was on my way to help Stiles with the finishing touches, but he called and told me he had already left. I decided to come by anyway. I wanted to see for myself what I need to do to help make your new place comfortable for you."

"That's mighty kind of you, but I think I have everything I need. The Lord has been good to me. Real good." Pastor didn't sound overly receptive to Detria, but he wasn't rude to her either.

Detria placed both hands on her lap. The two of them watched the remaining case on Judge Judy. When the television show ended and a commercial came on, Detria spoke up.

"Pastor, I want to talk to you again about what I did to—"

Pastor raised one hand toward Detria. "No. Stop it. No need to go there. We've already talked about it. As far as I'm concerned, that's over and done with. I'm not going to sit here and pretend like I don't think about what you did. I'm human, and what you did hurt me more than physically. But I'm also a man of God. I have to forgive. God commands me to do so. I've been a preacher since I was a youngster. I've heard confessions from people that you wouldn't believe. I've had to keep confidences of people who've done and said awful things. But if God can forgive us, then who am I not to find it in my heart to forgive you? You're my daughter-in-law and I still love you. I won't allow a wall of anger to keep me from receiving all that God has for me." His words still came out slowly, but he spoke clearly.

Detria shed tears that she quickly wiped

away with her fingers. "Thank you, Pastor. I don't see how you do it. I don't understand it. God knows you're a better person than I ever could be. If I were you, there's no way I could forgive a person who treated me the way I treated you. But I don't know what to do from here."

"What do you mean?"

"I don't know what to do about Stiles. I've been wrestling with whether to tell him that I was the one who hurt you. I don't want to deceive my husband. I don't want someone else taking the blame for something that I am responsible for doing."

"That's a decision you're going to have to make. As for me, as far as I'm concerned, it's over. I'm fine. There's no need for me to go running to Stiles and telling him what happened. To be honest, I can't believe he hasn't brought it up to me himself. But if he should, then that's when I'll tell him that it's something that you and I have already handled. He may not like that, but that's the way it's going to be. Plus, I know you're sorry, Detria. You didn't mean to hurt me."

"Oh, Pastor," Detria dropped to her knees beside him. "Would you do that for me?" Detria started to cry.

"I know you were going through a lot back then, Detria. I just wish I could have done something to help you, but I couldn't. I was too sick myself."

"That's what I'm talking about" She got up and sat back on the sofa. ." I took advantage of your sickness to abuse you. I was wrong. I know God has forgiven me. I know I've begged and pleaded with Him enough."

"Honey, you don't have to plead with God. You ought to know that, child. God stands ready to forgive us when we sin. He not only forgives us, but He. . .," Pastor stopped for a moment like he had to catch his next breath. "As far as the east is from the west, so far hath He removed our transgressions from us." Pastor still knew the Bible like the palm of his hand. Just like Stiles, Pastor could quote the scripture verbatim, stroke or no stroke.

"Yes, you're right. Part of me wants to leave what I did in the past. The other part of me wants to confess to Stiles." Her face appeared firmly set like she was in deep thought.

"All I can tell you is silence holds many words. Don't say anything to Stiles until you've heard from God. As for me saying anything to him, that's something you don't have to concern yourself with. Truthfully, I don't know if Stiles can handle it right now. I mean, it would be like another act of betrayal to him, I'm afraid."

"That's exactly what I'm talking about, Pastor. If he finds out that it was me, then he will look at me as betraying him, just like Rena did. I don't want to do that to him. I love him too much to deceive him. Then again, I love him too much to tell him. I just want us to move on with our lives together, Pastor. I want to prove to him that I can be the wonderful wife he thinks I am. I don't want to walk around pretending to be someone that I'm not. I'm just me," Detria said.

"That's who you should be. God made you unique. His Word says that we are fearfully and wonderfully made. Let me tell you this."

"What is it?"

"If you ever decide that you want to tell Stiles, let me know. We'll tell him together. How about that?"

Detria popped up from the sofa again. She ran back over, got on her knees, and hugged Pastor gently around his waist. She rested her head on his lap and cried. "Thank you, Pastor. Thank you so much."

Detria looked up and wiped her tears away. "How can you be so forgiving after I was so terrible to you? How can you still love me and accept me as your daughter-in-law?" she cried.

"Because, my child, we all fall short. We're all imperfect beings. That's why our Lord and Savior had to die for us. We couldn't save ourselves, so He did it for us. You have to trust Him, baby. If you decide to talk to your husband, trust that God will work it out. There is nothing too hard for Him."

Detria got up off her knees. She looked at Pastor with watery eyes. "Thank you, Pastor."

"You have nothing to thank me for. All the times I've made mistakes in my life, and yet God saw fit to forgive me. Shucks." He laughed. "All of the times I made Audrey upset, but one thing about her, she wouldn't hold a grudge against me. Not once. I miss that woman." His bold, black eyes revealed a look of intensity and longing.

"I know you miss First Lady Audrey. I do too. I hope I can have the strength and fortitude she had one day. I hope I can be as good a wife to Stiles as she was to you. That's what I desire, Pastor."

"God will give you the desires of your heart. You have to ask Him, and then you have to believe that He will do that which you ask."

"I will. It's time for me to move forward with my life. I can't keep holding on to my hurt either. If I do, then I'll find myself stuck with no place to go."

Pastor struggled to get up from his chair. Detria reached out her hands to help him steady himself, but he refused her help.

"I won't have you and Stiles around here. I need to learn how to get around this place by myself."

Detria stepped back. "Excuse me, then," she said. She stood back and watched him maneuver until he stood straight.

Detria clapped her hands. "Great job. You're going to be over in the recreational area dancing with the ladies soon."

"I just might," Pastor laughed.

They walked to the door. Detria turned and embraced Pastor again. "Thanks, Pastor. I love you."

"I love you too, baby."

"I'll call and check on you later tonight before we go to bed. And I'm going to bring some things over here to spruce up this place."

"Sounds good. Sounds real good."

Detria opened the door and stepped outside onto the porch. "Is there anything you need before I leave?"

"No, I have plenty of everything. You go on

home and be with your husband. I'll be just fine."

They said their final good-byes before Pastor closed the door and returned to his favorite chair.

On her way home, Detria thought about the frank conversation she'd had with Pastor. "God, I need you. I need your guidance and direction," she prayed. "I can't live a life of deceit. I want to tell Stiles everything. Help me. Give me the words to say. Let him be receptive and not close me out, Lord. I love my husband. I want things to work out between us. Amen."

Detria continued the drive home. She stopped at one of the grocery stores she frequented that was close to home. At the spur of the moment, she decided to prepare a special meal for herself and Stiles. She chose two nice thick rib eye steaks, the fixings for a Caesar salad, two acorn squash, dinner rolls, and a bunch of fresh broccoli.

She arrived home. Stiles wasn't there, which was fine with Detria. She went upstairs and changed into her favorite pair of house sweats and a T-shirt, then returned to the kitchen to prepare a delicious meal.

While her steaks were broiling, Detria called and told Pastor about her decision to talk to Stiles. He reassured her that he believed she was doing the right thing, and he said he would be there if she needed him. She followed up by calling Brooke.

"Brooke, I'm going to tell him," she said as soon as Brooke answered her phone.

"Tell who what?" Brooke asked.

"Uggg, I'm going to tell Stiles about, you know . . . Pastor," she reminded her.

"Oh that. Are you sure you want to do that? You may be opening up a can of worms, Detria. Like I told you, I think Stiles would forgive you; it may be hard for him initially, but something in my spirit tells me that he loves you too much to lose you. Then again, you know him better than I do, and telling him the truth could backfire and put your marriage in jeopardy. The bottom line is that it's your call."

"I know, which is why I'm so confused. I talked with Pastor again. He's settled into Kirby Pines, so I went to see him."

"How is that place?" Brooke asked. "I've heard people say it's really nice."

"Yeah, it is. I think Pastor is going to enjoy being on his own again. Plus, they have care providers round-the-clock."

"I can't believe that Stiles went for him living in an assisted-living community after everything that's happened."

"Pastor has his own mind. He wasn't about to come back and live with us. And you know how I felt about it."

"I hear you," Brooke remarked.

"I think it'll be better for our marriage, and it'll give Pastor the independence he needs. But anyway, we'll talk about that some other time. I'm cooking a nice dinner for Stiles. While we're eating, I'm going to just come out and tell him. I will not be another Rena. I'm not going to hide anything from my husband."

"I heard that. I'll tell you what, girl. I admire

you. You're a bigger woman than me because I don't know if I could confess something like that to John. I'd be too scared that he'd walk out on me. Whatever you decide, you know I've got your back. You are a wonderful person. I know that. Pastor knows that, and Stiles knows it too. If Pastor Graham could find it in his heart to forgive you, why wouldn't Stiles do the same? I believe he will."

"Don't think I'm not terrified because I am. This could be the end of my marriage. But I have to take the chance. I don't want to suffer the consequences of keeping this from him, only for him to find out one day what I did, you know?"

"Yeah, I hear you. I can understand that. I'm praying for you, for real. I don't wish what you're about to do on my worst enemy, not that I have one," Brooke mused.

"Ha, ha, ha. So funny. Seriously though, please pray. I'll try to call you later tonight if I can. If not, I'll call you when I get to work tomorrow."

"Okay. Bye."

"Bye," Detria replied. She hung up the phone and finished preparing dinner, then went upstairs to bathe and put on more clothes. She texted Stiles to let him know there was no need to stop and get something to eat because she had cooked dinner. She also told him that she had something important she needed to talk to him about.

Stiles responded to Detria's text: `"Is everything okay?`

Detria texted back: "Yes just need 2 tlk."

The last text message from him simply said: "K."

Stiles would be home from his evening class soon, so Detria took extra care to make sure everything was ready. She prayed another prayer, asking God for the proper words to say. On her way back downstairs, she saw Stiles at the foot of the stairs.

"Hey, you," he said with a broad smile that perfectly accented his chocolate skin.

Detria bounced down the stairs and into his outstretched arms. She kissed him fully and passionately on his lips.

"Now that's the kind of welcome I like. And something smells mighty good in here too. Did I forget something?"

"No, you didn't forget a thing. I just thought I'd prepare a nice meal for the two of us. Then we can talk."

"Talk? Umm? Now you've got me worried," Stiles said. "I didn't know what to think about that text message."

"No need for you to worry about a thing. Now, why don't you get comfortable, and I'll fix our plates."

"Okay, I'll be right back," he said and took the stairs two at a time.

Stiles returned moments later dressed down in a pair of blue pajama pants and a white tee. "Everything looks good," he said.

"Thank you. I hope it tastes as good as it looks," Detria responded.

"I know it will. You always have been a great cook." Stiles sat down at the table, followed by Detria. She extended her hands toward Stiles. He held them, the two bowed their heads, and Stiles blessed their food.

Stiles used his knife to cut a piece of steak. "This is delicious," he complimented her.

"Thanks, baby."

"Tell me, what is it you want to talk to me about? It must be pretty major to warrant such a great meal." Stiles stopped talking momentarily to chew his food. "Let's hear it," he said.

Detria cleared her throat. "Stiles, what I'm about to say is not going to be pretty. I already know that you're going to hit the roof. That's expected. But when I finish telling you what I have to say, promise me that you will go before God and pray for His spiritual guidance before you do anything else."

Stiles held the forkful of salad in his hand. He immediately swallowed what he had in his mouth. "What's going on? This doesn't sound good."

"It isn't good," Detria said. "As a matter of fact, it's terrible, and I'm responsible."

Detria shifted her eyes slightly away from Stiles then sucked in a deep breath before she began to confess what she'd done to Pastor. Detria ignored the changed expression on her husband's face. The urge to tell the truth was stronger. Detria got to the part about her abuse of Pastor. She jumped suddenly when both of Stiles' fists landed with monstrous force on the dining room table.

Stiles jumped up from the table. Like a tiger about to attack, the back of his foot kicked his chair from behind him.

Detria felt hot tears rolling down her face. Stiles stood before her with a look that revealed she'd hurt him. The realization that Stiles was deeply disturbed by what she'd told him could not quench the sudden sense of peace that fell over her. The truth, as bad as it was, had fought the battle and won the war. What Stiles would do was yet to be seen.

Stiles bolted from the dining room. He rushed to reach what was once Pastor's bedroom and closed the door behind him.

Stiles grabbed his head with both of his hands. He could still hear Detria's words replaying in his mind. She was the one who had hurt his father. Each footstep Stiles took in the room seemed to cause the pine hardwood floors to rumble.

"Not this again," he mumbled. "No, no, not betrayal." Stiles looked upward. "Father God, I don't understand what's happening." Stiles wailed like a baby. At first, he wanted to tune out the words spewing from her mouth. *Pastor, you need to talk to Pastor.* The inner voice pricked his spirit again. *Talk to Pastor.*

Detria ran up the stairs as soon as Stiles dashed from the dining room. She trembled with fear and cried over the realization that her marriage was probably coming to an end.

Stiles remained in Pastor's bedroom, his

mind jumbled with confusing thoughts. He held his head like he was desperate to keep away the words Detria confessed. He then whipped around and left the room. He raced to the bedroom upstairs where he quickly changed into a pair of trousers and a shirt. From her chair in the corner of their bedroom suite, Detria watched in utter silence as her husband moved around the room like a mad man. If he saw her, he acted like he did not.

Stiles kicked off his lounging shoes and replaced them with a pair of basketball sneakers. He looked inside the pocket of the slacks he had on earlier in the day and pulled out his keys.

"Stiles, are you going to be all right?" Detria asked. Her tears had dried on her face. She hated to see her husband in this state. But Detria believed there was no other way, not if she wanted a truthful relationship with her husband.

He looked shocked to hear her voice. Stiles turned and looked at his wife. "Am I going to be all right?" A look of disdain toward her was on his handsome face. "You ask me if I'm going to be all right? Are you serious? Who are you? What kind of person are you? Who am I married to? How can you even expect me to be all right after unloading this kind of bombshell on me?" Stiles rubbed his head over and over again.

Detria stared at him, her mouth partially opened. He had every right to be upset. She'd give him that much. Even if she wanted to answer his questions, it would not have been possible because Stiles turned and left the room in a hurry. His heavy feet pounded down the steps.

Detria's body stiffened when the downstairs door was slammed shut. She reached for the Bible parked on the table next to her chair. Detria pressed the brown leather Bible against her chest. "Lord, I surrender all," she said.

24

Francesca continued to feel better each day. She had a renewed strength about her and a determination to live a full, complete life dedicated to God. The doctors reminded her that it was crucial that she see her primary doctor regularly, something Francesca had neglected to do practically since she was initially diagnosed with HIV. Now that she had been diagnosed with AIDS, she realized that if she planned to live many more productive years with the incurable disease, she had to take care of herself and do what her doctors instructed.

She sat in her chair and went through the pile of messages, get well cards, and letters she'd received since her illness. She ran across Rena's phone number and saw the messages that Rena had called. Francesca looked at the clock on her table and decided to give Rena a call. It was early midday Saturday, and if Rena was still the same woman Francesca had known for so many years, then she was probably busy tidying up her home or out running errands.

She dialed the number listed on the paper.

The phone rang several times, but then went to voice mail. Francesca started leaving a message, but her phone rang while she was in the middle of leaving it.

Francesca clicked over. "Hello."

"This is Rena. Someone just called from this number."

"Hi, it's Francesca. How are you, Rena? I was sitting here going through my messages when I saw the notes that you had called. Thank you for thinking about me." Francesca's voice rang with humility.

"Francesca, oh my goodness, you sound great. I'm fine. How are you doing?" From Rena's voice, it was easy to discern that she was happy to hear from Francesca.

"I'm blessed. God is good. Now that I'm home, I'm going through tons of cards, notes, letters, and all kinds of things people sent to me. I tell you, it really feels good to know that there are people out there who care about me and who are praying for me. You're one of them. Thank you for your prayers and concern, Rena."

"Of course, I'm concerned about you. I know we've had some extremely rough times, but I still care about you, Francesca. It's good to hear from you. How is your friend, Brother Tim?"

"Oh, he's great. Have you heard?"

"Heard what?" asked Rena.

"Well, Tim and I have taken out friendship to the next level."

"The next level? What do you mean?" Rena asked.

"We're actually going to get married. It won't be a big wedding. We've decided to let our pastor marry us at the church. We're going to do a small reception in the fellowship hall."

"Did you say you and Brother Tim are getting married?"

"Yes, that's what I said," Francesca answered.

"I can't believe it. I'm . . . I'm," Rena stammered. "I'm shocked, but I'm happy for the two of you. I guess my mother doesn't know about it because she hasn't called to tell me. Usually someone from Holy Rock calls her and fills her in on the latest news."

"Well, I just told Stiles about our plans earlier today. He wished me well and told me he would call me back. He already guessed that there was something more to our relationship than mere friendship. And he was right."

"He didn't have anything else to say about it?" Rena queried.

"When I called him, he said he was in the middle of something, so I didn't get a chance to tell him our wedding plans. He said he would call me back as soon as he could. And Pastor, well, I talked to him last night and told him. So I'm sure the news will find its way through Holy Rock pretty soon." Francesca giggled into the phone.

"I don't know what to say—" Rena sucked in her breath and paused—"except congratulations. I can't believe this."

"I know. I can't either. Who would have thought that I, of all people, would end up with a husband. Girl, life is a trip, and God is definitely a comedian." Francesca laughed, and then coughed.

"You okay?" Rena asked.

"Yep. I still have some problems with my lungs, but I'm doing better. But this coughing gets to me every now and then."

"Are you sure you want to marry this man, Francesca? Does he know about . . . you know?"

"He knows everything, Rena. I wouldn't think of going through with this if he didn't. I didn't leave a thing out about my past. In spite of everything, the man still loves me, and he wants me to be his wife. I asked him if he had a mental problem or something." Francesca laughed again. Rena was quiet. "I know what you're thinking, Rena. How does someone like me deserve a wonderful man like Tim? Well, I've asked myself that question too."

"No, I wasn't thinking that. To be honest, I can't envision you with a man, that's all. So this is taking a little time for me to digest."

"Think about how I feel about it. This is definitely a newbie for me. But I have to admit that I love myself some Tim."

"Ooh wee, God is so amazing, Francesca."

"Rena, I've screwed up so many other people's lives that I can't understand why God decided that He'd bring an awesome man like Tim into my life, of all people. I don't know, but I'm tired of trying to figure God out. I'm just going to let Him be God. That way, I know my life will be fine."

"That's good, Francesca."

"How's your life going? How are Mr. and Mrs. Jackson doing?"

"Mom and Dad are fine. As for my life, I'm still seeing Robert. He wants to marry me."

"And? When is the date?" asked Francesca.

"I don't know what I'm going to do. I've been putting it off for some time. I did tell him that I would marry him, but I can tell that he didn't believe I was serious."

"Were you?"

"Francesca, frankly, I don't think so. I've been hurt, and I've hurt other people, like you, your brother, your entire family. And I've hurt myself. How can I live with a man, give myself to him as a wife when I have—"

"Stop. Don't even go there. Did you hear what I said earlier? I have AIDS. Not just herpes, not just HIV, but AIDS. And I have Tim. He loves me, Rena. He doesn't care that I could pass on a death sentence to him. He loves me. For the first time in my life, I know for myself what true love looks like and what it feels like. Whenever I see Tim, I'm reminded of unconditional love. When I hear his voice on the phone, I'm reminded of love. I'm a changed person inside and out, Rena. I hope you don't let yourself be the cause of ruining your own future."

"It's different for you. Robert knows about my past, but it doesn't make me feel better. But I guess I have you to thank for that, huh?" Rena said without sounding like she resented Francesca. "But anyway, just like Tim told you, Robert says it doesn't matter about my past or about my STD, but it's hard for me to believe and accept that he means what he says."

"If God can bring a man into my life, a good man at that, why do you feel like He can't do the same for you? It's a desire of your heart. As for me, I had no idea I would ever be with a man, let alone marrying one. But you . . . Rena, you loved my brother. I know you did, and he hurt you. I thought he would have been able to forgive you and that the two of you could move on together with your marriage. But it turned out not to be that way. Some people say that since he's a preacher he should have forgiven you, but they don't understand that Stiles is still made up of flesh. And who's to say that he hasn't forgiven you. People are so quick to judge others, especially preachers. This body, our thought process, everything about us needs work. That's why God had to die for us. There was no other way to get us cleaned up enough for us to have a chance at eternal life. The first time I met your friend, Robert, even though it was at my mother's funeral, I sensed that he was a great guy. I'm sorry I tried to come between the two of you. I think it was a last-ditch effort on my part to get back at you for moving on with your life. In some way, I think it was a way of me getting back at Audrey too, even though she was dead. I was still confused back then, Rena. But even after everything I told Robert about you and me, he loves you. The question is, do you love him, or are you still hanging on to memories of Stiles?"

"Stiles? Where did that come from? Stiles is married and has moved on with his life," Rena explained.

"That's not what I asked you. I said are you still in love with him?" Francesca repeated. She pushed some of her cards and papers to the side.

"No, I am not in love with Stiles anymore. I love Robert. I love his kids. I love everything about him."

"Then I suggest you have a little talk with God, honey. Get your stuff together and walk on down that aisle."

"I'll keep praying about it. Well, I guess I need to go. I'm glad to hear from you. I'll call and check on you from time to time. Oh, and please give Tim my love. Congratulations to the two of you."

"Thanks for caring, Rena. Bye."

Rena hung up the phone. She thought of Francesca and the fact that she was about to get married. That practically blew Rena's mind. She fought against Robert, didn't trust that he could love her despite all of her imperfections, yet Francesca had accepted love into her life without the least bit of hesitation. That was Francesca. She was a warrior. A soldier. Anything she did, she did it wholeheartedly. She served God with that same fervor and determined spirit.

Rena worked throughout the day at her house, and then did some grocery shopping. When she returned home later that afternoon, she called Robert. She didn't expect him to answer. Their relationship was troubled, and it was all her fault. Robert deserved more. He deserved someone who loved him as much as he seemed to love her. If Francesca could allow love into her life, surely she could too.

Rena prayed, drew in a deep breath, and called Robert. She was nervous. She had no idea how he would receive her, or if he would talk to her at all. She listened to the phone as it rang. She thought about hanging up, but then his little girl answered the phone.

"Daddy," the little girl called out, "Miss Rena is on the phone." Rena heard her giggling into the phone, and Rena couldn't help but laugh also. She found it made her feel more at ease.

"Hi," Robert said; then he fell silent.

"Hi," responded Rena. "I wanted to know if you and the kids would like to come over later this evening. I thought we could do some grilling. It's so nice outside."

"Uh, I don't know, Rena. I had some other plans."

Rena's heart fluttered. "Oh, I see. What about tomorrow after church? That might be even better. Whaddaya say?" she asked again.

"Are you sure that's a good idea? I don't want you to feel pressured. You've made it quite clear where our relationship is headed, which is nowhere."

"Robert, I know I was mean to you. I said quite a few things that I didn't mean. But, please, I really want to see you and the kids. We need to talk. Please." Rena could hear him sigh. Lord, please let him say yes.

"I guess tomorrow will be good. What time?" he asked.

"Around three?"

"Three it is." His tone was nonchalant. "We'll see you then. Anything else?" he asked.

"As a matter of fact there is." Rena began to speak extremely fast. "I love you, Robert Becton. I want to spend the rest of my life with you. I understand if you don't want to marry me anymore, but I can't keep fooling myself. I can't—"

"Whoa, hold up. Slow your roll. Are you serious?" Robert interrupted. "Don't play with my heart, Rena."

Rena heard the children playing in the background. "I wouldn't dare. I've done that far too long."

"Give me an hour. The kids and I will be over there. I suddenly feel like grilling," he said and started laughing over the phone, as did Rena.

"But I thought you said—" Rena halted. "Never mind. I'll see you when you get here." Rena hung up the phone. She couldn't help herself and burst out in uncontrollable laughter. "Ahhh," she screamed. "Thank you, God. Thank you, thank you, thank you."

25

"If any of you lacks wisdom, let him ask of God, who gives to all liberally and without reproach, and it will be given to him." James 1:5 NKJV

Stiles looked at the clock on the car's instrument panel. Nine forty-five. He disregarded the time of night. Pastor was more than likely already in bed reading his Bible, something he did almost every night around this time. Stiles had already surmised that this was one of those situations that couldn't wait until morning. He had the security code and a spare set of keys to Pastor's residence. He was set on talking to his daddy tonight.

Along the way, Stiles chastised himself for not seeing the truth of what had happened to his father. The one time his spirit tried to instruct him, Stiles had ignored it. He didn't understand what was going on in his life. Why did he keep making mistakes when it came to women? He was a man in his early thirties, articulate, God-fearing, yet it seemed he didn't have an ounce of wisdom. At least, that's how he felt. He'd been blind to Rena's indiscretions, and now he was experiencing the same betrayal from Detria.

He pulled into the gated community, used his security pass card, and drove to Pastor's apartment.

Stiles knocked on the door and rang the doorbell more than twice. He waited anxiously for Pastor to answer. After several minutes, Stiles decided to use his door key. Just as he was about to put it inside the lock, Pastor opened the door.

"Stiles." Pastor looked concerned and rightfully so. "What's going on, son? Is everything all right? Is it Francesca?"

"Francesca is fine. Everyone is fine. I know it's late, Pastor, but this couldn't wait until morning. I believe you know the real reason I'm here, whether you want to admit it or not." Stiles did his trademark head rub, and then sat down on the living room sofa.

Pastor moved toward his chair and sat across from his son. "Talk to me. Is this about your sister accepting Tim's proposal to get married? Son, God can change the hardest of hearts, you know. His ways are not our ways and His—"

"Hold on, Pastor, before you go any further," Stiles interjected, "this isn't about Francesca and Brother Tim. Francesca did call and tell me about her engagement, and I'm really happy for her. I have no problem with that. I'm grateful for the way God is moving in her life. She has a major testimony about the majesty of God. But this isn't about Francesca or Tim. This is about my wife and what she did." Stiles laid his hand against his chest. "And I need you to tell me the truth," Stiles insisted.

"What do you want to know?" asked Pastor.

"Did Detria physically abuse you?"

Pastor looked away, and then looked back

at Stiles. Pastor's words became shuffled more than likely because he was nervous about how to handle Stiles' inquiry.

"Pastor, please, no antics tonight. I just need you to tell me if my wife is the one responsible for beating you."

"Yes, but listen to me, son. As far as I'm concerned what Detria did is in the past. It's over. I'm trying to move on with my life, and you need to do the same thing."

Stiles reared his head back, and a guttural sound came up and out of his throat, and filled the small living room. "Move on? Oh, God, no," he screamed. "How can I move on? Who is the woman I married? How could she be so evil, so violent, and I not see it? Don't get me wrong, we've had some tough battles, she and I. And now that I look back on our marriage, I do recall a time or two when I questioned her temper, but for her to do something like this. . ." Stiles stood up and rubbed his hand over his head. "Pastor, what's wrong with me? Where is my spiritual discernment? I've gone all of this time believing that the agency staff was responsible for harming you, and all the time it was my wife? My God, how much more can I take?"

"Stiles, this is not your fault. As for Detria, I've talked to her, and she's settled her account with me. But more importantly she said she's gone before God and asked His forgiveness. I told her that if you came to me with this, I would tell you to talk to her about it because it's part of my past."

"So, you and Detria have already discussed

this? When? Did she fix you a nice meal and get you in a good frame of mind before she confronted you, like she did me?"

"No, quit it, Stiles." Pastor's weak voice raised at least an octave. "Detria has been tormented by what happened more than you or I will probably ever understand. What she did was wrong, but I'm glad it was me she took it out on."

"What are you talking about? How can you sit there and act like she's the one who got the short end of the stick? How can you talk like she's the victim? My wife physically and emotionally abused you, Pastor. What part of that are you missing? The woman is somebody I don't even know. Thank God Audrey isn't here to witness this. What Detria did to you is despicable, cruel, and insensitive. There is no way a woman of God, a true woman of God, could do what she did and then act like nothing has happened. That's the ultimate deceit." Stiles' hands flew in all directions. "Then she has the audacity to tell me how sorry she is with all of that game talking. I thought I had the woman God wanted for me. I thought she was the one, Pastor." Stiles hung his head and cried.

Pastor leaned on his walker until he was able to stand. He balanced himself, and then he walked over to where Stiles was and sat down next to his son.

"Stiles, the wounds that were inflicted upon me are healed. They were temporary. I couldn't speak at the time it happened. I was helpless, so to speak. But God understood. What you see as being evil and wrong is not what I experienced. Detria was hurting. She lost her child, son. A child she wanted to give you so badly. She looked at me and saw me as the enemy. She saw me as the man who stole life away from her. The wounds inflicted upon Detria are still open and fresh. I understand why she did what she did. It may not make sense to you, but you know the Word, son. Lean not to your own understanding. Trust God fully, and He shall direct your path. The physical pain I endured was nothing compared to the emotional abuse Detria has gone through these past few months."

Stiles looked and listened. He couldn't comprehend how Pastor could be so compassionate toward someone who had purposely harmed him. The love Pastor had for his daughter-in-law and his forgiveness of her hurtful act were present in every word he spoke. Stiles felt calmness entering into his spirit. The anger he felt started to disappear.

"You and your wife lost your baby. You moved past the loss; you worked through your grief. Your wife carried the loss with her every day. Think about it. There were hormonal changes in her, mental changes, physical changes—all of that combined with the fact that she miscarried, and you have a ticking time bomb. I know she shouldn't have done what she did to me, but I shouldn't have done what I did to her."

Stiles frowned. "What did you do to her?"

"I moved in with the two of you. You were newlyweds trying to start a new life together. I never should have agreed to move in with you all. When I had the stroke, you weren't there. It was Detria who strained to pick me up. How do you think she felt when she turns around shortly after and miscarries?" Pastor's voice grew stronger with each word he spoke. "For a while, Detria wasn't herself. She's just beginning to get over the loss of her child. She came to me and poured her heart out, Stiles. She asked me to forgive her. Who am I not to forgive when God forgives us? Who are you not to love and forgive your wife? She is not Rena, son. You are not reliving your past. Now, I can't tell you what to do, but I can tell you something I heard someone say years ago, and I've never forgotten it: 'You can't undo anything you've already done, but you can face up to it. You can tell the truth. You can seek forgiveness. And then let God do the rest.' That's what Detria has done. She came to me with a spirit of sorrow, needing my forgiveness. She can't change what happened. Neither can I, and neither can you. But we can learn from what happened. We can move on, and we can learn to forgive. I know there are times when you've thought that maybe you should have given Rena a second chance. But you didn't. You did what you believed was right at the time. God gave you an opportunity to love again when Detria came into your life. All I want to say to you is, pray. Pray and ask God for His guidance and for His will. Don't look at this through physical eyes, son." Pastor moved his hand to Stiles' shoulder.

Stiles grabbed hold of his father and cried

into his bosom. He felt like a lost little boy, unsure of which direction to go, which path to take. When he raised his head moments later, Stiles looked at Pastor. "I need some time to think and pray. You mind if I camp out on your sofa?" Stiles asked.

"Yes, quite frankly, I do mind. You have a home to go to. I suggest that's where you return. If you don't want to sleep in the same room with your wife, that's your decision, but I will not be an enabler for you, son. You have plenty of room at your own place. Go home and face your problems like a man."

Stiles was shocked at his father's answer. "I can't believe you're telling me to get out."

"Believe it," Pastor said and smiled.

Stiles stood, and then helped Pastor get back on his feet. "Let me walk you to your bedroom, and I'll lock up."

"Sounds like a good idea, son."

Before he left his father's home, Stiles made sure Pastor was comfortable and back in his bed. He thanked Pastor for his words of wisdom, and then he left.

Stiles replayed the words Pastor had fed him. "God, I need your help," Stiles prayed out loud. "This time I don't want to act on my own accord, Father. I want to do your will. I want to do what's right for my wife and for my marriage. I don't want to run away this time like I did when I was married to Rena. But I need you to help me through this, Father. I'm asking you to help my wife. I was blind to her hurt."

Stiles continued the drive home. His cell

phone rang. He touched the button on the steering wheel to answer the call.

"Hello," he said. "Hello," he said again. He looked at the instrument panel to see the caller's number. Before he could digest whose number it was, Stiles heard the sweet voice on the other end.

"Stiles? Did I catch you at a bad time?" Rena asked.

Stiles sort of shook his head in disbelief. "Rena? Is this you?" he asked. "How did you get my number?"

"Of course, it's me, silly. And you were the one who gave me your number, remember?"

"Oh, that's right. Sorry 'bout that. I've got a lot on my mind this evening."

"You concerned about Francesca?" Rena asked.

"Oh, so you heard, huh?"

"What? About her and Brother Tim?" Rena responded.

"Yeah," replied Stiles.

"She called me and told me the great news. Isn't it great, Stiles? Francesca is about to embark on a new life. I'm so happy for her."

"I am too," Stiles said as he tried to push away thoughts about his own sinking marriage.

"Look, I know it's late there, and to be honest, I wasn't expecting to reach you. I thought I was going to get your voice mail. I hope I'm not disturbing you and Detria. That was not my intent," Rena apologized.

"No, I'm on my way home. I just left Pastor's apartment."

"Apartment? Pastor has an apartment? I thought he was living with you and Detria."

"He was, but he decided it was best that he had his own place. He's still renting out Emerald Estates, but he lives at Kirby Pines Community." Stiles then flipped the subject. "So, what about you and your fellow? He still can't convince you to marry him, huh?" Stiles laughed and then his voice turned serious. "Maybe it's divine intervention of some sort. I know my life has certainly changed in the last twenty-four hours."

"Stiles, what are you talking about? Are you okay? What's going on?"

"Oh, nothing. I'm just babbling. Anyway, what's up? To what do I owe the honor of a call from my ex-wife?"

"I thought I'd let you know that I'm getting married," Rena said.

"What?"

"The last time we talked, I remember telling you that you would know when or if I decided to marry Robert. So, for the record, I want to let you know that Robert asked me to marry him and I accepted."

Stiles paused before saying, "Good. . . good for you. I'm glad to hear that. I hope you two have a happy life."

"Like you and your darling wife?" Rena commented.

Stiles stiffened in his seat. Flashes of his troubled marriage made him shake his head to clear his thinking. A car horn honked and Stiles jumped.

"Sounds like you need to get off those

Memphis streets." Rena laughed into the phone.

"You're probably right. I'm almost home now."

"You didn't answer my question," Rena commented.

"Oh, about me and Detria? I hope you and Rob will be just as happy as me and Detria." Stiles would never give Rena the benefit of knowing that he was unsure about his future with his wife. "Seriously, Rena, you're a great person. Things didn't work out for us, but that's the way it is sometimes. I'm glad that God brought someone into your life. And I'm not just talking. I'm being for real."

Rena cleared her throat. "Thanks." She paused for a moment. "Anyway, it was good talking to you. I only wanted to call and mess with you."

"Hey, before you go, I do have something to say," Stiles added.

"Go for it."

"I'm sorry."

"Sorry? Stiles, what's going on with you tonight? What are you talking about?" Rena sounded concerned.

"I don't know if I've ever told you that, but I truly am. For our marriage failing, for not having a forgiving heart when things first went awry, for everything I did that hurt you, Rena, I'm sorry. You were my wife, and I should have given our marriage a chance to work, but I didn't. I ask that you forgive me for giving up on us."

"Wow," Rena replied. "I don't know what to

say. That's the last thing I expected to hear from you."

"I know. But I mean it. And one more thing."

"What's that?" Rena asked. She sniffled over the phone like she may have been crying.

"I want to ask you if you will forgive me for the way I treated you."

Rena replied in a choked voice. "If you can forgive me, then my answer is yes."

"Then it's done. Now maybe God can do what He wants to do in both of our lives and our futures. I wish you and Robert nothing but the best, Rena. Take care of yourself, you hear?"

"Yes, I will. You too. Bye, Stiles."

Stiles pushed the END button on the steering wheel. "Father God, you made your will for my life clear right away. I didn't see that coming," he told the Lord as he made the left turn onto his street. "That definitely was a sign that I need to make things right with my wife. Help me to go inside this house and tell her that I forgive her. If Pastor can understand, and he was the victim, surely I can have a heart of forgiveness."

Stiles pushed the garage remote and pulled inside. For a few seconds, he remained in his car and whispered a final prayer to God for direction. He then went into the house to face his wife.

"Detria," he called out to her, but there was no answer. "Detria," he called again. Still no answer. He walked upstairs and found her curled in a ball like a kitten, asleep in her chair. He quietly walked over to her and leaned down to pick her up and carry her to their bed.

Detria woke up startled. She jumped in Stiles' arms.

"It's me. I'm home," he whispered into her ear and lay her on the bed. He pulled back the covers on the opposite side. Detria moved over and pulled back the covers on the side of the bed where Stiles had laid her. She sat up in the bed and watched Stiles remove his clothes down to his boxers.

"Where have you been?" she asked him.

"I went to see Pastor."

"Oh," Detria remarked.

"Detria, we need to talk. Well, let me rephrase that. I need to talk. You've done all the talking so far, so I guess it's my turn."

Detria remained quiet. She pulled her knees up to her chest and waited to hear what Stiles had to say.

"Detria." Stiles positioned his shirtless body on the bed so that he was face-to-face with her. He propped his legs underneath him Indian style. "What you told me tonight struck me right here." Stiles laid the palm of his hand over his heart. "I can't begin to tell you my first thought, my first reaction. It was like being swished away to another time. What you laid on me was so heavy."

"I didn't want to hurt you, Stiles. But I didn't want to deceive you either. The only right thing to do was to tell you. I know I stand a chance, a huge chance," Detria stretched her words, "of losing you, of destroying our marriage."

"You say you didn't want to deceive me, yet you didn't come to me and let me know what you were feeling. It's like you didn't trust me, Detria. I experienced a loss too, and I hurt too. We are husband and wife. You should have talked to me before things got out of hand like they did."

"How could I come to you, Stiles, when you wouldn't even touch me? You didn't make love to me. You barely kissed me, and we never talked about the miscarriage."

"And I wonder why?" Stiles grew agitated. "You think it had something to do with your rush to get back to work, not giving you or me time to talk about our feelings? You aren't the only one who suffered a loss, Detria, but you sure acted like it. If you weren't at the office, you were working out at the gym."

Detria fired back. "And if you weren't hiding away at Holy Rock, you were taking on extra classes at the university. So who's the one with the most blame?"

Stiles snapped. Sarcasm dripped from his thick lips like honey from a honeycomb. "Wow, things were so bad that you would rather beat on my father and blame him?"

Detria sat frozen.

Stiles watched. "Look, I'm sorry. I didn't mean to sound so cruel. It's just that I can't wrap my brain around the fact that you did what you did to another human being. That makes me question everything about us, Detria. What's going to happen the next time things don't go your way? If we do have children, will you beat them when they spill a bowl of milk?"

"Of course not," Detria screamed. "I am not like that, and you know it. How could you think I would abuse my own children?"

"But you are like that, Detria. That's what's so scary about this. You are capable of violence. Have you forgotten that you've gotten physical with me a couple of times too?" Detria looked shocked and her face turned pale. Frankly, I want things to work out between us. I love you. But this is so out there."

Detria started to cry. "Stiles, I know I need help. I'm going to seek some professional counseling. But until then, I want you to know that I love you. I'm sorry for what I did. I begged Pastor's forgiveness. He's the one who helped me work through this. I thank God for him." Detria wiped her runny nose with her hand.

"All I'm asking is that you give me another chance. Forgive me, please. I'm so sorry. I'm so sorry," she continued to repeat.

Stiles watched her tears flow. He could hear the anguish in her voice. He reached out to her and pulled her into his arms. Stiles began kissing her tear-streaked face. "I forgive you, Detria. I want this to work out for us. I'm not saying it's going to be easy. I may be a preacher but I'm not perfect, and I'm telling you that it's going to take time for me to get over what you did to my father. But if Pastor can find it in his heart to forgive you, then who am I not to do the same?" He continued planting kisses along her face and neck. "And I'm sorry too. I'm sorry for not being the husband you needed. I'm sorry you felt that you couldn't come to me. Will you forgive me?" he asked. He pulled away from her slightly so he could see her face.

"Yes," Detria answered. She fell into his arms again and rested her head against his bare chest. They held each other and cried together. "I promise you that I'm going to spend the rest of my life trying to make up for all of the pain I've caused and the wrong I've done. I will not let the devil steal my joy and ruin my marriage. Whatever it takes to make this right, I'm willing to do it," Detria sobbed. "I don't deserve a man like you."

"I'm here for you. Please know that you can always come to me, Detria. Always."

Their desire for one another escalated from a spark to a blaze. Stiles smothered her in kisses and Detria fully reciprocated. Enthralled in desire, passion, and love between a husband and wife, they rode the waves of fulfilling each other's needs and wants.

Stiles looked down on the woman beneath him. "I love you. I love you," he said over and over again as their bodies became one.

26

*"Love . . . it's a missing puzzle piece waiting to
be found and when you do find it you can
finally figure out the picture life has to show
you."* Paige

Pastor heard the daily mail drop into the
basket underneath the inside mail chute. He
had settled into his new home, and during the
three months he'd been there, he was
fortunate to meet new friends. He also
discovered that there were two other members
from Holy Rock who lived at Kirby Pines. He
felt good about his life, and his health was
continuing to improve. Without the aid of his
walker, he walked over and retrieved the mail.
He carried the pile with him to the kitchen
where he stuck his lunch in the oven. It was
almost time for Judge Mathis. While he waited
on his pre-prepared meal from the facility's
kitchen to warm up, he scanned the pieces of
mail. An envelope addressed to him from
Francesca caught his eye. He opened it and his
mouth turned upward.

The invitation read:

> Celebrating Our Love in Marriage
> Francesca Graham
> and
> Timothy Swift
> at two o'clock
> Saturday, the twenty-sixth of March
> Cornerstone Community Church
> Newbern, Tennessee
> Reception
> immediately following the ceremony
> Cornerstone Banquet Hall

Pastor's eyes grew moist. He looked up, raised his hands, and began to praise God. His joyous cries could probably be heard from outside. He didn't care. He wanted the world to know that God was a good God.

"Thank you, Lord. Thank you for being good. Thank you for hearing my prayers. Thank you for the good times and the bad. Thank you for it all, Father."

He read the invitation one more time before he took it to his bedroom. He sat on the side of his bed and propped the invitation on the nightstand. "God, I can't stop thanking you," he cried.

The telephone rang. Pastor wiped his tears away before he answered. "Hello," he said.

"Pastor, it's Detria—"

"And Stiles," he heard both of them say into the phone.

"Hello. Guess what, you two?" Pastor said. Excitement resonated in his voice. "I just received an invitation to your sister's wedding." He started laughing.

"We received ours in the mail today too. Isn't it great?" Stiles said.

"It sure is," Pastor answered and laughed into the phone.

Detria spoke up next. "Pastor, the good news doesn't stop there," she squealed.

"There's more? Let's hear it then," replied Pastor.

"We're pregnant," they both screamed in unison into the phone. "We are pregnant," they screamed again.

"Praise God. Hallelujah. That is so wonderful to hear. I'm so happy for y'all. My first grandchild. I can't wait," Pastor exclaimed.

The doorbell rang at Pastor's apartment. "Hold on, let me get the door." He walked to the door with the phone to his ear.

"Who is it?" Stiles asked.

"Come on in, Sista Josie. Have a seat. I'm talking to my son and daughter-in-law. Give me just a minute," Pastor said and walked toward the kitchen.

"Sista Josie? Who is Sista Josie?" Stiles asked.

"Josie? She's one of the ladies who lives in the complex. She comes over to watch Judge Mathis with me."

"Ohh," said Stiles. "Is that right? Well, well, well. God certainly is good and full of surprises too."

Pastor could hear Stiles and Detria laughing. "Stop it, you two." Pastor chuckled.

"Don't let us keep you from Sista Josie," Detria said and laughed into the phone again.

"Congratulations again. You two make me

proud. And your sister getting married? Now that's one that the Lord sneaked in on us. I don't think even Francesca saw it coming." Pastor chuckled. "A father couldn't ask for more. I love y'all," he said.

"We love you too," Stiles replied. "Go on and watch Sista Josie, oh, I meant to say Judge Mathis."

Pastor laughed out loud again. "Good-bye, son. Good-bye, Detria." He hung up the phone, removed the food from the oven, and proceeded to divide equal portions on two plates. "Sista Josie, is it on yet?"

"It's about to come on now," answered the attractive, thick hipped woman with long gray locks. "Let me help you," she said and walked in the kitchen to meet Pastor. She hummed to the tune of "Amazing Grace" while pouring glasses of juice for them.

Pastor walked over to where she stood by the refrigerator. "Thank you, sweetie," he said. He squeezed her around the waist and kissed her on the cheek.

They carried the food and drinks back to the living room. Judge Mathis was just starting. They placed the food and drinks on two food tables before they sat down next to each other on the sofa. They clasped hands, and then listened to the television moderator.

"The honorable Judge Greg Mathis is presiding. . ."

Continue following this family saga in Book 4, "My Sister My Momma, My Wife."

Words from the Author

"And when you stand praying, if you hold anything against anyone, forgive him, so that your Father in heaven may forgive you your sins." Mark 11:25 NIV

Forgiving someone or asking for forgiveness isn't always. Yet we are *commanded to do so in God's Word. The My* Son's Wife series reveals how deep unforgiveness can go and how harmful it can be. We, who call ourselves Christians are taught that we should forgive. Does that mean that we are to forgive any and everything? Do we forgive everybody who wrongs us? What about someone who has molested our child or raped us or abused us like the woman in My Son's Next Wife?

Is there ever a time when we are given a break from forgiving? If you expect me to let you off the hook and tell you that there are some wrongs that should not be forgiven, then you're wrong. If we want others to forgive us, then we have to forgive others. If we want God to forgive us for our constant mess-ups, then we have to forgive others. I know, I know, you are probably saying that you haven't done anything really bad to another person like murder, rape, or abuse. Maybe you simply told a lie on someone or caused friction in someone's relationship like many of the people in the *My Son's Wife* stories. You may think these are small, insignificant sins that are not going to be held against you if you don't forgive. But that's not true.

For most of us, our natural instinct when we are mistreated, injured, or wronged is to seek revenge, get back at the person(s) who wronged us—make them pay. We usually don't automatically overflow with love, forgiveness, mercy, and grace. But God requires forgiveness, or He will not forgive us. If we are unwilling or unable to forgive, then there's no need to ask God to forgive us. God stands ready to forgive us for our sins. He sent His son Jesus Christ to die for our sins of yesterday, today, and tomorrow. He says in His Word that we are to forgive seven times seventy—in other words, there is not a time when we are not to forgive.

Think about those who have hurt you and those whom you have hurt. If you are the one who has wronged someone, seek their forgiveness. If you are the one who has experienced the wrong, forgive as Christ Himself forgives you. You'll be so much better for having done so.

Discussion Questions

1. Why would Detria invite Pastor Graham to live with her and Stiles?

2. How is Detria different from Stiles' ex-wife, Rena Graham?

3. Does Stiles still love his ex-wife? If you think he does, discuss why you believe this.

4. Is Rena in love with Robert Becton, or is she still in love with Stiles?

5. What are your feelings about Francesca and Brother Tim? Is it a realistic relationship?

6. Do you know anyone who has been the victim of elderly abuse?

7. Do you know someone who abuses the elderly? If so, what have you done with the information?

8. What is your opinion of Detria's personality?

9. Do you believe Detria's miscarriage was God's way of saying she needed to get help before He gave her a child that she might end up abusing? Why or why not?

10. Should a husband and wife tell each other everything that happens during their marriage? If so, why? If not, why not?

11. Does Stiles make the right decision about his marriage to Detria? Why or why not?

To arrange signings, book events, or speaking
engagements with the author,
Contact sheliawritesbooks@yahoo.com

To send your personal comments
to the author:
Web site – www.sheliawritesbooks.com
Email – sheliawritesbooks@yahoo.com
Twitter: @sheliaebell
Instagram:sheliaebell
www.facebook.com/SheliaEBell

If you enjoyed this book or if you have enjoyed reading any books by Shelia E. Bell, please go to your favorite online site and **leave a review.** Reviews help determine the success of an author. It is the ultimate display of support you, as readers, can give.

Whether this is your first time reading a book by me or whether you have followed my literary career from the beginning, I say THANK YOU!

There is no Me without You!

Shelia E. Bell

More Books by Shelia E. Bell

Beautiful Ugly Series

Beautiful Ugly (1)
True Beauty (Book 2)

My Son's Wife Series

My Son's Wife: The Beginning (Book 1)
My Son's Ex-Wife: Aftershock (Book 2)
My Son's Next Wife (Book 3)
My Sister My Momma My Wife (4)
My Wife My Baby...And Him (Book 5)
The McCoys of Holy Rock (Book 6)
Dem McCoy Boys (Book 7)
My Brother, Father, and Me (8)
My Truth, My Time, My Turn (9)

The Real Housewives of Adverse City series

The Real Housewives of Adverse City 1
The Real Housewives of Adverse City 2
The Real Housewives of Adverse City 3
The Real Housewives of Adverse City 4

Standalone Novels

Always, Now and Forever
Show A Little Love
Into Each Life
Sinsatiable
What's Blood Got to Do With It?
Only In My Dreams
The House Husband

Forever Ain't Enough
Cross Road

Young Adult/Teen Fiction
Fairley High Series

House of Cars
Life of Payne
The Lollipop Girl

Anthology Contributions
Bended Knees
Weary to Will
Learning to Love Me

Nonfiction
A Christian's Perspective: Journey Through Grief

.